CALI BIRD

Tales Of The Countess

To Jenny
Enjoy!
Cali Bird
xx

Contents

Prelude

The Countess was dancing on a podium on a stage in X-Ray. She wore a gold lamé halter-neck top, a short charcoal-coloured skirt and black over-knee boots. Her arms were above her head, moving in time to the pounding techno beat. The cropped top revealed her slender midriff. Tucked into the waistband of her skirt was a six-inch square, fake fur leopard-print bag.

Lost in the pulse of the music and the atmosphere of the club, she danced for two more tracks. As the vibe of the music slowed, she decided it was time for a drink. After running her hands through her hair and wiping the sweat from her forehead, she sat on the edge of the podium and swung her feet onto the floor of the stage. Her hand touched the bag to make sure it was still lodged in her skirt. Then she pushed her way through the gyrating bodies, down the steps and made her way around the edge of the main dance floor.

On the way, she spotted her friend, Marie, and made a gesture that she was going for a drink. Marie nodded. Still dancing, she started moving towards the Countess. "You okay?" she mouthed as she got closer.

The Countess nodded and shouted, "Fucking brilliant. Let's get a drink."

The girls were regulars at X-ray and fully agreed with a recent *Time Out* article where it was listed as one of the top ten London clubs in 1998.

They made a beeline into a gap at the long bar which ran along the back of the club. The Countess took the leopard-print bag out from her skirt and held it by the handles. She was standing next to a man in a white T-shirt, easily ten years her junior.

"Cool bag," he shouted. "I was watching you dancing. You're pretty wild."

"Thanks. He's my pussy," said the Countess as she turned to face him. "Would you like to stroke him?" She offered the bag to the young man.

He put his right hand out towards the bag then hesitated.

"Go on," said the Countess. "He doesn't bite."

"It's a he?" said the man as he stroked the bag.

"Yes," said the Countess. "He's called Pussy Original. My friend here bought him for me one Christmas."

"I can't believe you go around asking people to stroke your pussy," said the man, laughing.

The Countess shrugged. "Why not? As you say, he's a cool bag."

* * *

Ten hours later, the Countess awoke. She was sprawled across her bed, fully clothed. A chink of the midday sunshine shone through a gap in the curtains, making a long diamond shape on her wardrobe door. The outfits that she had tried on and rejected the previous evening lay scattered around her bed.

"Bugger," she said as she came to. Still half asleep, she took off her boots and her clothes. She pulled back the quilt, got into bed and grabbed her teddy bear who had been sitting on the other pillow. She snuggled with the bear and slept for another two hours.

Next time she woke, feeling very dry in the mouth, she turned over and groped around on her bedside table for a glass of water, nearly knocking it over. Had it been full, it would have sloshed everywhere. She lifted her head and drank what remained in the glass. Then she sat up, got out of bed and staggered to the bathroom.

She looked in the mirror, licked her finger and tried to wipe away the previous night's mascara that was smudged under her eye. She took a breath inwards, stared at herself and slowly shook her head.

* * *

Back in her bedroom, the leopard-print bag, Pussy Original, had bounced up onto the bed to where the teddy bear lay. The bear was a medium-sized brown bear with a dusky purple-coloured ribbon around his neck. He had recently come into the Countess's possession, having been a gift from one of her colleagues in New York. She had been given him when she finished her assignment at SC Radcliffe, one of the world's biggest investment banks. For this reason, she had called him American Ted, though there was nothing particularly American about him. He spoke and carried himself in exactly the same way as the finest of English teddies.

"Looks like it was a rough night," said American Ted.

"You can say that again," said Pussy Original. "Boy, can she drink. Probably stores it in those long legs of hers."

3

The Countess once had Yellow Ted, who was very old and battered. One day, he was swept away in the linen at a five-star hotel when she was on a business trip and was never seen again. At the time, she figured it was a sign for her to grow up and find a decent man with whom she could share her bed. However, that plan had still not come to fruition, so when American Ted came into her life, she was secretly overjoyed.

"Do you think she'll ever settle down?" asked American Ted.

"I'm sure she'd love to," said Pussy Original, "but it never worked out with the MSL in New York, so she's still clubbing, drinking too much and chatting up the wrong men."

"The MSL," said American Ted. "Let's see if I've got this straight. He's called Ed. The one she used to work with?"

"That's him," replied Pussy Original.

The MSL was an abbreviation that the Countess had concocted with Marie. At the time, both of them were suffering unrequited love, and both used to jokingly refer to these men as *The Man I Love And Want To Marry.* They rolled the two men up into one imaginary character and named it in the third person, *The Man She Loves And Wants To Marry.* That got shortened to *The Man She Loves,* which got shortened to the MSL.

Marie eventually got to go out with her MSL, but he developed an aversion to spending any quality time with her, so she dumped him. That left the Countess still pining for hers.

"But she doesn't work there anymore," said American Ted. "That's why I'm here. So, will she ever see him again?"

"Who knows," said Pussy Original. "I think she was hoping for a fairy-tale ending when she had her leaving drinks in New York. You know, where she fell into his arms at the end of the night, and it was all stars and roses. Didn't happen though."

"Oh, no wonder she's hurting," said American Ted. "She's cried a couple of times at night. I bet that's why."

"Yep, she's hurting bad," said Pussy Original. "That's why it's great to have you around. She needs a teddy. Her old one kept her on the straight and narrow and frequently patched her up and put her back together when she fell apart. We have to look after the Countess. To the outside world, she is a beautiful, fantastic and lively businesswoman. But we see what's really going on in her life, and it ain't pretty."

"Oh God!" said American Ted. "I'm going to have my work cut out to look after this owner."

"You said it, Ted!" replied Pussy Original.

See You Next Tuesday

"Emergency drying procedure?" asked Pussy Original, who was sitting on the wooden blanket box situated under the Countess's bedroom window.

"Yep," said the Countess as she put a wet cream-coloured, lightweight blouse on a coat hanger and hung it on the second bar of the clothes horse.

She plugged in a fan heater, set it two feet away from the structure and turned it on. Realising she needed to tilt the heater upwards, she went over to her bedside cabinet and grabbed a book to put underneath it.

American Ted was sitting on the bed. He touched the sleeve of a navy blouse which the Countess had discarded on the unmade bed. "Don't you want to wear this one?"

"I can if necessary, but I love the cream one with my new suit," said the Countess. "I'm so annoyed for not noticing that spot on the front."

"But Madame, it's nearly eight thirty. What time do you need to be at your new job?" asked the bear.

"Bugger. It's still not the right angle." She walked around her bed and took two more books. Then she bent down at the heater and worked out the best combination of reading material that would direct the heat to the optimal place. "It's my first day, so they don't want me there until ten. Trust me, this won't take long to dry. Thank goodness it's sleeveless."

She stood back and looked at the heater and the blouse. Deciding that it was safe, she went to the bathroom and showered. A few minutes later, she returned to the bedroom wrapped in a towel and felt the blouse. "That's coming along nicely," she said as she turned the hanger around so the other side was closest to the heat.

Just after nine fifteen, she tottered up the steps from her basement flat into the early September sunshine. The blouse felt slightly damp under the armhole on the left-hand side where the fabric was doubled over, but otherwise, it was dry enough. She was about to walk to the tube station when she saw the orange light of a taxi coming up the road.

"What the heck," she said to herself as she held out her hand to hail it. "It's my first day. I'll arrive in style."

* * *

At five minutes to ten, the Countess entered the office of Periculum Software Solutions, a consultancy in Mayfair that dealt in risk systems for banks. Three weeks had passed since she had completed her assignment at SC Radcliffe in New York.

She loved her new suit and felt that she could conquer the world in the right tailoring. The fabric was a dark navy with a faint white pinstripe running through it. The jacket was single breasted and nipped in at just the right place. The skirt was long, below the knee and very elegant. When the Countess moved, one noticed that it had a clever front split, high enough to show off a suggestive hint of her fabulously long and well-toned legs but not so high that it was indecent or unprofessional. Together with her hair, which had been recently cut into a very precise bob, the Countess projected every inch the immaculate and capable businesswoman. No one would have guessed her unusual laundry habits of the previous hour.

She strode up to the reception desk. "Hello. It's my first day here. Aidan Kennedy said to ask for him."

"Ah yes," said the receptionist. "Aidan is expecting you. I'll just give him a buzz. Take a seat over there please, and he'll be out soon."

The Countess perched on the edge of the low-slung leather couch. She took hold of the skirt material that was to the right of the split and pulled it across her left knee. Then she put her handbag flat on her lap to ensure that she wasn't flashing anything.

She watched as a lady in high heels clipped her way across the marble floor of the reception area. The lady smiled at her as she punched in a security code for the glass door that separated the reception area from the main offices. The Countess returned the smile.

Thirty seconds later, Aidan Kennedy, one of the company's directors, appeared. She saw him press the door-release button on the other side of the glass. He wore a dark blue suit with a pink open-necked shirt and looked more like he belonged in the creative department of an advertising agency than being a director of a software consultancy.

"Good morning," he said with a smile. "Come on through." He held the door open and beckoned her in.

The Countess got up. As she reached the door, Aidan shook her hand. "Great to meet you again."

"Likewise," said the Countess. "It's good to be here."

Once she was through the door, she paused and waited for him.

He motioned her to walk ahead. "Go straight ahead to my office. It's the glass box just down there."

The Countess followed his direction and made her way through the open office. The lady from earlier was nowhere to be seen, but she did catch the gaze of one of the male twenty-something consultants who was sitting with other workers, all huddled over their laptops.

As the office gangway widened out, Aidan caught up with her. "It's really great to have you here. We have so much new business and stuff in the pipeline."

They went into his office. Aidan sat behind his desk, and the Countess took the chair in front. Despite all the modern glass fixtures of the office, she liked the fact that the arched stone window surrounds of the original building were still intact.

"Right, let's get down to the nitty-gritty," he said. "We've got Deutsche Landesbank in Frankfurt that would be ideal for you. Some of our work there has got a bit out of hand and we need someone to get in there and sort it out. You've come along at just the right time. I also need you to keep an eye on what's going on in one of our London banks. Their systems are so antiquated, they are barely part of this century, let alone ready to cope with the new millennium."

"Okay, the pressure is on for them then," said the Countess.

"They say they are ready for the Euro," said Aidan, "but I'm not sure if that means they've just hired a lot of monkeys with two sets of abacuses."

The Countess laughed. "It's amazing sometimes how

businesses manage to function when their systems are so old."

"Very true, but at least it keeps us in a job when they are forced to change them." Aidan leaned back in his chair and ran his hand through the front of his hair. "It seems hard to believe that all those European currencies are going to disappear in three years' time."

The Countess observed a few grey hairs at his temple and the beginning of a receding hairline. "I know," she replied. "It will feel weird to not have Deutsche Marks or French francs when travelling in Europe."

"It will be a lot more convenient just to have one currency to deal with," he said, "but I can't help wondering whether a single central bank and one set of interest rates will work for all those countries."

"Yes, I've wondered about that too," said the Countess. "I guess we'll know in a few years. Then we can see whether we should join too."

"Yes, that will be the big question." Aidan sat forward again. "Anyway, back to today's issues. At Deutsche Landesbank, we've got a project manager out there, but they're floundering a bit, so the client's getting twitchy. I think that if you give our manager a steer and sweet talk the client, then hopefully it will all smooth over very quickly."

"Sure," said the Countess. "When would you need me to go there?"

"Let's see, what day is it today?" said Aidan. "Wednesday. I think it would be a bit mean of me to send you out there this week, so why don't you go early next week for a couple of days? Give them a shout today on the phone. They'll get you up to speed and let you have access to all the documentation and stuff. I've got a laptop waiting for you out there somewhere.

10

Our IT guys assure me it is all fixed up and ready to go."

"Okay, no problem," said the Countess. "If you can give me the number for your travel agent, then I can fix that up straight away."

"Fantastic," said Aidan. "That's what I like to hear. It's going to be so good having you around."

They discussed a couple of other possibilities for the Countess, including a bid that was currently in progress for a bank in Vienna. As their meeting drew to a close, Aidan said, "One last thing. Please forgive me, but I'm such a nosy parker. I understand from one of my fellow directors that you're a countess. Is this true?"

"Yes," said the Countess. "The title was passed down to me when my father died."

"Ah right – sorry to hear about your father," said Aidan.

"Thanks. It was a while ago now," replied the Countess.

"Still, it must have been tough for you. Um, so, er… we've never had blue blood in the firm before. Do we have to address you in any formal way?"

"No," laughed the Countess. "Please don't feel obliged. I don't use my title like that. I prefer to just get on with my life and live and work."

Actually, in saying this, the Countess wasn't being strictly honest. For starters, she loved being a countess, and once she was comfortable and better acquainted with a work situation, she usually ended up larking around with her title. As for being addressed correctly, whilst it was true that she did not insist on this at work or with her friends, her beloved accessories back at Kennington Mansions always called her Madame. Why she had ended up with a French salutation, no one quite knew, but the Countess liked it so much that

11

American Ted and Pussy Original used it consistently.

"And your colleagues? The other employees here. Does it matter if they know who you are?" asked Aidan.

"No. I'm just here to get on with the job. The fact that I'm a countess usually comes out in conversation as I get to know people. It's no problem for me."

"Right. That's good," said Aidan.

The reality was that the whole company knew that the new recruit was a countess because he had let the cat out of the bag at a recent company drinks evening. Since then, everyone had been dying to meet her.

* * *

That evening, Marie waited for the Countess at their favourite cocktail bar, tucked around the back of New Bond Street.

"Gosh, it's busy in here for midweek," said the Countess as she squeezed in on the red velvet seating between Marie and the people at the next table. "Sorry I'm late. I thought I'd better look keen on my first day. I got caught by one of the bosses on my way out, so I had to engage in intelligent conversation with him."

"That's okay," said Marie. "How did it go?"

"Good," replied the Countess. "I'm about to get dispatched to Frankfurt to sort out one of their messy clients. I've been there before. It's not the sexiest place on earth, but as long as they put me in a decent hotel, then I guess I can grin and bear it."

Marie smiled. The Countess did a lot of business travel and much preferred it when her clients paid for business-class flights and a nice hotel.

"I'm sure they will," she replied. "They're based in Mayfair, so hopefully, they don't do things on the cheap. Anyway, what are you drinking?"

"Don't know. G & T? Jack and Coke? Or shall we have a glass of champers to celebrate my new job?"

"Champagne," said Marie. "I was hoping you were going to suggest that."

The Countess had known Marie for a few years now. They had once shared a house together when they were both new to living in London. Initially, Marie had been wary of the Countess because she obviously came from a well-heeled background. It was only a few months on that the Countess revealed to her that she had left home for a while aged seventeen and had still managed to get through her 'A' levels. The Countess subsequently refused family money from her father and went on to gain a first-class degree in Business and Mathematics. As her prejudices dropped away, Marie became firm friends with the Countess.

"How are you?" said the Countess.

"Pretty good," replied Marie. "It was fairly low stress today. One of my horrible weekly meetings was cancelled, so I had a much better afternoon than I'd anticipated."

"Is that the meeting with that silly man who shouts and rants a lot?" asked the Countess.

"Huh-hmm," said Marie, nodding her head.

"I hate people like that," said the Countess. "The bottom line is that they're incompetent and cover this by shouting and screaming. It makes them so bloody difficult to work with."

"Oh yes," said Marie. "He ruins my day at least once a week. I hate him. Let's order that champagne."

They managed to flag down one of the waiters who

crouched down next to them so he could hear their order over the hubbub of other people's conversations and the slow bass beat of the chillout background music.

When the drinks arrived, the Countess took a sip of hers and said, "Ahh, that's better. Now the world is a better place. I just love this stuff!"

"Me too," said Marie. After a couple more sips she set her glass down and then asked the Countess, "Have you heard from the MSL recently?"

"I got an email from him last week," said the Countess. "He said that my leaving party was so wild, it was still being talked about and will be for years to come!"

"That's pretty impressive. It's a shame though that he didn't make it wilder by actually having the courage to make a move on you!" said Marie.

"Yeah – he really kept his distance from me that night. It's quite ironic that he writes about what an outrageous party it was. I've been thinking about him a lot. I just can't get him out of my head. It's so annoying. But maybe this new job will help. Today was the first day that he has disappeared from my mind for a couple of hours. I've really enjoyed being free of him."

"That's good," said Marie. "I think you've done the right thing by taking this opportunity. You'll get over him eventually. If he didn't have the guts to make a move on you at your leaving drinks, then you're better off without him."

"I know," said the Countess. "But it feels so hard. I really thought that something was going to happen once we weren't working with each other. He is The Man I Love And Want To Marry. Making a fresh start back here probably was the right thing to do, given that it was going nowhere – but I've geographically taken myself away from him. Perhaps I should have hung out there just a little longer."

"No," said Marie. "You were starting to get really unhappy, and it was making you crazy. One day, you'll meet someone else. Someone better than him, who won't be afraid to love a countess."

"I hope so," said the Countess. "It is good to be back at Kennington Mansions though. I love my house, and I've been away from it too much in the last year or so."

"Aren't you going to end up in Frankfurt all the time?"

"Hopefully not," replied the Countess. "I'm going to be managing it rather than doing all the work, so with a bit of luck I can pick my own schedule. When I've seen others in this role, they seem to fly in and be on-site for a couple of days a week and then do the rest from the office."

"That sounds good," said Marie. "Working in Mayfair is going to be a real treat."

"Yes. I loved walking up from Piccadilly this morning. Berkeley Square is so wonderfully civilised."

"Did you hear any nightingales?"

"No," giggled the Countess. "But I'll listen out for them tomorrow!"

* * *

After that initial meeting on her first day, the Countess regularly communicated with Aidan by phone and email, but she did not see him again in person until three weeks later. She had begun to spend two days a week in Frankfurt and was working there late one night. All of the Periculum workers had left for the day, except for Aidan, who had made the trip over to check how things were going. The two of them had been reviewing progress on the whole project and the Countess had been going through everything she had achieved since starting there.

"Blimey, it's just gone eight," said Aidan. "Time we were out of here. Let's go and find a drink somewhere."

"That sounds good," said the Countess as she unplugged her laptop, placed it in her desk drawer and locked it away. "It's been a long day."

"Follow me," said Aidan. "I know this great place that's trendy, does fabulous cocktails and is not full of people from this bank. Let's go!"

They went into the main shopping area but then turned off down a side avenue. The Countess had never been this way as she was only familiar with the walk from her hotel to the office. She liked that the buildings had changed from the faceless glass towers of the finance industry to a boulevard with shops and restaurants. There was also something about European cities that smelled different to London.

Fifteen minutes later, they were still walking. Her new-found love of Frankfurt was waning as her shoes were starting to hurt.

"Are we nearly there yet?" she asked.

"Keep with me," said Aidan. "I can tell you are a lady of great taste, and you won't be disappointed with where we are going."

Better not be, thought the Countess to herself.

They took a couple more turns and then came into a small street that was full of restaurants and bars. It had a bohemian feel about it; somewhere where the city's cool people could hang out. Aidan stopped outside one of the establishments.

"This is my favourite," he said. "Though they're all good on this street. We can try another one later if you don't like it here."

The Countess was impressed. The interior was light and modern but not stark. Down one side, in booths, were tables that formed the restaurant section. People sat at the other tables drinking and chatting. At the far end was a long bar which looked as though it contained every possible liquor under the sun. The crowd was mixed and thirty-something. Some wore suits, but most were casually dressed.

"Looks good," said the Countess. "They do food too, but let's have a drink first."

"Ah, we are in luck. Two empty stools at the bar just for us," said Aidan and strode forward to claim them. "They do rather fine martinis," he added as he passed cocktail menu to the Countess.

"Is that what you're having?" asked the Countess.

"Yes. It's a wonderful drink for winding down from the pressures of the day," said Aidan.

"I'll have the same then," said the Countess.

Aidan attracted the attention of the barman and ordered their drinks.

While they were being prepared, the Countess asked, "How did you find this place? I've never been here with the others."

"I worked over here quite a few years ago," Aidan said. "This street has always been a good place to come. I like it because, on the whole, it's not full of business people. I don't tell anyone about it at work. I like to come here to get away from all of that."

"But you brought me here," said the Countess.

"You're different," replied Aidan. "I like you. There's

17

something fascinating about you."

"You don't like the others?" asked the Countess.

"You know what I mean," said Aidan. "Of course they're okay, and everybody works well together, but you know how it is. There are people you work with and there are people you like to spend your free time with. Most of the time, the two don't cross over that much. But you're not like the normal run-of-the-mill office person."

"Thanks," said the Countess. "I've never been normal or run of the mill, and I certainly don't intend to start now."

"Let's drink to that," said Aidan. He passed her one of the martinis, "No normal people here, please! Now. Down the hatch."

He took a large gulp of his martini. The Countess just sipped hers. It was a perfect gin martini – strong enough to cut diamonds and bring a hint of a tear to your eye but with just enough of a pleasing tang as an aftertaste.

Aidan took another gulp, leaving only a small quantity left in the glass. The Countess had never seen anyone knock back a martini in this way. "I hope this is okay for you," he said. "It's quite nerve-racking, deciding where to take a countess, you know!"

The Countess laughed. "This is great. Fabulous martini. There's no need to be nervous. I won't have you beheaded or anything like that."

"Phew," said Aidan. "Can I ask you something? I'm really fascinated by this title thing."

"Sure," said the Countess. "Anything you like."

"Okay," said Aidan. "Tell me if I have got this right. Your dad was the Earl of Kennington?"

"Yes," said the Countess.

"So, do you come from a long line of landed gentry?"

"No," replied the Countess. "My father was a self-made man. He was made a peer for his services to business and to charity."

"What did he do?" asked Aidan.

"Frozam – frozen foods. My dad set that up," said the Countess. "It started with one shop in Northampton, and then he opened them everywhere."

"I remember that. Didn't they make a point of taking on younger people who were unemployed?" asked Aidan.

"Yes," said the Countess. "Especially during the recession in the early 1980s. That's the main reason why Dad got the peerage. And the Earldom of Kennington was created."

"But those shops have gone now," said Aidan.

"Yes," said the Countess. "After he died the other directors sold out to one of the big supermarkets. The branding disappeared, but the factories are still there making frozen pizzas and stuff like that."

"Wow. How fascinating. So, can you sit in the House of Lords?"

"Yes, but not for much longer," replied the Countess. "I think Tony Blair is well on the way to axing the hereditary peers. Going ahead, there will only be a few seats and you'll probably have to get elected by the other peers."

"Would you like to be one of those?" asked Aidan.

"I'm not that bothered at the moment," said the Countess. "It might be quite good when I am older, but given that the average age of the Lords seems to be a hundred and two, I think I'll wait a while."

Aidan smiled. "Yes, I imagine that it's quite a fusty old place." Aidan paused and looked at her curiously. "But there's something else I've been trying to figure out."

19

"Go on. Just ask me," said the Countess.

"So, if your dad made all of that money, why do you work?"

The Countess smiled. She had heard this question so many times. People around her in the workplace could never fathom why she bothered to work so hard and was so driven by her career when she had no financial need to.

"Because I want to," she replied.

"Yes, but why?" asked Aidan.

"Basically, I made a decision many years ago that I would pay my own way in the world and not just live off the family," replied the Countess.

"That sounds very noble," said Aidan.

"It wasn't at the time," said the Countess. "It was all a bit of a mess, and I wanted to spite my father. He was really upset about something I did, and he told me that I was on my own and that he would never support me."

"Ouch," said Aidan.

"It didn't take long before he crawled back to me and tried to patch things up, but I just thought, 'Fuck him! I'll do it my own way anyway.'"

"Impressive," said Aidan. "I guess a lot of young women in that position would have let Daddy install them in a nice flat in Chelsea and become a nanny or take a cookery course or something like that."

"Exactly," said the Countess. "And that just wasn't for me. I wanted to make more of myself. So, even though I was back in favour and he was willing to chuck money at me, I refused it all. I left college, took up residence in a bedsit in a shared house in Finchley and got a job as a trainee accountant."

"And what was his reaction to that?" Aidan asked.

"Ironically, I think he was quite proud of me," replied the

Countess. "My mum hated it though because I didn't earn much money to start with, and I was living in this horrible shithole. She worried that I was losing my old friends and connections, but, as you say, the girls from my school were all doing cookery courses in Chelsea, and I no longer had much in common with them anyway. I didn't have much time either because I had to study so much."

"Accountancy is hard," said Aidan. "I thought about doing it, but I couldn't stand the thought of all those exams."

"It was hard," said the Countess. "And distinctly unsexy too but totally worth it. As soon as I qualified, I got the hell out, got myself a real job in the City and started making decent money. I'm proud to say that I bought my lovely house in Kennington with my own money. Money that *I* had made. It's definitely more satisfying that way."

"So, you actually live in Kennington," said Aidan. "Do you have to because you're the countess there?"

"No, that's just coincidence," said the Countess. "Actually, I was reluctant to because of all the associations with Dad. But property is such good value there, and it's really central, so four years ago I bought a house there. I call it Kennington Mansions. It's a big Victorian townhouse divided into two flats, so I live in one and rent out the other."

"I love those old townhouses. They are so big and have so much character," said Aidan.

"They do," said the Countess. "Even though I took the lower flat for myself it's still a good size and split over two floors."

"Does that mean you get to go upstairs to bed, like in a proper house?" asked Aidan.

"I do," said the Countess. "The living room and kitchen are in the basement and then my bedrooms are on what would

21

be the ground floor. It's a really good layout."

"It sounds like you've been very smart," said Aidan. "What does your mum think of your life now?"

"She's much happier now I'm living somewhere decent. And she's proud of what I do workwise. But having said that, I think she is still waiting for the day that I give all this up, get married and start producing babies."

"Would you give it all up and have babies?" he asked.

"I don't know. I don't think you ever know exactly what you would do until that moment arrives. It would have to be with the right person," the Countess replied. "Unfortunately, I haven't had much luck in that department."

"Don't panic. You'll find your Prince Charming one day," said Aidan. "I'm sure there's no shortage of volunteers to team up with you at our place." He knew this to be true, as practically every man at Periculum had been talking about the Countess. They were attracted by her spirit, the length of her legs and, surprisingly, by the handbag she carried.

The Countess had bought a new handbag at the airport when she made her first trip to Frankfurt. She noticed it at the back of the duty-free shop, hidden away behind the designer sunglasses and Hermes scarfs. It was an old-fashioned style with just a carrying handle and no shoulder strap, creamy white in colour and had crocodile-style indentations in the patent leather.

The Countess was immediately drawn to it. As she examined the bag, she joked with a lady who was standing next to her about its quaint nature.

"It's a bit Maggie Thatcher, isn't it?" said the lady.

"Yes, I guess it does resemble her, and the Queen Mother too," said the Countess. "I think it is fabulous though. I'm very tempted."

The lady obviously did not want to follow the style set by the former leader of the Conservative Party and walked away to browse at other things, but the Countess was transfixed by the design and the unusually pale colour of the bag and decided to buy it. She considered that the colour would be very versatile, as it could be used with any colour of outfit, and the style, though very traditional, would be fitting for her new job. She bought the bag and named it, obviously, the Queen Mum bag.

The Queen Mum bag seemed to have an unusual effect on men. Many of them in the Countess's work environment, both at Periculum and in Frankfurt, commented on it. Surprisingly, it was the quieter, conservative ones – not the more sartorially aware, such as Aidan – who spoke about it. Aidan couldn't work out why the bag had such an effect on these men. The only thing he could think of was that in some strange way, it must have reminded them of their mothers; either that or it elicited some strange Margaret Thatcher fantasy in them!

* * *

One martini became three, and then Aidan suggested champagne. Of course, the Countess needed no persuasion on this one, despite the fact that she felt hungry. Once they were settled with their bottle of Veuve Clicquot, the Countess decided that it was time to probe for the details of Aidan's life.

"What about you?" she asked. "Are you married?"

Aidan laughed. "No, darling. I'll never be married. It's not legal for people like me, and I can't see it changing any time soon."

"I thought so," said the Countess. "But I just wanted to check. Is there a special man in your life?"

"No. Not at the moment. I'm footloose and fancy-free. I was in a grand relationship for five years, but it finished a year ago."

"And how does that feel now?"

"Terrific," said Aidan. "He's gone and is well out of my way, at last. And I got to keep the flat in Notting Hill, so it all turned out very well."

"That's not bad," said the Countess. "At least you have something to show for your heartbreak. What about work? How long have you been at Periculum?"

"A couple of years now," replied Aidan. "I was one of the first team of people who set up the London office. It's been fun. I like the company, and I just love working in Mayfair. It's one hell of a classy place to do business."

"Isn't it?" replied the Countess. "I like that too. It's a very different feel from the City. It has a relaxed opulence about it that the City doesn't. The City has to be go-go-go in order to make all the money, whereas in Mayfair, the money is just there – and people are just playing with it – because they can!"

As the champagne continued to flow, the conversation between the Countess and Aidan rapidly descended from its reasonably polite, getting-to-know-you level to something of a naughtier nature. With dinner long since forgotten, the pair were soon bragging about various sexual exploits and recounting stories of past partners and outrageous events in their lives.

"I have a fancy title too, you know," said Aidan.

"Oh yes, what's that then?" said the Countess as she took a sip of her drink.

"I'm the High Priestess of all Cunts," he replied.

On hearing this the Countess sprayed her champagne across the bar and then almost choked as she tried to swallow what was left in her mouth, whilst laughing at the same time.

"The High Priestess of all Cunts?!" she said as she coughed and spluttered and had to accept a wallop on the back of her shoulders from Aidan. "Fuck me! Where did you get a title like that?"

"It was after a drunken night like this one," said Aidan. "You know that feeling when you've had far too much booze the night before and your skin feels as if it has dirt, grease and a general filth oozing out it? I was so bad that I had to pull a sickie from work. I was croaking away to one of my equally hung-over friends, and I just came out with it. I said to him, 'You know, I feel like a cunt. In fact, I feel like the high priestess of all the cunts in the world.' And that was it. My new name was born, and most of my friends now call me High Priestess."

"I love it," said the Countess. "Can I call you High Priestess?"

"Of course you can, dear. Though you'd better not scream the C-word at the top of your voice across the office."

"No, don't worry, I won't. That word upsets some people, doesn't it? I find it fascinating. People either say it or they don't. And the people who don't get so offended by it."

"I love the C-word," Aidan said. "Cunt! Cunt! Cunt!"

* * *

Around midnight, they realised that they had not eaten, so they ordered food. However, they were so drunk by then that it was wasted on them. Sometime after two o'clock, they staggered back to the hotel and decided to have one final drink in the bar. Of course, this became two drinks, so they did not retire to their rooms until almost four.

The next morning, the Countess awoke just after eight o'clock with a raging hangover. "Shit! Shit! Shit!" she said to herself as she looked at the time. She would usually be arriving at the office by this time. Her hung-over state meant that progress in getting ready for work was slow, so she did not arrive at the office of Deutsche Landesbank until nearly ten. On her way from the lift to her office, she bumped into Aidan, who was looking equally worse for wear.

"You made it in then," he said.

"Of course," she replied. "I've never missed a day of work due to alcohol consumption. How are you?"

"Well, I'm here, in body at least. I'm not sure about mind or spirit though!"

The Countess laughed, "Are you having a High Priestess moment?"

"Partially," said Aidan. "You?"

"Same," said the Countess. "I can't wait to get that plane home tonight though. What flight are you on?"

"The four o'clock," he replied.

"Me too," said the Countess. "Thank God the later one was full when I booked it. This way, we only have to last until just after lunch, then we can get the hell out and find somewhere to quietly die."

"Nonsense, my dear. I expect you to be fully recovered by then and ready for hair of the dog in the British Airways lounge."

"I'll do my best," said the Countess, "but right now, I urgently need the coffee machine or I'm going to collapse."

* * *

That night, back at Kennington Mansions, the Countess was feeling overjoyed at having found a playmate at her new job. "His friends call him High Priestess," she told American Ted. "Or the High Priestess of all Cunts, to give him his full title. Isn't that fabulous?"

American Ted didn't know what to say. He'd heard about this appalling name from the Queen Mum bag, who was severely unimpressed at the whole escapade between the Countess and Aidan.

"It's not very becoming of a countess," the Queen Mum bag had said to American Ted when they were back at Kennington Mansions. "I'm not sure that I can live here if she's going to carry on like that. It is a shame, as she is such a capable woman at work. I'm very impressed with her professionally, but I really can't accompany someone who uses such foul language."

American Ted sympathised with the Queen Mum bag. She was obviously not that kind of bag, but on the other hand, now that she had been purchased by the Countess, she really had no say in the matter. Ever the diplomat, American Ted responded to the bag by saying that he would try and have a word with the Countess about the matter. As her teddy, he did have a duty to advise her if he considered she was acting inappropriately, but this was not going to be an easy task. The teddy bear training that he had received prior to being sold had been geared at comforting children and steering them back to their parent's wishes if they had been naughty. It certainly did not cover how to deal with a strong-minded, capable countess who had a liking for offensive language.

Now that the Countess was putting him on the spot, he had no choice but to speak out.

"It certainly sounds like a fun name, Madame, but to be honest, I wouldn't call it fabulous."

"I think it's great," said the Countess. "The High Priestess of all Cunts. It does have a certain ring to it."

"Yes, Madame, that's for sure – it does have a ring to it. But I can't help thinking that it's not quite the ring that is suitable for a Countess," said American Ted.

"Why not?" asked the Countess.

"Madame, it's quite a vulgar word, and a lady such as yourself really ought not to be using it," he replied.

"You've been talking to the Queen Mum bag, haven't you?" said the Countess.

"Yes, Madame, I have. She is very worried about this development and can't bear the use of that word," said American Ted.

"I thought she had a bee in her bonnet about something. She was very curt with me earlier today," replied the Countess. "Okay, where is she? I'm going downstairs to get her."

The Countess went down to the kitchen where she had left the Queen Mum bag on the table. "Come with me," she said to the bag. "We need to have a chat."

The Countess took the bag back upstairs and sat on her bed. She rested the Queen Mum bag on one knee and American Ted in the other.

"I need to nip this in the bud right now," she said. "Queen Mum bag, you're not happy about Aidan and something we said last night, are you?"

"No, Madame, I'm not," said the bag. "It is a terrible, vulgar word, and a young lady such as yourself should not be using

28

it."

"Don't worry," said the Countess. "I'm hardly going to scream it out loud in the middle of the office. But you need to know this. I've built my career on being able to drink with the right people, and I am not about to stop now. That was a really good night with Aidan last night. Now, I have an ally in my new workplace. That's really important."

"But, Madame," said the Queen Mum bag.

"Please let me finish," said the Countess. "Having him in my back pocket is going to make work a lot easier. I want to do well at this company. I want to have control of the projects that I work on. Being mates with him is going to help that. And, most importantly, he's a really good guy, and I think we can be genuine friends."

"I understand that, Madame. I can see that you are very capable at work. I just…"

The Countess interrupted her, "You just want me to act like a lady."

"Yes, Madame," said the Queen Mum bag.

"Well, I am a lady," said the Countess, "but I'm a modern lady, and we do things differently. I hope you can understand that."

"I do, Madame," said the Queen Mum bag.

"Ted?" asked the Countess.

"Yes, yes, I do, Madame," said American Ted. "You're the boss, and you know what you are doing."

"Thank you." The Countess smiled. "Right, let's get ready for bed. I had hardly any sleep last night, and I'm exhausted. I have to be back on form again for work tomorrow."

The Arrival Of Pussy Deluxe

"You cannot go out on the town with the SC Radcliffe lot," said Marie.

It was a Friday night, and the Countess had just returned from two days in Frankfurt. The project at the Deutsche Landesbank was stalling and the Countess could see that part of the problem was in the way they communicated with their North America division. She had suggested that their key players went to the New York office to exchange ideas and information and build better personal links with the staff there.

When making this proposal she had not intended that she would be part of this delegation, but the client had insisted that she was the best person to facilitate the whole assembly. Aidan had also decided that he would go, as he was keen to meet the senior management in New York. They were due to fly out on Tuesday evening and then have meetings until Friday lunchtime.

"But it would be weird going and not seeing them," said the Countess.

"Have you heard anything from the MSL recently?" asked Marie.

"No," replied the Countess.

"Then don't meet up with him," said Marie. "You need to leave it."

"But it would be really good to see all those guys and go out on the town on the Friday night like we always used to. I could fly back Saturday."

"But if you do that," said Marie, "you'll get drunk, do something daft and be crying over the MSL again. Please don't do that to yourself."

"But it's so much fun there," said the Countess. "I bet Aidan knows some cool places to go. He's pretty wild underneath his immaculately suited exterior."

"Aidan can look after himself," said Marie. "He'll only be interested in gay stuff, and he can do that on his own."

"What about shopping? I won't get time to do any," said the Countess.

"If you go out on the Friday night, you'll be too hung-over anyway. Just this once, come straight home."

"I suppose you're right," said the Countess. "I wish I didn't have to go. It's too soon."

"Apart from this trip, how are you enjoying your new job?" asked Marie.

"It's a good company," said the Countess. "There is so much business at the moment because everyone is under pressure to upgrade their systems. I've discovered that I've become a bit of an expert in banking risk. Some of the other consultants really have no idea about it. They know about implementing software and being a consultant in general, but they don't know anything about the subject matter. It makes me feel kind of smart when I have to explain all the financial products and do all the calculations for them.

"You are very smart," said Marie.

31

"Ah, thanks, so are you," said the Countess. "The new thing for me is the consultancy side. I've never had to juggle clients before, and also, I have to remember that they are the client, and I have to be polite with them – even when they talk complete bullshit, which happened earlier today. I'm having to develop my diplomacy skills."

"I guess you can't be rude to them," said Marie. "Whenever we have consultants in, we always give them such a hard time. I've never really thought about it from their point of view."

"Ah, well now you know that we consultants are human too," said the Countess, teasingly. "Try being nice to them next time."

"Okay," said Marie, smiling. "Do you fancy another cocktail?"

"I'd quite like a glass of bubbly," said the Countess.

"Yes, lovely. Shall we get a bottle?" said Marie.

"Now who's trying to lead me astray! Go on, twist my arm," said the Countess.

"We can celebrate the fact that you're now a fabulous and very expert senior consultant," said Marie.

"Good idea," said the Countess. "I'll get it. My treat." She reached down to the floor and picked up the Queen Mum bag.

"Is this the new bag?" asked Marie.

"Uh-huh," said the Countess as she took out her wallet. Then she held the bag up by its handle in front of Marie. "Do you like it?"

"Very unusual," said Marie. "It looks like something my granny might carry."

"Then she must be a very chic and sophisticated granny," said the Countess. "I was going to name it after Mrs Thatcher but in the end decided she was more like the Queen Mother."

* * *

The next day, the Countess surfaced at around midday. Feeling hung-over, she went downstairs and opened the fridge door in search of something for breakfast. Inside were two bottles of Veuve Clicquot champagne, a butter dish and some cheese. Behind the bottles, she found what she was looking for – a pack of bacon that she had opened the previous weekend.

She took it out, sniffed and examined it. "Thank goodness I bought smoked," she said to herself and put the remaining rashers under the grill.

She took the butter and the milk that was in the door and closed the fridge. She made a cup of earl grey tea, buttered two slices of bread then sat down at the kitchen table while she waited for the bacon to cook.

"Did you enjoy yourself last night, Madame?" asked American Ted. He liked to sit and chat with her on a Saturday morning.

"Yes, we had a brilliant time. I met Marie and we ended up having two bottles of champagne," replied the Countess.

"Gosh – that sounds like rather a lot," said American Ted. "How's your head?"

"I'm hoping that it will feel better when I've had brekkie," said the Countess. "It was nice to just relax together and let our hair down a bit."

"Did you meet any nice men?" asked American Ted. "Marie could do with meeting someone as well."

"Well we did get chatted up quite a bit," said the Countess. "And I vaguely remember snogging some bloke as we were leaving."

"That was most unladylike," came a voice from under the

table. It was the Queen Mum bag.

"Oh, that's where I left you," said the Countess. She picked the bag up and put it on the table. Despite today's lecture on morality, it was always a relief to confirm that she had managed to bring her handbag safely home after a drunken night out. "I don't think I was that bad. Sleeping with him might have been unladylike, but having a snog is pretty harmless."

"A lady would not have been as drunk," said the Queen Mum bag.

The Countess stood up to check her bacon. "Well, that's pretty rich coming from someone who is named after a grand old lady who spends a good part of her life sipping gin and Dubonnet."

"I'm sure that the dear old Queen Mother would never be seen as drunk in public as you and Marie were last night. And she seemed such a sensible girl when you met up earlier in the evening."

The Countess shrugged. "I don't care – it was Friday night. A girl has to have a bit of fun in her life."

"Yes, you do need to have fun, Madame," said American Ted, "but we always like it when you get home safely without experiencing any mishaps along the way."

"Very diplomatically put, Ted," said the Countess, picking him up and giving him a kiss on his head. "Is this bloody bacon ready yet? I'm starving."

* * *

The night before her departure for New York, the Countess packed her things at Kennington Mansions. Even though she would have loved to have stayed the weekend to go shopping and hang out with her SC Radcliffe friends, she carried through on her promise to Marie and had booked her flight home for the Friday evening.

Given that she did not have a night of clubbing planned, there wasn't any need to take Pussy Original, but it felt mean to leave him behind when he had accompanied her on so many trips in the past.

She also decided to take American Ted. "Are you feeling all right about the trip, Madame?" he asked her.

"Mostly," said the Countess. "I've spoken to many of the North American staff from the Deutsche Landesbank on the phone, and it is always good to put faces to names. It just feels weird going there and not meeting up with the MSL."

"I think you should trust Marie's advice," said American Ted. "She knows you well. If he hasn't shown enough interest up to this point, then it's probably best to leave it."

"I know," said the Countess. "But going all that way and not seeing him just feels like a wasted opportunity. What if this were the moment?"

* * *

The trip got off to a very good start. The Countess liked the staff at the Deutsche Landesbank's New York office, and they, in turn, had a lot of respect for her skills and knowledge. As is usual in implementation projects, they felt that they were having a computer system imposed on them from head office and that the German section of the bank did not understand the type of business they were doing in North America. The Countess was easily able to demonstrate the various modules of the software developed by Periculum and show them how it could be tailored for their needs.

As the Countess was packing up her laptop, Aidan came up to her.

"Well done," he said. "You've had this lot eating out of your hand."

"Thanks," said the Countess. "I'm pleased it went well."

"They're not your only fans," said Aidan. "I spoke to Bill Shankey over at SC Radcliffe this afternoon. He was singing your praises too."

"Really?" said the Countess. "I didn't know that you knew him."

"Yes, I worked with him yonks ago," replied Aidan. "Did you have much to do with him when you were there?"

"I didn't work directly with him. He was the project sponsor of the work I was doing, but he wasn't involved day to day," replied the Countess.

"Well, you must have made quite an impression on him because he spoke very highly of you," said Aidan. "Anyway, he's going to round up some of his chaps and meet us for drinks in the bar of The Warwick Hotel tomorrow at six thirty."

"Me as well?" asked the Countess.

"Yes, naturally. You'll know more people than me there," said Aidan. "Why, did you have something else planned?"

"Oh no, nothing like that," said the Countess. "It's just er… you just caught me on the hop that's all. Did Bill say who was coming?"

"No, but you'll probably know some of them," said Aidan. "He said that they missed you there. It will be useful meeting with them because their project is coming to an end, so we can find out what some of their consultants will go on to next."

"Um, yes," said the Countess. "It's a shame he didn't say who was coming. It would have been nice to, you know, prepare."

"I love how diligent you are," said Aidan. "Don't worry, let's just go with the flow and see how the evening pans out."

"Indeed," said the Countess raising her eyebrows. She took a long intake of breath through her nose and then blew the air out through her lips. "Let's see how it pans out."

* * *

That evening, throughout dinner with the staff from Deutsche Landesbank, all the Countess could think about was whether the MSL would be attending the following evening. It took all that she could muster to keep smiling and saying the right things to the right people.

At the end of the meal, Aidan was deciding whether to go on for drinks.

"Do you mind if I bail here?" said the Countess. "I think the jet lag might be catching up with me. If I don't sleep soon, I'll be fit for nothing tomorrow."

"Of course," he replied. "Though I'm surprised at you. I thought this was your town."

"It is," said the Countess. "But if you want me to be productive and polite to the client tomorrow, you're going to have to let me go now."

The Countess walked back to her hotel. She enjoyed being free of everyone and having some time to herself. She turned the corner of Fifty-Fourth Street and headed down Lexington Avenue. However, instead of going straight back to the hotel, she decided to take a small detour as she was only a couple of blocks away from the apartment hotel she had stayed in when she worked at SC Radcliffe.

She loved the way that New York mixed apartment blocks among office buildings with nail bars and tiny coffee shops sandwiched in between. She stopped at a convenience store on the corner of Second Avenue and bought a bottle of water and some fruit before continuing on to her hotel.

Once inside her room, she sat on the bed.

"How's it all going?" asked American Ted.

"It was going great," said the Countess. "Until Aidan told me that we are going to meet up with people from SC Radcliffe after work tomorrow."

"SC Radcliffe?" said Pussy Original. He bounced from the bedside cabinet across the bed to the Countess. "Is the MSL coming?"

"I don't know," said the Countess. "He might be. It is people from Bill Shankey's team."

She picked up Pussy Original. "It's a shame I can't take you with me. I'm sure they would love to see you again. You were quite a star on our nights out. But I don't think it would be a good idea this time."

"That's okay, Madame," said Pussy Original. "I'm sure they will love the Queen Mum bag, even though they can't stroke her, like me."

"Maybe it is not so bad seeing the MSL," said American Ted. "At least you can see how you feel about him now."

"Well, I was starting to get over him," said the Countess. "Now, I just don't know. He might not come though. That's the worst part, not knowing."

"I wonder if *he* knows you'll be at the drinks," said Pussy Original.

"Oh yes, I hadn't thought of that," said the Countess. "Now, that could be interesting. Would he come because he hoped that I would be there, or would he not come because he wanted to avoid me?"

"You could always phone him tomorrow and find out," said Pussy Original.

"I could, but if Bill hasn't invited him, then it would be awkward. And then it will seem like I'm desperate to see him," said the Countess.

"But you are, right?" asked Pussy Original.

"I don't know," said the Countess. "I had got used to the idea of not seeing him this trip, but now, everything has changed. I feel I can't win either way."

"Then leave it to fate," said American Ted. "If he's there, he's there. And if he's not, he's not."

"Easier said than done," said the Countess. "How am I supposed to sleep tonight and function tomorrow? I wish I didn't feel this way."

* * *

It took a while for the Countess to fall asleep. All she could think about was whether she would see the MSL the next evening.

Aidan greeted her the next morning at breakfast. "So how was your beauty sleep? Are you all ready and refreshed to face another day?"

"Yes. That's one way of putting it," she replied. "Where did you go after dinner? Was it a late one?"

"That depends on your definition of late," said Aidan.

"Hmm. Two o'clock?" she asked.

"Just after," replied Aidan.

"That's not too bad," said the Countess. "It could have been worse. How are you feeling? Is it a High Priestess morning?"

"No, actually I'm okay, not too bad. I drank a lot of water throughout the meal, and this breakfast is giving me some much-needed ballast. I can't be out late tonight though. This old queen needs some beauty sleep too. If the SC Radcliffe lot want to rave until the early hours, you'll have to lead the charge."

"Okay, sure," said the Countess. "I'll see what I can do."

Thankfully, she didn't have a further opportunity to worry about the drinks that evening as her meetings were very hectic. There was some friction between the European and North American staff members at the bank, and she spent all day facilitating tense debates. The formal meetings finished at five fifteen, but she stayed behind, chatting with two of the directors from the New York office.

At six o'clock, Aidan interrupted her conversation. "Excuse me, gentlemen, but I'm afraid we'll have to continue this discussion tomorrow. I need my chief of staff here to go to another meeting."

The Countess rounded off the discussion, and the gentlemen left the room. "Thanks for rescuing me," she said. "That was getting a bit much."

"I noticed," said Aidan. "I bet you could murder a drink now."

"Yes," replied the Countess. "A cool G&T with a nice wedge of lemon in it. That will be just the ticket. Have you talked to Bill today? Do you know who's coming from SC Radcliffe?"

"No. He emailed me to confirm and said he'll bring a few of his people with him," replied Aidan. "Have you been in contact with any of your crew there?"

"No," replied the Countess. "I was going to phone them, but I've been too busy here. I suppose we'll just have to get down there and see who shows up."

The Countess and Aidan walked the couple of blocks down Sixth Avenue from the Deutsche Landesbank's offices to Fifty-Fourth Street. Even though it was October, the weather was still mild, and the Countess carried her Burberry raincoat.

"I love this bar," she said as they went into Randolph's at The Warwick Hotel. "It's still got that old-money New York feel about it."

"I know what you mean," said Aidan. "I don't think those old wooden panels have ever been redecorated. It's good for having conversations too. As much as I love the nightlife of this town, it's really hard to schmooze people when you have to shout to be heard. Why don't you grab that area down there, and I'll sort you out a well-earned drink."

The Countess went and sat in one of the dark brown leather tub chairs at a table in the far corner of the bar. From there, she could see the length of the bar and would immediately know when the SC Radcliffe group arrived. Trying to calm herself, she took a couple of breaths and blew them out slowly. Then she decided to pull the neighbouring table a little closer, so it adjoined the one she was at. She laid her coat across another two chairs.

She sat forward in her seat, her legs crossed and with her top leg bouncing on her knee. She bit her lip as she repeatedly looked around the bar. Would the MSL show up tonight?

* * *

Aidan arrived with drinks and sat at the other end of the table in a bid to claim more space. "We're a bit early," he said as he looked at his watch. "How's that G&T?"

The Countess stirred her drink, removed the monogrammed plastic stirrer from the glass and took a sip. "Perfect," she said. "Just what I needed."

They reflected on the day's meetings, the Countess all the time keeping an eye out for their guests. Eventually she saw them. "There's Bill," she said as she spotted him at the entrance of the bar.

"Brilliant," said Aidan as he stood up. "Bill! Over here."

The Countess stayed seated. She recognised two people who sat near Bill's office, Mary, who had brought American Ted for her, a couple of guys she didn't recognise, Dan with whom she had also worked closely; and then, bringing up the rear, was the MSL.

She felt an immediate relief that he was there, but at the same time, her heart lurched. He looked the same as ever, taller than the others, still slim. His dark brown hair was neatly cut, and he was scanning the bar, looking for them. She looked away, not wanting it to appear as though she was waiting for him.

Mary approached first. "You're looking well," she said and came forward to hug the Countess.

"Thanks," replied the Countess, standing up to greet her. "So are you. How are things?"

"Oh, you know," said Mary. "The same as ever. Busy. Dealing with these crazy guys."

"Hey, who are you calling crazy?" said Dan. "Hey you," he said to the Countess and hugged her.

"Hiya," said the Countess. Over his shoulder she looked at the MSL. He was looking down at the ground. The little mark

42

in his skin on his left cheekbone was visible to anyone who bothered to look for that level of detail. Then he looked up. His blue eyes met hers and he smiled.

She finished her hug with Dan and then stepped towards him. "Hey, how are you?" she asked.

"I'm good, very good," he replied. He reached forwards towards her, touched her on the side of each arm and gave her a kiss on the cheek. "You look great. How are you?"

"I'm okay, thanks," she replied, loving the feel of his touch. She also loved that he appeared to be blushing. It was an excellent sign.

They stepped back from each other. "We've been in meetings for the last couple of days with our client. It's nice to get out and see some people that I know," she continued.

"It's good to see you," he replied. "Can I get you a drink?"

"Oh no," she replied. "Drinks are on us tonight. Let me sort that out."

She took everyone's drinks orders and went up to the bar. While waiting, she turned around and looked over her shoulder at the group. The MSL was staring at her, but he looked away as soon as she caught his eye. She smiled and felt warm inside. Perhaps the evening wouldn't be a disaster after all.

* * *

It was an endless hour before the Countess got to speak with the MSL as he was talking with Bill and Aidan. She spent the time chatting with Mary. She was desperate to find out from Mary if the MSL was dating anyone, but she didn't want to come across as needy. While telling Mary about how great it was to be living in her house again and how cute the teddy bear was, her mind was urging, *Go on. Do it. Just ask her.*

She was just about to pluck up the courage when Dan came and stood with them. The conversation veered towards recent projects at SC Radcliffe. The Countess didn't feel she had much to contribute and looked up to see where the MSL was. He had just sat down. Without excusing herself from the conversation, she went and sat next to him. She was pleased that she had brought her favourite navy suit to New York, as it was the best skirt for showing off her legs.

"Hi again," she said.

"Hey," he replied. "Judging by how good you're looking, I think being back in London agrees with you."

"It is nice to be at home," she said crossing her legs towards him. "I'm travelling back and forth to Frankfurt at the moment, but it's only for one or two days at a time. I like being a bit more settled."

"That's good. You had been away from home a lot when you were here. It must be nice to have your life back," said the MSL.

She studied the perfectness of his face and longed to reach out and touch him. "It is," she replied. "I get to see my friends more often. And it's nice not living in a hotel like I used to here. I like my own bed."

He smiled as she said that. "Yes, there's no place like home."

There was a brief pause in their conversation. "So, er... how are things at work since that big risk project ended?" she asked.

"Busy as ever," he replied. "You know how it is. There is always more to do. I'm thinking of moving on too. With the millennium fast approaching, there is so much Y2K work around. Everyone is racing to get their systems ready. I've been a consultant here for over two years now. I told them that I would stay to the end of the next phase of the project, but then I really ought to go."

"So that'll be what, another three or four months?" said the Countess.

"Probably," replied the MSL. "Six, tops."

"What will you do then?" she asked.

"Look for another client. I know people at Clayton's, Bank of America, Chase, UBS. There's bound to be something. And I decided that I'm going to splash out and go to the annual Risk conference next year. It's in Berlin, in the spring."

"I love Berlin," said the Countess. "I haven't been there for ages. Have you been before?"

"No. I've only been to Zurich, London and Paris. And all of that was for work."

"You'll love it there," said the Countess. "Berlin rocks."

"You can show me around," said the MSL. "Presumably Periculum will be there. They are making quite a name for themselves in the risk world."

The Countess noticed that he was leaning in towards her. Did he really want her to show him around Berlin? "Yes, we are doing well as a company," she said. "I don't know who gets to go to those conferences though. It will probably be the directors."

"That might be you by then," said the MSL. "I was chatting with Aidan earlier, and he said you were doing really well."

"Did he?" asked the Countess. "That's good. I'm glad to know that I made the right choice and that I won't get the boot anytime soon."

"I very much doubt that," said the MSL. "You're really good

45

at what you do."

"Thank you," said the Countess. "From you, that is quite a compliment."

"Hey. You know that I've always admired how you work," said the MSL.

The Countess smiled at him. It was a now-or-never moment. "Do you admire me beyond work?"

He paused before replying. "Of course. I think you are amazing. But… err… I think we should just keep talking about work."

"We don't work together anymore," she said.

"I know," he said. He shifted back in his seat. "But it's a small world, and we might in the future."

"Oh. I was just wondering…"

He leaned in again. "I know what you are wondering. But let's just keep things as friends. I think it works best like that." He turned his head and looked into his drink.

"Friends," said the Countess. "Sure." She uncrossed her legs, sat back and took a sip of her drink. She looked around. Bill was deep in conversation with Aidan. Mary and Dan were standing with the other people from SC Radcliffe. Two businessmen were laughing about something at the bar.

The MSL picked up his glass and drank from it. "So, are you here for the weekend?"

"No, I'm flying back tomorrow evening," replied the Countess, still looking up at the others.

"That's a shame. There's a bunch of us going out tomorrow night. You could have met up with us again," said the MSL.

She returned her gaze to him. "I have to get back."

"Big weekend planned?" said the MSL.

"I'm out with my friends on Saturday. I'm not sure what

we're doing yet."

"Somewhere cool and trendy in London?" he asked.

"Probably," said the Countess. "There's a new bar opened in Clerkenwell that we might try. Maybe dinner. I'll find out when I get back."

He nodded. "Well, so long as you have fun. And stay out of mischief."

The Countess smiled. "Mischief usually finds me."

"Do you still have your pussy bag?" asked the MSL.

"Of course," replied the Countess.

"That's probably how the mischief starts."

"Maybe," said the Countess. "But it's fun. Harmless really. It's just a leopard-print handbag."

Their conversation paused again. The Countess took a large swig from her drink and then drained the rest of the glass. "Well, it's been lovely chatting. I'd better circulate though. You know how it is when you're hosting drinks. Can I get you another one?"

* * *

"Friends, fucking friends!" The Countess stormed back in her hotel room, worse for wear from drinking too much.

The Countess was undressing as she talked. She took off her shirt, screwed it up and threw it in the general direction of her suit carrier.

"I've got loads of *friends*," she continued. "What I need is a *boy*friend, but he doesn't want that."

She laddered her tights as she took them off, swore and threw them in the bin. "He is always so pleased to see me and a little bit embarrassed too. I can tell he likes me. Why doesn't he act on his feelings? He's so confusing! And it's so disappointing, so fucking... *disappointing!*" Then she stomped off into the bathroom to take a shower.

Back in the bedroom, American Ted, Pussy Original and the Queen Mum bag assessed the evening.

"See, Ted, I told you how she is when she's seen him," said Pussy Original. "She always gets so upset."

"She's not crying yet, but it can't be long before she does," said American Ted. "I don't think I've ever seen her rant like this. You've met the MSL. Is he worth all this heartache?"

"Yes and no," said Pussy Original. "There's definitely some chemistry between them, and he is very fond of her. From what I can make out, they had a very strong working relationship, and they went out a lot after work. He's an all-round nice guy and he'd make an ideal boyfriend for her, but for some reason, he doesn't want to take that step."

"Hmm," said American Ted. "Queen Mum, you saw it all first hand. What do you think of the situation?"

"The Countess was very well thought of by everyone who attended tonight's drinks," said the Queen Mum bag. "That particular gentleman was also popular within the gathering. She pushed him though. She tried to steer the conversation about whether he admired her outside of work, and he didn't want to go there."

"That's interesting," said American Ted. "So she tried to tell him how she felt."

"She shouldn't have done that," said the Queen Mum bag. "If a man is genuinely interested, he would say so. If he says nothing, then a woman should leave well alone."

"That's new too. She never spoken to him like that when she worked here," said Pussy Original.

"No wonder she's hurting," said American Ted. "It must have taken a lot of courage to do that. And it didn't work out."

"It's too bad she had to see him tonight. She has been trying so hard to forget him," said Pussy Original. "At least she took Marie's advice and isn't planning to stay the weekend and get hurt more."

"He asked her about that," said the Queen Mum bag. "He said it was a shame that she couldn't go out with her ex-colleagues tomorrow night."

"What did she say?" asked American Ted.

"She said that she had to get back to London," replied the Queen Mum bag.

"Good for her," said Pussy Original. "The Countess of old would have changed her flights and stayed anyway."

"That's encouraging," said American Ted. "Let's see how she is when she gets out of the shower."

The Countess emerged from the bathroom wrapped in a large white bath towel and sat on the end of the bed. Pussy Original, the Queen Mum bag and American Ted all looked at each other, then American Ted walked over to where she was sitting and spoke.

"How are you feeling now, Madame?"

"Like shit," she replied, and then, "Sorry, I'm just so frustrated by him. One minute he tells me I look good and he's pleased to see me and then he doesn't want to take it any further. What am I supposed to do?"

"Exactly what you're doing, Madame," said American Ted. "It sounds like you handled it really well."

"But it hurts so much. And I'm so fed up with having to cope with this. I just want to be with him. We'd make each other happy. And we could get married and have kids and live

49

happily ever after. But he doesn't want that, and it makes me so sad and so… ugh!" She thrust her head into her hands.

"It'll be easier when you get back home again, Madame," said Pussy Original. "Then you won't have to see him again and be reminded of your pain."

"But I will see him again," said the Countess, through her fingers. "He is going to the annual Risk conference next spring. Periculum is bound to be a big player there, and since I'm their star attraction at the moment, you can bet your bottom dollar that they'll send me. It feels as if I'm never going to escape from him. Just when a bit of time has gone by and I've started getting over him, I have to go through it all again. Either that or I'm going to spend the next few months yearning for him, and I'll never be free of these feelings." She banged her fist down on the bed.

*　*　*

The Countess woke up as agitated as the previous night. She wandered around her hotel room distractedly as she packed up her bags and got ready to check out.

"Good morning," said Aidan when he met up with her in the hotel lobby.

The Countess looked up at him, and he caught the haunted expression on her face. "Gosh, what's up with you? Did you have a bad night?"

"Sort of," said the Countess. "Come on, let's get a cab."

The Countess remained silent for most of the cab journey. As they approached the offices of the Deutsche Landesbank, Aidan spoke. "We've only got a couple of meetings. Hopefully, we can get done by lunchtime and have the rest of the day off.

What time is your flight back?"

"Seven o'clock," said the Countess. "I'll probably need to leave around three in order to get ahead of Friday-night traffic. When are you going back?"

"Tomorrow," said Aidan. "I thought I'd see if I could find myself some mischief tonight."

"There's plenty of that in this town," said the Countess.

"I was wondering whether you fancied having lunch together, if her ladyship feels a little happier by then," said Aidan. "I don't know about you, but I'm sick of wining and dining clients. It's been a pretty full-on trip hasn't it?"

The Countess smiled. "Sorry, yes, hopefully, I'll have cheered up by then. Lunch would be lovely. It would be perfect actually, as then I can get a cab straight off to the airport."

"That's a date then," said Aidan.

Their respective mornings went according to plan, and they were both wrapping up with the client by midday. They found a small Italian café just around the corner that they liked the look of.

"Fabulous," said the Countess as they stood outside, looking at the menu. "A big plate of creamy warm pasta is just what I need to see me through until I get fed on the plane later. Let's do it."

They went inside, ordered their food and then chatted about the time spent with their client in New York. Their food arrived, and they continued analysing how the trip had gone and also what the strategy should be once the Countess was back in London. As they were finishing up their pasta, the conversation turned to the drinks the previous evening with SC Radcliffe.

"They're a good bunch," said Aidan. "I can see why you had so much fun working there."

"Yes, it was a blast most of the time," said the Countess.

"They all spoke very highly of you," said Aidan.

"Ah, that's really lovely," said the Countess. "I enjoyed my time there."

"The client is really impressed too," said Aidan.

"Thank you. That's good to know," replied the Countess.

"There was one person last night who sang your praises most of all, and he didn't seem to be able to take his eyes off of you," said Aidan.

The Countess shifted uncomfortably in her chair. She assumed that Aidan was talking about the MSL, but if he couldn't keep his eyes off her all night, then why did he give her the brush-off? "Oh really," she said. "And who was that?"

"Ed Crawford," said Aidan. "Have you got something going on with him?"

"No," said the Countess. "We get on very well. People often think that."

"He's a decent bloke. Bit of all right too. He'd be a great boyfriend for you. You need someone who's intelligent and sorted in their life. He obviously likes you," said Aidan.

"I beg to differ with you there," said the Countess. "He doesn't want to be with me."

"How do you know that?" asked Aidan.

"Because I tried to steer the conversation that way last night, and he was having none of it," replied the Countess.

"How strange," said Aidan. "When I spoke with him, he talked about you the whole time, and later on, he kept looking over at you. I assumed that you both had a secret tryst lined up for later."

"I wish," said the Countess. "No, there is absolutely nothing going on."

"His loss," said Aidan. "Is that why you were miserable this morning?"

The Countess nodded. "Let's just say that I could have done without seeing him this week."

"Sorry," said Aidan. "I wondered what was wrong. Do you want to change the subject?"

"In a minute," said the Countess. "Last night, Ed mentioned the annual Risk conference in Berlin. Do we go there as Periculum?"

"Yes, we'll be there," said Aidan. "It's a riot. I've been the last couple of years. By day it's all talk about risk regulations and pricing models and boring stuff like that. Then by night, everyone gets totally shitfaced and some serious mischief goes on. I usually come back completely exhausted and in need of a liver transplant. I even managed to pull last year, which isn't bad considering it is a mainly hetero crowd."

"Well done," said the Countess. "Will I be going?"

"Definitely," said Aidan. "Actually, I was wondering if you would like to present one of the sessions. You were brilliant at demonstrating our software this week."

"Sure," said the Countess. "I've never done anything like that, but I'm sure that I could. It sounds like a lot of fun."

"You'll be great. You're a natural," said Aidan.

"It's a shame we can't use Deutsche Landesbank as a case study," said the Countess. "But I can't imagine them being happy with revealing all their proprietary data to the market."

"Don't worry. We'll figure something out," said Aidan. "Is Ed going?"

"He said he had decided to go," replied the Countess.

"Then maybe you'll get another bite at his cherry, so to speak," said Aidan.

"Yeah, maybe," said the Countess.

* * *

After lunch, Aidan disappeared off to start enjoying the delights of New York City. The Countess lingered around outside the restaurant and then half-heartedly looked in the window of the neighbouring antique shop.

She looked at her watch. It was one forty-five. She had just over an hour until she needed to get a cab to the airport. Bloomingdales, her favourite store, was only five blocks away. In her condition, there was only one thing that could help – retail therapy.

She loved wandering around Bloomies and thought of it as her New York "mother ship". She tried a couple of perfumes and bought some of her favourite skincare products. Then she went up to one of the womenswear floors and had a brief look around. She didn't really have time for any serious shopping, but the chance to relax and take in the atmosphere lifted her spirits.

On her way out she decided to check out the handbag section. Initially, nothing grabbed her attention but then her eyes fell upon a light brown fur bag, which was locked in a glass show cabinet. It was of a simple style, a rectangular body section, not dissimilar in size to a fur muffler, with a fur shoulder strap. The Countess was transfixed by it.

"Can I help you, ma'am?" said a sales assistant in the usual attentive American way.

"Yes," replied the Countess. "Can I look at this bag, please?

It's gorgeous isn't it?"

As the assistant fiddled with the key to the cabinet, she chatted with the Countess. "Yes, it's of a very high quality. Those stripes running through it give the appearance of real fur, but actually, it's fake."

"Really?" said the Countess. "It looks so real."

"It's from La Maison De La Fausse Fourrure in Paris. They're the best when it comes to fake fur," said the assistant.

The assistant handed the bag to the Countess. As she held it, its size and the softness of its fur made the whole experience reminiscent of stroking a long-haired cat. The Countess loved it instantly.

"It's beautiful," she said. "How much is it?"

"Let's have a look," said the assistant and turned over the price tag. "A hundred and thirty-five dollars, plus tax, of course."

The Countess kept stroking the bag. "It's lovely. I can't believe it's not real."

"I can assure you, ma'am," said the assistant, "that nothing died to make this bag."

The Countess held the bag up to her left cheek. A snap decision was required. She needed to get back to the office, pick up her bags and go to the airport. "I love it," she said. "I have to take it."

"Okay, ma'am. Please come this way."

The Countess paid for the bag and then went outside onto Lexington Avenue to hail a cab. She was very eager to admire her new purchase, and as soon as she was safely inside a taxi, she took it out of its brown carrier bag to stroke it. Now she had another pussy, and this time, an extremely upmarket one. She decided that the bag would be called Pussy Deluxe.

"Hello, my new pussy," she said as she stroked him.

"Hello," he replied. "I must say, I was very glad that you bought me."

"Oh fab, you talk. Then I must tell you your name. It is Pussy Deluxe."

"That's unusual. I like it. I hope you will enjoy my soft feline feel."

"Oh yes," said the Countess. "You're lovely. I've got another furry bag back at my hotel. He's called Pussy Original. You two will be able to hang out together now."

"These are interesting names for your bags. I look forward to meeting Mr Pussy Original."

The taxi pulled up at the offices of the Deutsche Landesbank. "I'll be two minutes," she said to the driver. "I just have to pick my stuff up from reception, then we can go straight off to JFK."

She dashed inside and picked up her suit carrier and laptop bag from behind the security desk. As she turned to leave, she bumped into Aidan who had just come out of the lifts.

"Hi," she said. "What are you doing here? I thought you were done for the afternoon."

"Hello," he replied. "I got all the way back to the hotel and realised that I'd left some of my notes here, so I had to come back and get them."

"What a bugger," said the Countess. "Are you going off to play now?"

"Yes. I thought I might have a disco nap and then go out and hit the town later. Someone's been shopping. What did you buy?" he said.

"A new furry handbag," she said, reaching inside the carrier to pull out Pussy Deluxe. "Isn't it gorgeous?"

"That reminds me," said Aidan. "Last night, they were telling me about one of your handbags and said that I should ask you if I could stroke your pussy. What's all that about?"

The Countess smiled. "I'll have to tell you that over a drink when we've got more time. Anyway, you can stroke this pussy if you like. He's called Pussy Deluxe." She offered the bag to him.

"It's been a while since I stroked one of those," said Aidan as he put his hand on the bag. "Oh, it's lovely and soft. Is it real fur?"

"No. It's fake. Good though isn't it?" said the Countess. "Have a lovely time tonight, and I'll see you next week in the office."

* * *

On arrival back at Kennington Mansions the following day, the Countess unpacked her bags and introduced her new purchase to her other accessories.

Pussy Original's heart sank. He took one look at the new bag and felt that he was about to be upstaged. How could he compete with this new, posh and exceptionally well-groomed specimen from a top department store in New York? Pussy Original had been bought by Marie from a market stall in Camden and was looking decidedly worse for wear after a year or so of hard clubbing and stroking with the Countess. Now, the Countess appeared to have replaced him.

His worst fears were confirmed when the Countess had finished unpacking and left the bedroom to go downstairs.

"I have no idea what this pussy thing is about, but since I have the word 'deluxe' in my name, I guess I outrank you," said Pussy Deluxe. "The Countess has just purchased me for a very large sum," he looked Pussy Original up and down, "and I can't imagine something as scruffy as you being anywhere near as expensive."

Pussy Original was horrified at this. "You stuck-up bastard," he said. "You'll never get away with this. You may be of a better quality than me, but you're new here, and you're named after *me*, so I remain the boss. As the Countess's accessories, we have to work together. The Queen Mum bag takes care of the Countess's formal needs, whereas she uses me for all informal occasions. Your role will probably be somewhere in between, so you had better be nice to both of us."

"You're out of business now," said Pussy Deluxe. "You're old, scraggy and dirty. She won't use you anymore. She has me now, and she adores me. Look how happy she was to show me to you. You should have seen the way she stroked and fussed over me in the taxi after leaving Bloomingdales."

Pussy Original retaliated, "She may like stroking you, but you are too big to go clubbing. And that's what the Countess does most weekends. For that, she needs a small bag, and I am of perfect size."

Pussy Deluxe would not let up. "She has to hold you in her hands though. With me, she can hang me on her shoulder, thus leaving her hands free for whatever exploits she wishes."

"No," said Pussy Original. "You are too big. She dances wildly, and she needs the minimum of clutter. It's really hot in those places. Your fur would be too warm against her."

"Well I guess we'll have to see who she chooses," said Pussy Deluxe.

Pussy Original raised his voice, "*I* am the Countess's pussy. You'll never be as popular as me. Without *me*, she would never have been inspired to buy *you*."

"Whatever," said Pussy Deluxe. "I can't help it if I find it hard to associate with someone of such a ragamuffin look and background."

This was the last straw for Pussy Original. He gave Pussy Deluxe a hard shove in the side. Pussy Deluxe struck back with his shoulder strap and before long, a full fight ensued. The Countess, on hearing the commotion, came back upstairs.

"What is going on here?" she said as she bent down, picking up both bags and prising them apart.

"Nothing!" they both said, almost in unison as if they were two naughty children caught fighting in the playground.

"Well, it didn't sound like nothing to me," replied the Countess.

"It was Pussy Deluxe, Madame," said the Queen Mum bag, who had been watching the brewing commotion. "He was saying very cruel things to Pussy Original."

"Is this true?" she said to Pussy Deluxe.

"He hit me first," said Pussy Deluxe.

The Countess turned to Pussy Original. "Did you hit him first?"

Pussy Original said nothing.

"I paid good money for him, you know," said the Countess. "I don't want him ruined before I've had a chance to use him."

"Sorry, Madame," said Pussy Original.

"And you," she said, giving Pussy Deluxe a gentle shake, "you need to learn some diplomacy. This is a peaceful household, and I won't have you upsetting my other accessories. Now, get back in your Bloomingdales bag and stay there until I choose to use you." She lobbed Pussy Deluxe, with a perfect shot, into the brown paper carrier bag which was still standing by her wardrobe.

As she put Pussy Original back down on the bed, she said, "And I expected better of you."

The Countess went back downstairs, lay down on the sofa and took a nap. She hated flying back from New York and trying to get through a whole day of jetlag. Normally, she didn't let herself sleep, but she was meeting her friends later that evening and knew she wouldn't make it through without getting some rest.

She awoke three hours later and found Pussy Original curled up at her feet.

"Oh, hi," she said. "What are you doing down here?"

"I'm sorry, Madame," he said. "I shouldn't have started that fight. I was just worried that's all."

"Worried about what?" she asked as she sat up and put Pussy Original on her lap.

"Pussy Deluxe. He's so posh and perfect and new," said Pussy Original. "And I'm looking a little worse for wear these days. Does this mean it's the end of the road for me?"

"What do you mean, the end of the road?" asked the Countess.

"Well, now you have your new bag, you won't need me anymore," said Pussy Original.

"Don't be so silly! Of course I need you. Pussy Deluxe might be more upmarket, but that doesn't make him any better than you. Anyway, he's too posh to take out on the town. Do you want to come out with me tonight?"

"Yes, Madame, I'd love that," said Pussy Original.

"Okay, well I'm glad that we've got that sorted. Now, let me give Marie a ring and find out the plan for later."

Two More Pussies

Time passed, and the Countess settled into her job at Periculum. She had to make a couple more short trips to Frankfurt and had flown out to Basel and Vienna with Aidan in an effort to win new business. Her attendance at the Risk conference in Berlin had also been confirmed by Periculum, and they had managed to secure her a slot on the official programme where she would combine a demo of their software with her at-the-coalface experience of risk systems implementations.

One evening in November, she had arranged to meet Marie after work at their usual haunt behind Bond Street. She left the office with time to spare and decided to pop into Fenwick's. Now that winter had begun to arrive, she knew that they would have their new fur collection out; fake-fur stuff, of course.

She walked through the main door and cast her eyes around, looking for the right section. Then her eyes fell upon it, a whole display next to the escalators with everything from fur cushions to slippers to throws to handbags. The area resembled a pet shop rather than retail finery. The Countess walked straight over and, trance-like, walked around touching, stroking and examining everything. There was so much there that she hardly knew where to begin. She particularly liked some slippers that were in a long-haired dark blue and black fur. The fur stuck out and up in a way that resembled a Peruvian guinea pig. She searched for her size but sadly, could not find it. In an attempt to ease her disappointment, she told herself that a young career-countess was far too trendy to wear slippers at home when deep down, she just knew that her life would not be complete without the furry footwear.

After giving up on the slippers she decided that she had better leave the store and continue on her way to meet Marie. Just as she was leaving, she noticed a handbag in the same fur as the slippers. It was absolutely delightful. A ball of fluff with two small navy leather handles protruding from the top. The fur and its crazed sticking-out nature, as well as the unusual dark blue tone, reminded the Countess of a marvellous coat she had once tried on in a shop in New York. It had been made from Mongolian sheepskin and resembled a long-haired rug that had had a corkscrew perm. The colour of the coat had been the same dark blue and black colour as the new bag. She picked it up and stroked it across her cheek. Then she held it from its handles in front of her and admired it.

"Mongolian Sheep Pussy," she said to herself. "It has to be."

She immediately took the bag to the cash register.

Mongolian Sheep Pussy was excited that she had been purchased. She had been sitting in the shop for quite a few days and had started to panic that nobody liked her. *Oh, I wish I wasn't such an unusual colour*, she had thought to herself. *Why can't I just be a brown or black fur bag like those ones over there? That's what people expect from fur, and that's what they seem to be buying. Why am I blue? Whoever heard of a blue fur bag?*

When Mongolian Sheep Pussy had seen the matching blue slippers and cushions arrive in stock, she had become excited, no longer feeling alone in the strange colour. Unfortunately, that excitement soon turned to dismay as the slippers sold like hotcakes and she was still left alone, unwanted. When she had seen the Countess getting excited about the slippers, she'd had bitter thoughts – *Another one who wants slippers and not me!* This turned to an almost spiteful glee as the Countess had rummaged through them but had been unable to find her size.

At the eleventh hour, when the Countess turned and spotted her, Mongolian Sheep Pussy could not believe her luck. Suddenly, her heart was pounding with the anticipation that someone was going to buy her. *I take it back about the slippers*, she thought. *You're obviously a lovely lady. Please buy me. I'll be really good. I promise. Please buy me!* Her willing the Countess towards her had worked. Mongolian Sheep Pussy was beside herself with joy. *I'm being purchased, I'm being purchased!* her heart sang out as the sales assistant removed her security tag and packed her into a Fenwick's carrier bag. The Countess, as usual for a handbag purchase, was enthusing with the sales assistant about the unique and very cute design of the bag and how it reminded her of a coat she had tried on in New York. The sales assistant agreed with her and asked if she had seen the slippers. "Yes, they're lovely," replied the Countess, "but I couldn't find my size."

Thank goodness, thought the bag.

* * *

The Countess now needed to hurry for her date with Marie, so she rushed out of the shop and arrived five minutes later at the nearby bar.

"I'm sorry I'm late," she said as she found Marie and sat down across the table from her. "I've just been in Fenwick's, and I've bought a fabulous new pussy. Check this out." She took the bag out of the carrier and held her up for Marie to inspect.

"She's called Mongolian Sheep Pussy," she continued, "because it reminded me of that crazy coat I once tried on in New York."

"It's very sweet," said Marie. "It looks more like a guinea pig or some other small fluffy creature though. Are you sure it's not alive?"

"I don't think so. Perhaps we should get it a bowl of water and a lettuce leaf just in case," laughed the Countess.

"In that case, we had better get two bowls because I have something for you," said Marie.

"For me?" asked the Countess.

"Yes," said Marie as she handed the Countess a bag. "I saw it at the weekend, and I immediately thought of you. I know you've not been too happy recently, so I thought you might like this as an early Christmas present."

The Countess thrust her hand inside the bag and pulled out another furry handbag, but its style was quite different to Mongolian Sheep Pussy. It was a small grey knapsack-style bag with grey fur pom-poms on the end of its drawstrings.

"It's fantastic!" laughed the Countess as she jiggled the bag about to make the pom-poms bounce. "Pussy With Balls."

"It has to be," said Marie.

"Thank you so much," said the Countess. "I love it. Now I have two new pussies today. Amazing." Then, taking a bag in each hand she played with them saying, "Mongolian Sheep Pussy, this is Pussy With Balls. And Pussy With Balls, this is Mongolian Sheep Pussy. I hope you'll both be very happy with me at Kennington Mansions."

After thanking Marie profusely, she took the bags off the table, put both of them into the Fenwick's bag and turned her attention to the cocktail menu. While the two friends were chatting, the two new bags began to whisper to each other.

"We've been given names then," said Pussy With Balls. "I like yours. I've never met a Mongolian sheep. Have you?"

"No. Can't say that I have," replied Mongolian Sheep Pussy. "Your name is funny. But it makes you very strong and masterful. I'm sure that no one will mess with you."

"Thanks, love," replied Pussy With Balls. "I'll make sure that no one ever messes with you, either. If you're ever in trouble, you just let me know."

"Thank you. That's very kind of you. Did you know that we now belong to a countess?"

"Really?" said Pussy With Balls. "How do you know that?"

"At Fenwick's just now, when she bought me, the Fenwick's woman said something about a countess on her credit card."

"Now you say that, I have overheard something like that from Marie. I've been sitting in a carrier bag in her house all week and a countess was mentioned a couple of times. So that's her then?"

"Yes. It must be. Isn't it exciting? I wonder if she lives in a palace," said Mongolian Sheep Pussy.

* * *

"Oh, that's a good martini," said Marie as she sipped her drink. "Have you heard from the MSL since your New York trip?"

"No," said the Countess. "I emailed him in New York to say that I'd be at the Risk conference next year, and he replied to that. But I haven't heard anything else."

"So, he knows you're going," said Marie. "How do you feel about the conference now?"

"From a work point of view, it's really good," said the Countess. "But as far as he's concerned, it's a bit mixed. Sometimes, I just can't help being excited at the prospect of seeing him again, but I know that I shouldn't read that much into it. It's only going to be four days and he'll probably come out with all that friends crap again."

"You'll have to make sure that you give a stunning performance at your presentation so he is deeply impressed with you and decides he just can't live without you," said Marie.

"If only it were that easy," said the Countess.

"Why is he being so clueless?" said Marie.

"That's the sixty-four-million-dollar question," said the Countess. "Even Aidan said that he looked like he was really into me, so I just don't understand why he doesn't want to do anything about it."

"Maybe he isn't ready. It has to be the right time for a bloke," said Marie.

"And when it is the right time, they settle down with the first girl that they meet," said the Countess. "Given that I'm not in New York anymore, that girl is unlikely to be me."

"Unless it's the right time for him next spring," said Marie.

"Hm, along with those flying pigs," said the Countess. "I can't keep getting my hopes up for him. I've got to move on. I need a nice man who lives here in London. You do too."

"That would be lovely," said Marie. "Let's go looking for one next weekend. You could take Mongolian Sheep Pussy out clubbing. She's the perfect size, just big enough for the essentials. And then you can use her to reel in a nice bloke for

66

both of us!"

"Okay," said the Countess. "It's a plan."

The Countess and Marie decided to stay and have another cocktail, and then they made their way to a nearby restaurant for dinner. Before going their separate ways, the Countess once again thanked her friend for the gift of Pussy With Balls.

* * *

Pussy Original was sitting on the Countess's bed, enjoying the fact that she had recently got into the habit of making her bed every day. She used to leave it in a mess until one day, she noticed American Ted struggling to climb out from, and walk over, the heaped-up quilt.

"It's easier when I make the bed isn't it?" the Countess had said at the time to Pussy Original.

"Well, Madame, yes, it is nicer for us. But you know, we understand that you are a busy lady," he had replied.

"No, that's a poor excuse," said the Countess. From then on, most days, she shook out the quilt and straightened it.

Pussy Original heard the Countess arrive home. A couple of minutes later, he heard her footsteps coming up the stairs. She entered the bedroom, and he noticed she was carrying a bag.

"Hello, Madame," he said. "How was your evening?"

"It was lovely, thanks," said the Countess. She sat on the bed and put the carrier bag on the floor. Then she put Pussy Original on her lap and stroked him. "I met Marie for drinks and then we grabbed a bite to eat. How's life been at Kennington Mansions today?"

"Oh, you know," he replied. "We sit around and ponder the

meaning of life together. Pussy Deluxe likes to think he has an answer for all the world's problems."

"That's because I do," said Pussy Deluxe who was on top of the blanket box.

"Really?" said the Countess. "In that case, what do you think about the millennium bug?"

"I think those computer programmers should have written the date properly back in the 1960s and 70s," replied Pussy Deluxe. "If only they had used four digits instead of two, then we wouldn't be worried about what will happen as we approach a new century."

"I agree with you," replied the Countess. "But if they had, then there wouldn't be this scramble to correct all the computer systems, and I wouldn't have as much work. Then I wouldn't earn as much money..."

"And you wouldn't be here," said Pussy Original, glaring at Pussy Deluxe. It was always nice to get one over on him.

"I doubt that," said Pussy Deluxe. "Quality will always win in the end."

"Okay, you two," said the Countess. "Let's not get started on that again."

"What have you got in the bag, Madame?" asked Pussy Original.

"Yes, that's what I came to talk to you about," said the Countess. "I want you to know that I have a couple of new pussy bags. One I bought myself, the other is a gift from Marie. They're both very lovely, and I hope you will get on well with them."

Pussy Original braced himself. It was inevitable that the Countess from time to time would buy other bags. Sometimes, as in the case of the Queen Mum bag, it was no threat to him, other times he knew that he would gradually be replaced.

"Madame," he replied. "That's exciting. Let's have a look at your new specimens."

The Countess reached into the bag and pulled out Marie's gift.

"Okay," she said. "This is Pussy With Balls, and he is an early Christmas present from Marie. Isn't he fabulous? I do love his furry balls."

"Yes. Nice. He is very practical too, Madame," said Pussy Original. "He's big enough for your book as well as your usual wallet and things. He'll be very useful for travelling too because you'll have space for all those extra travel documents," said Pussy Original.

"Yes, you're right," said the Countess. "You're so thoughtful."

"And what about the other one, Madame?" said Pussy Original.

The Countess once again fished inside the Fenwick's bag and took out Mongolian Sheep Pussy. "This little ball of fluff is Mongolian Sheep Pussy."

Pussy Original liked this bag. She was an unusual colour with very long fur, but she looked classy too. "Very cute, Madame. She looks quite expensive and cultured."

"I guess she is," replied the Countess. "She is made by La Maison De La Fausse Fourrure, same as Pussy Deluxe."

Pussy Deluxe heard this and immediately piped up, "Oh, a cousin of mine. Thank you so much, Madame. It's nice to have a bit of class around here."

Pussy Original's heart sank. He dearly hoped that the new bag didn't have the same temperament as his arch-enemy. His mind was put at rest though as Mongolian Sheep Pussy immediately spoke.

"Good evening," she said in a very sweet voice. "I understand that my name is Mongolian Sheep Pussy, and this is my friend, Pussy With Balls. What are you called?"

"I am Pussy Original; you're all named after me. Welcome to Kennington Mansions."

"Thank you," said Mongolian Sheep Pussy. "And who are you?" she asked Pussy Deluxe.

"I am Pussy Deluxe. Like you, I am from the *superior...*" he glanced at Pussy Original, "...La Maison de la Fausse Fourrure. It is a pleasure to meet one of my own kind."

"Were you purchased at Fenwick's too?" asked Mongolian Sheep Pussy.

"No. I was bought by the Countess on her most recent business trip to New York City. She purchased me in Bloomingdales of Lexington Avenue."

"How exciting," replied Mongolian Sheep Pussy. "You are very well travelled then?"

"Yes. I like to think so."

Pussy Original was not happy about this exchange, as Mongolian Sheep Pussy had unwittingly walked straight into the trap of letting Pussy Deluxe talk himself up. Thankfully, it seemed as though he might have an ally in the other bag.

"'Ello, mate," said Pussy With Balls. "I'm from London, born and bred."

"Yes. Me too. I'm from Camden Market," said Pussy Original.

"Oh. I'm from just up the road from there. I was bought from some craft shop in Chalk Farm," said Pussy With Balls.

"Looks like we've got a lot in common then," said Pussy Original. "Welcome to Kennington Mansions. I was bought by Marie as well. She has excellent taste."

Pussy Original saw that the Countess was smiling. He was relieved, as he didn't want the new bags to cause any trouble for her.

* * *

The following Saturday, the Countess went to Knightsbridge to return a blouse she had bought at Harvey Nichols. She decided to use Pussy With Balls and had filled him with all her bits and pieces, including a book that she planned to read while having a coffee.

As usual, she checked out the handbag section before leaving the store. Nothing in particular caught her eye, though she did pick up one or two bags and examine them. While she was doing this, Pussy With Balls slipped down her arm, so she repositioned him back on her shoulder. His pom-poms on the end of his drawstrings must have swung out as she did this because the next thing she knew, a man, wearing a tight black t-shirt said, "Hey! I'm being attacked!"

The Countess looked at him. Although she hadn't realised what had happened with the pom-poms, she did notice that he had rather lovely biceps.

"Your bag," said Mr Biceps. "One of these things hit me." He took hold of one of the pom-poms and showed it to the Countess.

"Oh. I'm so sorry," she said. "Are you hurt?"

"No, I think I'll survive. That's some crazy bag you've got there."

"Thanks," replied the Countess. "It's new. My friend bought it for me this week. It's the first time I've gone out with it, and already it's misbehaving."

"She chose well. I like it," said Mr Biceps.

"Yes, she is very good at buying me bags," said the Countess.

"Are you into handbags then?" asked Mr Biceps.

"Yes," said the Countess. "I love them."

"Well, you might be just the person that I need to help me. It's my mother's birthday tomorrow, and I thought I'd buy her a new bag."

"What a lovely present," said the Countess. "Have you chosen one yet?"

"No. They all look the same to me," he replied.

"Do you need some help?" asked the Countess.

"Yes, that would be great. Do you mind?"

"No," said the Countess. "I love handbags. Don't worry, you're in expert hands."

The Countess and Mr Biceps spent the next ten minutes or so browsing the bags. The Countess asked sensible questions about the style of his mother's existing handbags and the colour of her outfits. Eventually, they selected a duck-egg blue Osprey bag. It was rectangular shaped with a zip across the top and two matching handles, with a detachable shoulder strap.

"Ask them to gift wrap it," said the Countess as they walked towards the cash desk.

"Good idea," said Mr Biceps.

While the sales assistant packed up the bag, he added, "Thank you ever so much for helping me. Could I buy you a drink in return?"

"Um, yes, okay then," said the Countess. "There's a really good bar on the fifth floor. I do have one thing to ask you first though?"

"What's that?" asked Mr Biceps.

"Obviously, a girl needs to be careful before she accepts a drink from a man she's never met before. So, I just need to check that you're not an axe murderer."

"That's a very sensible thing to check for," said Mr Biceps. "And I can one hundred per cent guarantee to you that I have never murdered anyone, axe or otherwise."

"In that case, I accept your invitation," said the Countess.

"I've heard that there is quite a scene in the bar."

"Yes. It's really busy in the evenings," said the Countess. "Anyone who's anyone comes here."

"So, are you a regular?" he asked as he took the posh paper Harvey Nick's bag from the sales assistant and put his wallet back into his pocket.

"I come here sometimes," said the Countess. "I wouldn't call myself a regular though."

"Where do you normally go?" he asked as they started walking towards the lift.

"I quite like places in the West End. There are some lovely bars tucked around the back of Regent Street and Bond Street. At weekends, we tend to go to Clerkenwell or Islington."

"Clerkenwell is getting really trendy these days isn't it?" said Mr Biceps.

"It is. I like it there," said the Countess. "It used to be this nothing boring place, but now, there's some really interesting stuff happening around St John Street and south of Islington High Street."

They got into the lift, and Mr Biceps pressed the button for the fifth floor. "I love how London always changes. An area will go from really rough to really posh in no time at all. Look at Fulham."

"I know," said the Countess. "Ten, fifteen years ago, you

wouldn't dream of living there, but now it's the place to be. Where do you live?"

"I used to live in London, but now I live in Sydney. My family are there." The lift doors opened. "Wow, great view," he continued as they stepped out of the lift. "What can I get you to drink?"

"Er… I'll have a Jack Daniels and coke please," said the Countess.

The Countess had only ever been to the bar in the evening when it was rammed with London's trendy set. However, mid-afternoon on a Saturday, there was only a handful of people there.

They perched on stools as the barman busied himself with Mr Biceps' order. In no time, he was handing the Countess her drink.

"Thanks very much," she said. She held her glass up to his, "Cheers to handbags."

"And expert helpers," replied Mr Biceps, chinking his glass against hers.

"So, are you Australian, because you don't sound it?" asked the Countess.

"I'm not," replied Mr Biceps. "My family moved there ten years ago, and a couple of years later I decided to follow them."

"But it's your mum's birthday tomorrow. Is she over here as well at the moment?"

"Yes. My sister is getting married next week to an English guy, so we're all back for the wedding."

"Well, you can tell your mum that a countess helped you to pick out her handbag."

"You?" asked Mr Biceps. "A countess?"

The Countess nodded.

"Wow," he replied. "She'll like that. So, where do you live? In a palace or something?"

"No," replied the Countess. "In a flat in Kennington."

"Kensington?" he asked.

"No, Kennington," she repeated.

"Oh, yes. I know. Just over the river. I bet that's another up-and-coming area."

"It is," said the Countess. "Even though it is central, it used to be a wasteland in terms of places to buy a pint of milk on a Sunday. A couple of years ago, they began building swanky flats, and now, we even have one of those posh convenience stores."

"I'm impressed," said Mr Biceps. "Now, you'll never have to run out of milk again."

The Countess and Mr Biceps talked about their work and families before the conversation came back around to his sister's wedding. "You could come with me if you like," he said.

"Oh, that's really sweet of you," said the Countess, "but I think it might be a bit too much. You don't want to be hanging around with me when you need to be involved with your family. I bet your mother has a ton of jobs lined up for you on the day."

"Yes," he said. "You're probably right. But I'd like to see you again. Would you like to come out with me one evening this week?"

It was a tough one. He was a good-looking man, with a great sense of humour and bought nice presents for his mother. She couldn't deny that they'd hit it off, but he wasn't the MSL.

Mr Biceps sensed her hesitation. "It's okay," he said. "You're still worried that I might be an axe murderer."

"Well, you can never be too careful," said the Countess, relieved that he was letting her off the hook.

"That's true. Safety first. Okay, how about this. I'll write down the name and number of my hotel, and if you want to meet up, say, Wednesday night, why don't you give me a ring?"

* * *

Later on, back at Kennington Mansions, Pussy With Balls was regaling the tale to Mongolian Sheep Pussy. "So, I flung my pom-poms out as far as I could to see if I could hit the guy, and I did."

"And then what happened?" asked Mongolian Sheep Pussy.

"Well, he started chatting to our Countess and then he asked her out for a drink."

"Really," said Mongolian Sheep Pussy. "How romantic. The Countess needs a nice man. How did it go?"

"Not so good," said Pussy With Balls. "They were chatting along well and everything. And he was a decent man. Would have made her a nice boyfriend, but when he asked to see her again, she turned him down."

"Oh, no," said Mongolian Sheep Pussy. "And he sounded so lovely. Why did she do that?"

"I don't know," said Pussy With Balls.

"Didn't you ask her?" asked Mongolian Sheep Pussy.

"No," replied Pussy With Balls.

"Why not?" asked Mongolian Sheep Pussy.

"I didn't think it was my business," said Pussy With Balls. "She's her own woman."

"Of course it's our business," said Mongolian Sheep Pussy. "We need to look out for her interests at all times. And it would be really great if she was married to someone tall and handsome and lived happily ever after."

"*You* ask her then," said Pussy With Balls. "I'm a guy. I can't talk to her about things like that."

"Don't worry," said Mongolian Sheep Pussy. "I will. As soon as I can."

Mongolian Sheep Pussy's chance came later that evening. The Countess was putting away some of her clothes from where she had dried them on the radiator. Mongolian Sheep Pussy was bursting to talk to her, but there were too many of the other accessories lounging around in the bedroom. So she followed the Countess downstairs.

The Countess picked up a pile of her underwear and was about to head back upstairs when she nearly tripped over Mongolian Sheep Pussy.

"Mongolian Sheep Pussy," she said. "What are you doing there? I almost trod on you."

"I was just coming downstairs to get some peace and quiet," said Mongolian Sheep Pussy. "Pussy Deluxe is bragging about his life again, and I'm bored of listening to him."

The Countess laughed. "Yes, he does like to go on, doesn't he?"

The Countess put her clothes back on the kitchen table and picked up Mongolian Sheep Pussy. "Are you settling in okay?" she asked the bag. She sat down at the table and placed the bag on her pile of laundry.

"Oh yes," replied Mongolian Sheep Pussy. "I love it here. There's always something going on, and you have such a lovely house."

"Thank you," said the Countess. "I'm glad you're happy. Are those boys upstairs treating you okay? They're not playing you up or anything are they?"

"Oh no. They're lovely," said Mongolian Sheep Pussy. "I really like Pussy With Balls. I kind of feel an affinity for him because we arrived here the same day. And Pussy Original is such a sweetheart. And American Ted too. He's a real gentleman."

"So, just Pussy Deluxe who's a bit annoying then," said the Countess.

Mongolian Sheep Pussy giggled. "He's not so bad," she replied. "He just likes the sound of his own voice a bit too much."

"I'm glad that everything is okay for you. I like my accessories to be happy," said the Countess.

"It's nice having boys around," said Mongolian Sheep Pussy. "It's a shame you haven't got a man, Madame. Oh, I hope you don't mind me saying that."

"It's okay," said the Countess. "Yes, I'd love to have a man around here too. But it hasn't worked out that way yet."

"What about that guy you met with Pussy With Balls?" said Mongolian Sheep Pussy. "He sounded really nice."

"Yeah, he was a nice guy," said the Countess. "And he is obviously well brought up and thoughtful, buying his mother a decent handbag."

"Was there something you didn't like about him?" asked Mongolian Sheep Pussy.

"No, he seemed okay," said the Countess. "I just… well, it didn't feel like there would be any spark. He was nice. And if he lived here that might have been different. But…"

"But what, Madame?" said Mongolian Sheep Pussy. "Is there something wrong?"

The Countess sighed. "Well, there's this guy that I like. I

78

used to work with him. He lives in New York. I'm trying to forget about him, but I just can't get him out of my head, and I can't imagine liking anyone else as much as I like him."

"Oh, that's a shame," said Mongolian Sheep Pussy. "So, didn't it work out with him?"

"Sadly no," said the Countess. "I really wanted it to. And I could tell he liked me. But he had this thing about us just staying as friends. The last time we spoke I got very upset."

"Oh, I'm sorry, Madame," said Mongolian Sheep Pussy. "What's his name?"

"Ed," said the Countess. "But I always refer to him as the MSL. It's short for Man She Loves. It's this silly thing that Marie and I came up with."

"So, is there any chance with him, the MSL?" asked Mongolian Sheep Pussy.

"No, it doesn't look like it," said the Countess. "But I just don't seem to be able to get past him. And the bummer is, that when someone really nice like that Mr Biceps guy comes along, I'm just not interested. I can't be bothered. I just think I will always be wishing he was the MSL, so I might as well save us both the heartache."

"Oh, Madame. I'm sorry you're hurting so much. But one day you will stop thinking about this MSL chap and then you will meet someone else."

"I wish I could be so sure of that," said the Countess. "He just won't get out of my heart. I really wanted to give things a go with him. And of course, my mind worked overtime as to where this might have led. But despite the looks he often gave me and the chemistry we had, he just didn't want to take things further. In the end, I couldn't bear working alongside him."

"Wow, you really do like him a lot," said Mongolian Sheep Pussy. "Did you think he could be the one?"

"Yes, I did," said the Countess, "and deep down I still do. But he doesn't want to be with me."

Christmas

It was Christmas Eve, just before lunchtime. The Countess had been busy wrapping presents and packing up all the things she needed to take back to her mother's for Christmas. She took a break from her preparations, made herself a cup of tea and sat at her kitchen table, reflecting on what had passed in the previous twelve months.

The year, as usual, had been a busy one. She had left her job at SC Radcliffe and had established herself very successfully at Periculum Software Solutions in Mayfair. Although she had tried to cut her losses over the MSL and move on from him, she still could not shake him completely from her thoughts. It seemed that he was simply refusing to budge from her heart, no matter what she did to try and forget about him.

As she sipped her tea she thought also about her lovely accessories. They had mushroomed throughout the year, and now she had quite a collection. Though she did not use him as much, Pussy Original remained her rock, along with the ever-wise American Ted. The Queen Mum bag was her favourite formal handbag, though she often found the bag's old-fashioned lectures about morality to be a little tiresome. Mongolian Sheep Pussy was the most delightful bag she had ever owned, and she enjoyed her pure-hearted sense of romance. Pussy With Balls became great friends with Pussy Original and helped to defuse the tension between Pussy Original and Pussy Deluxe. Though she knew that Pussy Deluxe did not have the nicest of personalities, as the winter had closed in, she had started to use him nearly every weekend. Not only was he big enough to put all her bits and pieces in, but his fur was good at keeping her hands warm if she had to wait around outside somewhere. She frequently offered him to her friends for the same purpose.

Jesus, he thought one day as he was being passed around her friends, *It's bad enough being one of her pussies without turning into her muff!*

She smiled as she thought about them hanging out on her bed every day and wondered what exactly they got up to when she was out of the house.

American Ted appeared at the kitchen doorway.

"Hello, Ted," she said to him.

She picked him up and sat him on the table in front of her.

"Hello, Madame," he replied. "Are you looking forward to Christmas?"

"Not especially," replied the Countess. "There's nothing like being alone at this time of year and going to your parents like a waif and stray to make you feel crap."

"I'm sure your mother is pleased that you're going," said American Ted.

"Yes, she is," said the Countess. "She's alone too, and I can't leave her like that. I just hate all my nosy aunts and cousins who, without fail, will ask me if I've got a boyfriend yet and then give me the sad look when I say I haven't. That's the last thing I need at the moment, but once again, it is going to be the usual miserable ritual."

"Do you miss your father at this time of year?" asked American Ted.

"Sort of," said the Countess. "We had a weird relationship. Everything blew apart when I was seventeen. We patched it up, but we were never as close. Not like when I was younger. I was his little girl."

American Ted laughed. "At your height? Were you ever little?"

The Countess smiled. "Yes. I know it is hard to believe when you see me now. I was a little girl once, though I was always the tallest in my class at school."

The Countess paused, lost in her own thoughts for a moment. "Christmas used to be so much fun," she continued. "My dad would dress up as Santa on Christmas morning. He had this fantastic costume from when he ran Christmas parties at his company. Even when I was still young enough to believe in Father Christmas, I knew that there was a real Santa, and then on Christmas morning, it was just my dad larking about."

The Countess put her cup down and leaned back in her chair, smiling. "One year, I got a bike. We still lived on a normal street back then. This was before he made it big and we moved into the posh house. He came out the front with me, still dressed as Father Christmas, while I rode up and down on the pavement. He was always so jolly. He waved at all the other kids and at any cars going by."

"He sounds like quite a character," said American Ted.

"He was. He would do anything for me," said the Countess. "We used to spend a lot of time together. He would take me out for walks. Sometimes we took the train down to London, and he would show me the sights. Other times, I would go into his office. I loved it when we did that. I always felt like I was entering a grown-up world, and he trusted me enough to let me in."

"He must have been really happy to show you off," said American Ted. "You don't have any brothers and sisters, do you?"

"No, it's just me," said the Countess, picking up her tea and taking another sip. "I think they struggled to conceive because I was born quite late. Mum and Dad were in their early thirties, which was quite old to have kids in those days. When I did come along, I suppose I was like a kind of fortunc child to them."

"No wonder he loved to spoil you," said American Ted.

The Countess looked into the distance again as she held her mug. "Yes," she said as she nodded. "He did love to spoil me."

"When did he die?" asked American Ted.

"Six years ago," said the Countess. "It was such a shock. He was only fifty-nine. One day, he had a heart attack and just keeled over. They couldn't revive him."

"That must have been really hard for you," said American Ted.

"I suppose," said the Countess. "It was much tougher for my mum, obviously."

She took a last sip of her tea, looked at her watch and put her mug down decisively.

"Right," she said, standing up. "Enough chit-chat. I need to get a move on."

* * *

Her family duties were done for another year, and on the afternoon of 27th December, the Countess headed back to

London. She loved being in London in the days between Christmas and New Year and always booked this time off work. She enjoyed being able to lounge around at Kennington Mansions and get up late, as well as going to the sales. It seemed to her that for a few days, the whole of London was relaxed, as most people took holidays, left their suits in the wardrobe and went out to the shops in their civvies.

The day after her return to London, she happily took her place amongst the throngs of sale shoppers and explored the department stores in the West End. She had decided to take Pussy Original out on the shopping expedition. Since her other bags had arrived on the scene, she had barely used her faithful Pussy Original, so she decided to give him a treat.

"I'd be much more suitable for shopping, Madame," Pussy Deluxe had said as the Countess had plucked Pussy Original from the other bags that were, as usual, lounging around on her bed.

"Oh, shut up," said Pussy With Balls. "If the Countess wants to use Pussy Original then that is her choice. Have a lovely afternoon, Madame."

"Thanks," said the Countess as she smiled at the bickering between the bags.

"What are you going to buy, Madame?" asked Mongolian Sheep Pussy.

"I'd quite like a new winter coat," replied the Countess. "And whatever else takes my fancy."

"I'm sure that La Maison de la Fausse Fourrure makes coats in the same fur as me," said Pussy Deluxe. "If you bought one of those, then you would coordinate wonderfully when we go out at the weekends, Madame."

Pussy Original and Pussy With Balls groaned as Pussy

Deluxe said this, but Mongolian Sheep Pussy sought to have a more balanced approach. "She doesn't just have to buy La Maison de la Fausse Fourrure. She can have any coat she likes."

"Thanks for the suggestion," said the Countess. "I'll have to see what I can find." Though she would have loved a coat in the same fabric as Pussy Deluxe, she did not want to take the risk of it having the same personality.

She searched several department stores, looking for something which grabbed her attention. She saw two coats which fitted the bill, but they were either the wrong size or the wrong colour. The Countess became despondent and decided to take a break and have a coffee.

Pussy Original could sense her frustration. "Don't worry, Madame. Something will leap out at you. Perhaps today is not the day to buy a coat."

"But it's sale time," said the Countess. "It's the perfect time to buy something truly fabulous at a knock-down price. I usually do so well at this time of year. But yes, let's not be defeated. There is still Fenwick's."

"Madame, we've already been to four department stores. Aren't you exhausted?" asked Pussy Original.

"Yes," replied the Countess. "But we can sleep when we're dead. In the meantime, there's work to be done."

With that, she set off on the short journey to New Bond Street. Before entering the shop, the Countess decided to walk around it and look at the window displays. Normally, she would have just dived straight in, but something inside told her not to. Her intuition served her well, for in the last window she came across a very elegant sheepskin jacket.

"It's amazing," said the Countess. "It looks so soft. What do you think?"

"Lovely, Madame," said Pussy Original. "But it's white. It's not going to be very practical."

"I don't care," replied the Countess. "It's fantastic. Let's go in and have a look."

The Countess walked into the shop. "Right, coats section," she said to herself. "I think that's on the first floor."

She ran up the escalator to the first floor and walked around the coats. However, everything was dark in colour, and the beautiful white sheepskin was nowhere to be seen.

"Bugger," said the Countess. "I can't find it."

"Ask someone," said Pussy Original.

"Good idea," replied the Countess.

She cast her eyes around and eventually found an assistant. "Hi, excuse me, please," she said. "There's an amazing sheep-skin coat in the window, but I can't seem to find it."

"We've probably sold out then," said the assistant. "It's sale time. All of the stock's on the shop floor."

"Am I looking in the right place? Is this where it would be if you had it?"

"Yes, madam. This is the coats section." The assistant tried to dismiss the Countess and walk away.

"But I can't see anything like it."

"Then, as I said, madam, we've sold them all."

"Can I try the one in the window, please?" asked the Countess.

"No, madam. It's for display only."

"Really?" said the Countess. "I've just come back from New York, where the shop assistants fall over themselves to sell you something. Are you sure that I can't try it on? Please?"

The assistant sighed. "All right then. Wait here."

"Thank you," said the Countess.

"Well done, Madame," whispered Pussy Original to her as they waited. "I can't believe she didn't want to let you try it. She shouldn't treat customers like that."

Five minutes later, the assistant reappeared with the sheepskin coat.

"Brilliant, thanks ever so much," said the Countess. She slipped on the coat and looked in the mirror. "Wow, this is fabulous. I want it. It's a perfect fit."

The Countess took a minute or two to revel in the coat. It was so soft and delicate. She touched the soft suede hide on the sleeve then turned up the collar and rubbed the luxurious-feeling fleece against her cheek.

"How much is it?" she asked the Countess.

"Two hundred and ninety-nine pounds," said the assistant "knocked down from six."

"Mm, it's not cheap," said the Countess, "but I love it. And compared to six hundred, you could say that I'm saving money."

She thought for a moment as she continued to stroke the collar. "Where do I pay?" she asked finally.

The Countess reluctantly took off the coat so that it could be packed away in a bag when really, in the same way that she used to insist as a child on wearing her new shoes home, she wanted to wear it now.

"Mission accomplished," she said to Pussy Original when they got outside the shop. "Let's get a cab home. I'm knackered."

In the taxi back to Kennington Mansions, the Countess chatted with Pussy Original. The sheepskin coat remained silent in the bag.

"I think you've got something very special there, Madame,"

said Pussy Original. "But you'll have to make sure that you keep it clean."

"I know," said the Countess. "I can't wait to get it home and try it on again. We're going to have to come up with a name for him. The obvious is Dolly, after Dolly the cloned sheep."

When they arrived home at Kennington Mansions, the Countess took the sheepskin coat straight out of the bag and held the collar up to her face. She revelled in the soft feel of it. Then she buried her face into the furry sheepskin lining of the back of the coat. "It's just divine," she announced. "I could cover my face in it from now until the end of time."

* * *

The sheepskin coat looked around at his surroundings. There was a large white sofa standing on polished floorboards. On the glass coffee table were glossy magazines, one he noticed was in a foreign language. Above the fireplace was a large, gold-framed mirror. This place was stylish. Maybe it wouldn't be so bad living here.

That thought was short lived when the Countess took him upstairs to meet the other accessories.

"My darling accessories," she said. "We have a new member of our team today. This is Dolly, named after Dolly the sheep."

The new coat was aghast. He had a name, and it was *Dolly*!

"Isn't he just lovely?" said the Countess.

"Madame," said Mongolian Sheep Pussy. "He looks terrific on you. He's so soft. Where did you get him?"

"Fenwick's," replied the Countess. "We went all around every other shop, but there wasn't a decent coat in sight. Then, when I was so tired that it was tempting to give up, we popped down to Fenwick's, and this is what I saw in the window. But when we tried to find it inside, this really unhelpful sales assistant told us it was sold out and then was really reluctant to go and fetch the display one. I had to plead with her before she'd cooperate, but look – thank goodness she did!"

The Countess took the coat off to show Mongolian Sheep Pussy what he was like inside. "It's like a cat," said Mongolian Sheep Pussy. "Are you sure this is a sheep, Madame?"

"Yes, definitely," she replied as she sat on the edge of the bed and hugged the furry lining once again. "But you're right, it does look like a Persian cat. One of those posh long-haired things that sits on a cushion all day long."

"You'll have to get him a cushion then," said Pussy With Balls.

"And a saucer of milk," laughed Pussy Deluxe.

"Hello, coat," said the Countess. "Can you miaow?"

"No," he replied.

The Countess continued to stroke him.

"Maybe you should call him Persian Dolly?" said Mongolian Sheep Pussy.

"Persian Dolly. What a great name!" said the Countess. "I love the sound of that. What do you think, everyone?"

"Persian Dolly sounds good, Madame," said Pussy With Balls.

"Yes, Madame. Quite distinguished and exotic," said Pussy Deluxe.

"It was my idea. I'm clever," said Mongolian Sheep Pussy.

"Yes, very clever," said the Countess. She picked up Mongolian Sheep Pussy and gave her a kiss. "Well done, my lovely Mongolian Sheep Pussy. Hey, I wonder if you two are related?"

"No, Madame," said Mongolian Sheep Pussy. "I'm not really

a sheep."

"Oh yes," said the Countess. "Okay, Persian Dolly it is. Now, I have to go and get something to eat. I'm going to leave Persian Dolly here. Would you look after him for me?"

"Of course, Madame," said Mongolian Sheep Pussy.

The Countess left the room and went downstairs to make herself some dinner. Meanwhile, Mongolian Sheep Pussy began to initiate the new coat to life at Kennington Mansions.

"Well then, Persian Dolly. Let's introduce you to everyone," said Mongolian Sheep Pussy. "This is Pussy Original. You've met him already, no doubt. He was the first of us accessories, and it's thanks to him that we are all called pussy something or other. Anyway, that's another story which I'm sure you'll hear at some point."

"Yes, we've already met," said Persian Dolly.

"Over there is Pussy Deluxe," continued Mongolian Sheep Pussy. "We're the same fake-fur label. Incidentally, I'm from Fenwick's too. It's a lovely store isn't it?"

"Welcome to the madhouse," said Pussy Deluxe. "Don't worry, you'll get used to hanging out with the riff-raff."

"You mind what you say," said Pussy With Balls. "Just because you're posh doesn't make you better than us. And you, Persian Dolly, I hope you can show us that you've got better manners than that nasty piece of work."

"That's Pussy With Balls," said Mongolian Sheep Pussy. "He's a great friend to me. We arrived here at the same time. Now, this is the Queen Mum bag. She's lovingly made by Furla in Italy."

"Enchanted," said the Queen Mum bag.

"Likewise," said Persian Dolly.

Mongolian Pussy finished the introductions. "And last, but

by no means least, this is American Ted. As the Countess's teddy bear, he's the boss. We have to do what he says."

"A bear?" said Persian Dolly. "You want me to take orders from a teddy bear? I don't think so. If it's okay with you, I'll just keep myself to myself."

* * *

The Countess was very pleased with her purchase of Persian Dolly, and this put her in a good mood in the days running up to New Year. On New Year's Eve, it plummeted. It was just after three o'clock, and she had been relaxing on her sofa, leafing through the weekend newspaper which contained the usual round-up of the passing year. She was reminded of a conversation she had once had with the MSL where they talked about what they usually did at New Year. The Countess had told him that no matter where you were or whatever you were doing in Britain, everyone tunes into Big Ben.

"Same over here," the MSL had said. "Except everyone watches the ball drop at Times Square. Hey, you should fly back over for New Year this year. You'll love it."

So that had been the Countess's original intention. She was going to see in the new year in New York City with the man she loved. Sadly, it had not worked out like that. Her perfect dream of kissing her perfect man at the perfect moment as the ball dropped in the Big Apple was not going to happen. Despite having the most fabulous night lined up in one of the most exclusive clubs in London, it just could not compare to what might have been.

She started to cry. Then she got annoyed with herself for getting upset. *I've cried enough over that man this year,* she thought. *And I'm not going to give him any more tears.* She wiped her eyes and decided to investigate the contents of her fridge to see if there was any appealing food that would cheer her up. She cut herself off a lump of cheese and ate it while surveying her food cupboard. She found a box of chocolates that she had been given for Christmas and decided to open them. Then she went back to the fridge and took a bottle of champagne from it. Apart from the occasional gin and tonic, she never drank at home on her own. However, today, she decided to open the champagne and celebrate the fact that the forthcoming year could not possibly be as heartbreaking as the one just finishing. It felt very naughty to be opening a bottle of champagne just for herself.

She poured herself a glass, waited for the bubbles to settle and then topped up the glass. She took a sip and said aloud, "Ah, fabulous." She tucked the box of chocolates under her arm, picked up the bottle and the glass, returned to the living room and sat back down on the sofa. After stuffing a chocolate in her mouth and taking a gulp of champagne, she picked up the TV remote and started channel-surfing to see what was on. She came across *The Sound of Music* and decided to watch that. She arranged herself so that she was sitting on one half of the sofa with her legs up on the other half, box of chocolates in her lap and glass in her hand. There she sat, scoffing one chocolate after another and drinking champagne. Before long, half of the chocolates had disappeared and she was into her second glass of bubbly. She loved *The Sound of Music* and thoroughly enjoyed herself, singing along to all the songs.

After a while, and another glass, she felt chilly and went upstairs to get a cardigan. Singing *Doh, a deer, a female deer,* she went into her bedroom and rummaged around in her

93

wardrobe to find something warm to wear.

"Hello, my lovely handbags," she said as she opted for a hooded sweat top. "And hello, Ted," she added as she put the top on and zipped it up. Persian Dolly was hanging from the handle of one of her wardrobe doors on a coat hanger. "Ah, my darling coat," said the Countess to him as she took the hanger from the door, held Persian Dolly up to her face and snuggled against his soft white fur. "I'm going to wear you later. I can't wait to show you to my friends."

Pussy Original, Pussy With Balls and Mongolian Sheep Pussy were sitting together near the middle of her bed. American Ted was on the pillow and Pussy Deluxe was on the wooden blanket box next to the wardrobe.

"You're cheerful, Madame," said Pussy Original.

"We've been listening to your singing," said Mongolian Sheep Pussy. "I never knew you had such a nice voice."

"I'm not sure that I do," said the Countess. "But champagne certainly helps."

"Are you drinking, Madame?" said Pussy With Balls.

"I most certainly am," said the Countess. "And eating some lovely chocolates."

"What are you celebrating?" asked Mongolian Sheep Pussy.

"I'm celebrating the fact that the MSL is just not worth it, and I'm never going to cry about him again," said the Countess.

"Oh," said Mongolian Sheep Pussy.

"Anyway, I need to get back," said the Countess. "The captain and Maria are just doing their love song. It'll be the bit where they kiss any minute now and then they get married. See ya later."

The Countess went back downstairs and the accessories continued to chat. They could hear her singing *How Do You*

Solve A Problem Like Maria? which indicated that she was now watching the wedding scene.

"Does she always drink like this?" asked Persian Dolly, who was once again affronted that the Countess had stuck her face all over his clean, white fur.

"Not at home," said Pussy Original. "She likes to have a few when she is out with her mates. I've never seen her drink like this."

"She's pretty toasted. I wonder how much she's had," said Pussy With Balls.

"I wish the MSL had loved the Countess," said Mongolian Sheep Pussy. "Then she'd have her own wedding. I think she would be much happier if she could be with him."

"Yes, he's certainly caused her a lot of grief this year," said Pussy Original.

"And she's drowning those sorrows now," said Pussy With Balls. "Do you think we ought to go down and check that she's okay?"

"Not now," said Pussy Original. "Let's wait until she has finished watching the film and then we'll see what she does next."

"I hope she sobers up before she goes out tonight," said Pussy With Balls. "Otherwise, she's going to be trashed."

"Oh, listen to you lot," piped up Pussy Deluxe. "Who are you? The Samaritans? Just because she's having a glass or two, it doesn't mean that she's about to top herself. She's a big girl, and she can handle her drink."

"That's as may be," said Pussy Original. "We're just concerned about her, that's all."

"This will do her good," said Pussy Deluxe. "She needs to forget about the MSL and just get out there and find someone

95

else. Next time you're out with her, Pussy With Balls, perhaps you could hurl your pom-poms at a bloke who doesn't live in Australia. Maybe she'll score tonight."

"Oh, shut up," said Mongolian Sheep Pussy. "I notice that you haven't helped her find anyone."

"I'm staying out of her love life," said Pussy Deluxe. "It's an emotional minefield, and only she can sort it. Nothing that you lot do will make a blind bit of difference."

* * *

The Countess watched until the end of *The Sound of Music* and then dozed off to sleep on the sofa. When she awoke, it was almost seven o'clock. "Shit, shit, shit!" she said when she noticed the time, as she had only an hour to get herself ready for her evening out. She drank the small quantity of champagne that was left in her glass, grabbed a glass of water from the kitchen and then went upstairs to get showered.

"How's your head, Madame?" asked Pussy With Balls as she entered the bedroom.

"I'm not sure," said the Countess. "I still feel half asleep. Drinking in the afternoon is always fun at the time, but it makes you feel so crappy later on."

"Maybe you'll feel better when you've had a shower," said Mongolian Sheep Pussy.

"I hope so," said the Countess.

The Countess arrived only a few minutes late to the restaurant where she was meeting her friends.

"Fab coat," said Marie as the Countess settled herself. "Is that the new sale purchase?"

"Certainly is," replied the Countess.

"And its name?" asked Marie.

"Persian Dolly," said the Countess. "Dolly the sheep, but really, inside it looks like a Persian cat."

"Oh yes, it's lovely and soft," said Marie as she stroked the collar. "We've already ordered some fizz. I'm guessing that you don't have any problems with that."

"Not at all," said the Countess. "I've already had a few glasses today. I'm only just sobering up."

"Really?" said Marie. "Who were you with earlier?"

"No one," said the Countess. "I just saw a bottle in the fridge and felt like it. I ate a whole box of chocolates too, so I'm feeling a bit fat now."

"Never mind. We can get healthy in January," said Marie.

Following dinner, they all went to a private club at which the Countess had managed to secure everybody an invitation. By this time, as the champagne and wine she'd had with dinner accumulated on top of her afternoon drinking, the Countess was very drunk. It had just turned midnight, and she was trying to enjoy herself, but she was starting to feel mournful about her situation. She always hated being single at New Year as she never had anyone special to kiss at midnight. This year, it felt even worse. Marie noticed that her mood had dropped. "You look a bit down," she said. "Are you okay?"

The Countess screwed up her mouth and nose. "Not really," she replied. "I don't feel on form tonight." She didn't want to get into her earlier thoughts on the MSL, but they must have been apparent.

"You're not upset about that American again are you?" asked Marie.

"Yes," replied the Countess. "I don't want to talk about him now. But I just can't get him out of my head and it really pisses me off. I didn't want to take him into the New Year. I want to be free of him. I'm fed up with being upset about him. I'm fed up with being miserable on a great night like tonight. And I'm fed up that we are having this conversation, again! I've had too many of these conversations. It's very dull and very boring. I just want this bloody man who doesn't want to be with me out of my head and my heart so that I am free to find someone else. It's all so fucking tedious and I don't want another year of it. It's the new year now, and I want new emotions and a new man!"

Marie gave the Countess a hug. "It's okay. You'll get through. You've done so well the last few months. He'll go, eventually."

"I wish I could believe that," said the Countess. "This bloody conference is coming up in the spring which means that he'll always be sitting in the back of my mind. I'm not going to be able to completely flush him out until after then. So, I'm stuck with false hope for another four months, and I hate it." The Countess stamped her foot in frustration, spilling her drink over Mongolian Sheep Pussy.

"Hey, hey, steady," said Marie as she gently took hold of the Countess's wrists. "It's okay. You're going to let go of him despite this conference, but you're going to have to work really hard to choose to be free of him."

"I know," said the Countess as she slid her left hand free from Marie and wiped a tear from the corner of her eye. "I'm just so sick of it. I just want to be normal and meet a normal man who lives down the road and have a normal relationship with him. I want a relationship that isn't full of doubt, because this man, whoever he may be, will be so crazy about me, he'll tell me that he loves me all the time and then I'll never have to go through all this bullshit again."

"You and me both, honey," said Marie. "Come here."

The Countess and Marie gave each other a big affectionate squeeze, "Thank you, Marie," she sniffed

"We'll both get a man eventually," said Marie. "But in the meantime, it's New Year's Eve. Let's have some fun. Shall we go for a dance?"

Though she didn't feel like having fun, the Countess went along with Marie's suggestion and started to dance. She always got a trance-like type of relaxation from immersing herself in the music and just doing whatever moves came naturally to her. This soon had a therapeutic effect on her mood, and she enjoyed being lost in a world of her own.

She had not been paying any attention to the people around her, unlike Marie, who tapped her on the arm and said, "Look, those guys over there are eyeing us up."

Feeling a bit dazed, the Countess said, "Who?"

"Over there, by the bar."

The Countess looked over and saw two young men, one of whom smiled at her as he caught her eye. "They're very young," she said. "But very cute. The blonde one on the right is quite sweet."

"That's good because I think the other one is a bit of all right," said Marie. "Come on, let's go and talk to them."

"I don't know," said the Countess.

"The Countess, turning down a gorgeous young man?" said Marie. "That'll be a first. See, they're looking at us again. We'll just chat with them for a few minutes. And if they're complete prats, we'll move on."

"How old do you think they are?" said the Countess.

"Twenty-something," replied Marie. "Old enough." She grabbed the Countess by the arm and started walking across the bar area to where the two young men were standing.

"Happy New Year, ladies," said the blonde one as they approached. "Any chance of a New Year kiss?"

"Maybe," said Marie. "We haven't made our minds up yet."

"And what will it take to convince you?" said the man Marie liked.

"It depends," said Marie.

"On what?" he asked.

"Many things," she replied as she smiled playfully at him.

"Would you like a drink?" asked the blonde one. The Countess had already had plenty to drink and should have had a water, but she thought it would be too uncool to ask for that, so she went for her usual, Jack Daniels and coke.

"And you?" the blonde one asked Marie.

"Vodka and cranberry juice please," said Marie.

"Do we get a kiss now?" asked the other man.

"You can't bribe me with drinks," said Marie. "I don't even know your name."

"I'm Dave," he replied. "And this is my mate, Richard."

New Year, New Behaviour

The following morning, the Countess came to feeling extremely thirsty. Her head felt so heavy that, despite her need for water, she could not be bothered to raise herself up and get a drink. She kept her eyes closed, curled up a little more on her side and drifted off back to sleep.

At some point later, she woke again. She still had the heavy, dry, thumping feeling in her head. This time, she knew that she needed water. She was facing the direction of her bedside cabinet and hoped that she had placed a drink there the night before. She opened one eye and spied a glass with an inch of water left in it. Now all she had to do was prise herself up from her pillow.

Her quilt felt so cosy, but it was no good. She needed to rehydrate. She rolled onto her back, pushed the quilt down off her shoulder then levered herself up onto her elbow.

It was then that she realised she was not alone. Curled up on the other side of the bed was Richard.

"Shit," she said quietly. "Fuck, bugger, shit!"

Her movement caused him to stir. He opened his eyes and looked at her. "Morning beautiful," he said.

"Hello," she replied.

He reached his hand out to her and said, "Give us a cuddle."

101

Without moving, she replied, "I need some water. I'll be back in a minute." She drank what was left in the glass, then got out of bed, grabbed her robe from the back of her bedroom door and went to the bathroom, making sure she shut the door properly.

"Shit, shit, shit!" she said to herself as she sat on the loo. Then she thought, *What the fuck is he doing here, and how am I going to get rid of him?*

She went downstairs, filled up another glass of water and gulped it down. Then she ferreted around in one of her kitchen drawers and found some painkillers. For good measure, she also knocked back one of her multi-vitamin tablets and a thousand milligrams of vitamin C. She refilled the glass, and as she drank, she noticed Mongolian Sheep Pussy lying on the kitchen table.

"Mongolian Sheep Pussy," she whispered.

"Morning, Madame," said Mongolian Sheep Pussy.

"Shh!" whispered the Countess. "We need to be quiet."

"Did you have a nice time with Richard?" asked Mongolian Sheep Pussy, now speaking much quieter.

"He's here," said the Countess.

"I know," said Mongolian Sheep Pussy.

"How did it happen? I can't remember."

"You started off by bragging that you had the longest legs in London, then you kept asking him to stroke your pussy and waved me around in front of him," said Mongolian Sheep Pussy. "After you had snogged him for a while, he said that perhaps the two of you should go back to yours. And you said all right then."

"Fuck!" said the Countess. "Do you know if we... you know?"

"I don't know, Madame," said Mongolian Sheep Pussy. "But you were making a lot of noise."

"Bugger!" said the Countess.

"He's good-looking," said Mongolian Sheep Pussy. "And he seems keen on you."

"I don't care," said the Countess. "He's got to go."

She picked up her glass of water and headed back to the stairs. On the way, she caught sight of herself in the hall mirror. *I look awful*, she thought. She dipped her finger in the glass of water and tried to wipe away her smudged mascara. Then she continued up the stairs to her bedroom.

She paused at the entrance to the bedroom and looked at her bed. Richard appeared to have fallen back to sleep. Feeling like more sleep herself, she kept her robe on and got back into bed, hoping that he would not wake up. She curled up on her side with her back to him.

She awoke later when Richard got up and went to the bathroom. When he came back, he said, "Happy New Year."

"Er, thanks," she replied. "You too."

He got back under the covers. "You were a wild woman last night."

"Really?" she said.

He snuggled up to her and said, "I'd love some more of that."

"Not now," she said. "I have a category-four hangover." Her headache had actually improved, but he did not need to know that.

"It will make you feel better," he said as he kissed the side of her face and tried to reach for one of her breasts.

"I'm not sure about that," she said and blocked his hand before he could get it inside her dressing gown.

"Don't you want to?" he asked, still nuzzling against her.

She could feel that he had an erection.

"No, not really," she said.

"But you did last night."

"Well, that was last night."

He tried again to touch her breasts.

"Stop it!" she said as she caught his hand. "I said no." She raised herself up and rested on her arm.

"What's the matter?" he asked.

"Look, I'm really sorry. I was a bit drunk last night. I shouldn't have brought you back here. I'd like you to leave, please."

"That's a bit harsh," he replied. "I'm starving, is there any chance of having breakfast before I go?"

Even though the Countess wanted to get rid of Richard immediately and pretend the whole thing had not happened, she felt mean kicking him out without so much as a cup of coffee. It wasn't his fault that she had been so drunk and out of control.

"Okay. I'll make some toast," she said. "Let's get up now. There's another robe in the bathroom which you can use if you like."

She got out of bed and went straight down to the kitchen. She could hear him moving about upstairs and hoped that he'd either get dressed or at least cover up in the robe. A couple of minutes later, he emerged in the kitchen, fully dressed.

"It's okay," he said. "You don't have to feed me. I can see that you're really uncomfortable."

"No, it's all right. I'm sorry. I didn't mean to be horrible to you. Do you want some coffee?"

He smiled. "Well if you insist – white with two sugars please." He sat at the table and picked up Mongolian Sheep Pussy. "Last night was fun," he said as he put her down.

The Countess walked over near the table to put some bread under the grill. He reached up and stroked her hand. "You're very nice, you know."

"That's really sweet of you, but I don't feel very nice at the moment."

"It's my fault too," he said. "You were pretty drunk, and I shouldn't have taken advantage of that. But I just couldn't believe my luck. You're beautiful… and fabulous in bed!"

The Countess smiled at this last comment. She did not dare tell him that she remembered nothing of her night with him. She pulled her hand away from his and fiddled with the bread under the grill.

He kept talking. "Don't feel bad about last night. We can start again if you like. I could take you out for a drink one night next week, and you could get to know me better. How about that?"

The Countess turned to face him. Though he seemed to be a nice young man, she did not want to see him again. "Er, I'm not sure."

"Or what about over the weekend?" said Richard. "We could do something Sunday afternoon."

"Thanks, but no," said the Countess with more certainty. She turned back to the grill pan and stared intently at the bread, willing it to toast faster.

Richard's mood changed. "You women in your thirties are all the bloody same. You're just obsessed with sex – you have no interest in having an actual relationship with anyone."

"It's not that," said the Countess, who was taken aback by his change of tune. Now, even more, she wished that he would just disappear. "You're a lovely man. It's just…"

"What?" he said.

"It's just that I'm getting over someone at the moment, and I'm not sure about dating anyone else."

"Like I said, you can fuck, but you can't date," he said.

"I was drunk. Very drunk. I shouldn't have done it. Sorry," she replied.

"Thanks a lot," he said.

"Well, you said yourself that you took advantage of me. That's not very nice is it?" said the Countess.

"You were very willing," said Richard.

"You could have resisted," she replied. "You know, been a gentleman?"

"You were throwing yourself at me," said Richard. And then, a little more gently, "and I was really drunk too. I'm sorry. I'm trying to be nice and gentlemanly now. Go on. Come out with me again."

"Like I said, I was too drunk last night. I was upset about something and I shouldn't have done what I did. I'm sorry," said the Countess.

"So that's it?" said Richard, becoming irate again. "You're just going to toss me aside. Do you do that to all your men?"

"I'm not tossing you aside," sighed the Countess. "I'm just saying that I regret what I did, and I don't want to go out on a date with you. Look, this is really awkward. Maybe you should leave."

Richard stood up and went into the living room. He picked his jacket up from an armchair and then sat down to put his shoes on. He looked up at her as he tied his laces and said, "You're bloody weird, you are."

"Just go," said the Countess.

He stood up and went to the front door. The Countess

106

followed him, but he let himself out and slammed the door shut.

* * *

Persian Dolly had despised the previous evening. The Countess had been so drunk that she had been falling around and crashing into walls as she left the club with Richard.

He hated the thought that he might get dirty. At first, he'd been happy to be bought by a Countess, he felt this was fitting of his quality. Then he discovered that her house was full of fawning fur that sucked up to a teddy bear. And now, this drunken behaviour.

He had expected that a coat of his quality would have been treated correctly and hung up whenever they arrived back home. Instead, last night she just peeled him off and threw him to one side. He landed on the floor and skidded across it. Thankfully, he didn't crash into the corner where he could see that there were cobwebs.

Then he had to endure her goings-on with the young man. At last, they went upstairs, and he was able to gather himself and get off the floor. A hanger would have been nice, but there were none available, so he hoisted himself up onto the sofa and lay carefully over the arm.

When he heard them come downstairs the next day, he regretted his move lest the couple resumed their activities from the night before. His fear was unfounded as he listened to their conversation in the kitchen.

After the young man left, the Countess sat down on the sofa, picked up Persian Dolly and hugged him to her.

Oh no, she was going to bury her face in his fur again. He

hated that. "You've only yourself to blame, Madame," he said, trying to wriggle free of her teary grip.

"Pardon?" said the Countess.

"You've only yourself to blame for this," he repeated.

"What do you mean?" asked the Countess. "It's not my fault that everything goes wrong on me."

"You were too drunk," said Persian Dolly. "You shouldn't have brought him back here."

"I don't need you to tell me that," said the Countess. "I just drank too much. I was upset. If only the bloody MSL…"

"The MSL. Is that the man in America that I've heard the others talking about?" asked Persian Dolly.

"Yes," said the Countess. "I want to be with him, but it just hasn't worked out."

"I'm not surprised, if this is how you carry on when you go out," said Persian Dolly. "It sounds like a bit of a long shot anyway. He's in New York. You're here. You don't work with him anymore. It's never going to happen."

The Countess looked at Persian Dolly, "What?"

"It's never going to happen," said Persian Dolly. "You need to get over him. And sober up."

"How can you say that?" said the Countess. "Anyway, you're just a coat that looks like a cat. What do you know?"

The smell of burning toast wafted into the living room. "Shit!" said the Countess and stormed through the living room to the kitchen. Persian Dolly heard the sound of toast being scraped and the Countess muttering swear words. Then he heard her footsteps go back upstairs.

* * *

The Countess went back to her bedroom where she noticed a condom wrapper lying on the floor near to the side of the bed where Richard had slept. She picked it up and stared at it. It confirmed to her that they had indeed had sex together the previous night. The only crumb of comfort that she could get from the wrapper was that they had at least used protection.

She walked around to her side of the bed and dropped the wrapper in the wastepaper basket. She noticed American Ted lying on the floor by the side of the bed. She looked around the room. Pussy Deluxe was in his usual place on the wooden box. Pussy Original and Pussy With Balls must have tidied themselves away in the wardrobe with the Queen Mum bag.

"Are you okay, Madame?" asked American Ted.

"No, I'm not, Ted," said the Countess as she shook out her quilt to straighten it. "But it's nothing I don't fully deserve." She got back into bed and lay down.

"Can I help?" asked American Ted.

"No," said the Countess as she started to cry. "I think I might be beyond help."

American Ted climbed up onto the bed and sat by the Countess's face. Tears trickled down her cheek and landed on the pillow. "What's the matter?" he asked.

The Countess just shook her head and kept crying. American Ted went to stroke her hair with his paw.

"I'm sorry, Ted. I know you want to help, but I just can't talk right now," she said and turned over in bed to face the other way, leaving poor American Ted staring at her back.

Pussy Original and Pussy With Balls nudged open the wardrobe doors and looked over at American Ted and the Countess. American Ted shrugged his shoulders at them. The Countess cried on. From time to time she would reach for a tissue, half sit up and blow her nose then lie back down in the foetal position and continue crying. Eventually, she dozed off .

Pussy Original and Pussy With Balls bounced down from the wardrobe and met up with American Ted at the foot of the bed.

"What was all that about?" said Pussy Original.

"I don't know," said American Ted. "But I suppose it's to do with the MSL or that man she brought home last night."

"Or both," said Pussy With Balls.

At this point, Mongolian Sheep Pussy had made her way back upstairs and into the bedroom to join them.

"How is she?" she asked.

"Not good," said American Ted. "What happened?"

"She fell out with that Richard bloke. He stormed out and then Persian Dolly laid into her because she had drunk too much. He wasn't very nice to her. He said she was never going to make it with the MSL."

"That bloody coat," said Pussy With Balls. "He might be right about the MSL, but he should know better than to talk to her like that. He's so up himself. I didn't like him from the minute he turned up here the other day."

"Let's go down and have a word with him," said Pussy Original. "Ted, you'd better stay up here in case the Countess wakes up."

Pussy Original, Pussy With Balls and Mongolian Sheep Pussy ventured downstairs.

"Oi! Sheep!" said Pussy With Balls when they arrived in the living room. "What have you done to upset the Countess?"

"Hey, don't blame me for that," said Persian Dolly. "She was already upset."

"What did you say to her?" asked Pussy With Balls. "She's in a right mess upstairs."

"Well, I might have said something she didn't want to hear," said Persian Dolly, "but she was already in a state from getting in a fight with that man."

"What exactly did you say to her?" asked Pussy Original. "We need to know because then we'll know better how to handle her when she wakes up."

"God, you lot all fawn around her so much," said Persian Dolly.

"That's our job," said Mongolian Sheep Pussy. "We're here to look after her and make her happy."

"Well, if you ask me, you mollycoddle her. No wonder she's so weird," said Persian Dolly.

"Just tell us what you said," said Pussy With Balls.

"I told her she'd drunk too much," said Persian Dolly, "and that she only had herself to blame for how she's feeling today."

"The Queen Mum bag is always telling her to act more ladylike," said Pussy Original.

"She's right," said Persian Dolly. "If she really wants to be with this MSL person, then what is she doing bringing someone else home?"

"She does drink too much," said Pussy Original. "It is the source of all her mischief. She always gets too drunk and ends up snogging someone completely inappropriately. Once, in New York, she did this in front of the MSL."

"No wonder he doesn't want to be with her. A decent man doesn't want to be with a woman like that. What she needs is a bloody good telling off," said Persian Dolly.

"But you can't do that," said Mongolian Sheep Pussy.

"Why not?" said Persian Dolly.

"Because she is our mistress, and it is not for us to tell her what she can and can't do. Didn't they teach you anything at Fenwick's?" replied Mongolian Sheep Pussy. "And anyway, she loves the MSL. If she was with him and he wanted her, then she wouldn't be running around getting into trouble with other men. It is his fault. If she were with her man, then she'd be happy."

"I don't think it works like that," said Pussy Original. "I think she needs to be happy in herself first. I suppose that's what we need to help her with, or she'll never be in a fit state to meet anyone else."

"That's what I was trying to tell her," said Persian Dolly. "I said that she didn't have a chance with that man in America and that she needed to get over him."

"No wonder she's upset," said Pussy With Balls.

Pussy Original sighed. "It sounds like you were a bit too blunt with her."

Persian Dolly shrugged. "I might have been."

"And that doesn't work with the Countess," said Pussy Original. "She's sensitive. We're going to have to patch her up now and see if we can wean her off the MSL in a gentler way."

"But he's the love of her life," said Mongolian Sheep Pussy. "How can she give him up? How can she be happy without him if she wants him that much? She's going to see him again in a few months, and this might be the time that he falls for her."

"But if he's still not interested in her, then she'll face even more heartache," said Pussy Original. "You don't want that for her, do you?"

"No," said Mongolian Sheep Pussy. "I just want her to have her man."

* * *

The bags decided to go back upstairs. Persian Dolly was about to come up with them so he could be hung up properly in the Countess's wardrobe.

"Are you having a laugh?" said Pussy With Balls. "You can't come up with us. You're the last person she'll want to see when she wakes up."

Persian Dolly sighed. "See, there you go, being all soft on her again."

"Mate, we're not being soft," said Pussy With Balls. "Just sensible."

The bags made their way upstairs to the bedroom. The Countess was still sleeping. American Ted slid down from the bed to talk with them. They relayed their conversation with Persian Dolly to him.

"You know, I think he's right," said American Ted. "Though, like you, I find it difficult to be that tough with her. Let's see what she's like when she wakes up."

The Countess slept for another hour. American Ted was at the ready as she began to stir.

"Madame," he said. "How are you feeling now? What's the matter?"

"The usual," replied the Countess and then rolled over, curled herself into a ball again and closed her eyes. She dozed for a few more minutes and then sat up in bed and threw back the covers. Before she could get up, Pussy Original, Mongolian Sheep Pussy and Pussy With Balls bounced up on the bed, and Pussy Original spoke.

"Madame, we know Persian Dolly upset you. We want to help. Would you like to talk it through with us?"

113

The Countess looked terrible. Her eyes were puffy from all the crying, and there were still remnants from the previous night's make-up on her face. However, this act of kindness from her beloved accessories made her smile.

"Persian Dolly was wrong," said Mongolian Sheep Pussy. "He shouldn't have said those things."

"It's okay," said the Countess. "He was right. I didn't like what I heard, but what he said is true. I can't keep blaming the MSL for everything that is going wrong for me. It was really stupid to bring Richard back here last night, but I was so drunk. I've had one-night stands before, but I've never not remembered having sex with someone. That's really awful." She put her face in her hands.

"We can't change what's happened," said American Ted. "We just want you to start feeling better about things."

"That's the problem," said the Countess. "I don't know how to make myself feel better."

She started to cry again.

"Madame, we'll help you find a way," said American Ted. "Please don't cry."

"I feel awful," said the Countess.

"You didn't have any breakfast, did you, Madame?" said Mongolian Sheep Pussy. "Why don't we all go downstairs to the kitchen? You can fix yourself something to eat and we can help you come up with a plan."

"Okay," said the Countess. She pushed the quilt aside, got out of bed and retied her robe. Then she swept American Ted and the bags up into her arms and went downstairs. She set them down on the kitchen table and cut herself two slices of bread. This time she didn't bother toasting it but buttered it straight away and added some Marmite. She ate one of them whilst still standing at the kitchen counter. Then she refilled the kettle, put the other slice onto a plate and sat down at the table with the accessories.

"The problem is this bloody Risk conference," she said and took another bite of bread. After chewing it, she added, "There is no way I can forget about the MSL when I know that in four months' time, I'm going to see him again."

"Maybe you don't need to forget about him," said Mongolian Sheep Pussy.

Pussy Original shoved her in the side. Mongolian Sheep Pussy shoved him back.

The Countess spoke again. "I don't know if I'll even go to the conference. It's too painful."

"But you've got to go, Madame. You're presenting there," said American Ted.

"Well, I'll have to tell them at work that I've changed my mind. I'll get Aidan to do it instead."

"Madame," said Pussy Original. "This is not the Countess that we know. She would never give up such a marvellous opportunity to shine at her job. You're always so capable."

"Thanks," sniffed the Countess. "But I really don't think I can do it."

"Madame, don't let him affect you like this," said American Ted. "You need to get to that conference, be the glittering star that you always are and make sure that he gets a good look at what he is missing out on."

"But I'm just not going to be able to cope," said the Countess.

"Of course you will," said American Ted. "Right now, you feel really low because you're upset. But the conference isn't for another four months. You'll feel fine by then. Anyway, we can all come with you and give you all the support you need."

"I'd love to come," said Mongolian Sheep Pussy.

"Thanks, guys," said the Countess. "It just hurts. I'm so lucky on so many fronts. I love my job, I love living here with all of you, and I have amazing friends. But I'm useless when it comes to men. I don't seem to have the relationship gene. Other people meet someone nice, they get together, and there doesn't seem to be any drama. They just get on with it. Me, I don't seem to have any luck with men. I always fall for the ones who aren't interested. Then I get drunk and end up with someone far too young and totally unsuitable."

"Madame," said Pussy Original. "Do you think it might be an idea to drink a bit less when you go out? That way, you won't put yourself at risk of doing something stupid."

"After last night, I don't think I ever want to drink again," said the Countess.

"I don't think you need to go that far, Madame," said Pussy With Balls.

"Just cut back a bit," offered Pussy Original.

"That's a good idea," said the Countess.

The kettle clicked itself off, and she got up to make herself a cup of tea. "I'm always far too drunk by the time I realise I need to drink some water. Then it's too late, and I end up feeling awful and getting into messy situations."

"And then you end up feeling how you do today," said Pussy Original.

"Yes," said the Countess, sitting down again with her tea. "I think I'm going to have to take some kind of measures, especially judging by what Aidan says about the Risk conference being a huge alcohol fest."

"Don't worry about the conference now," said American Ted. "Just sort yourself out. Why don't you get up and do something nice like have a bath? Then give Marie a call and see how she is. Maybe the two of you can go and see a film or something."

"I'd like that," replied the Countess as she popped the last of her bread and Marmite into her mouth. "It will be good to have a chat with her."

The Countess took American Ted's advice. She cleaned herself up and sorted out her bed. Even though her sheets had only been on the bed a couple of days, she stripped them off and replaced them with clean ones. She was reminded of her mother who, if she had seen her, would have recounted an old wives' tale about not doing any washing on New Year's Day, lest one "wash one of the family away". However, desperate to get rid of the reminders of her night with Richard, she ignored this superstition and shoved the dirty sex sheets into her washing machine. Then she phoned Marie and arranged to go and spend the afternoon with her.

Calm After The Storm

The first couple of weeks in January were uneventful for the Countess. She avoided drinks with her work colleagues on the Friday evening and only had one glass of wine at dinner the following week when she had to go to Frankfurt. The next Saturday, when she met up with her friends, she decided to alternate an alcoholic drink with a soft drink. She ended the night only mildly tipsy, a lot less drunk than she would normally have been.

The accessories were pleased to see the Countess's dark mood evaporate. They had also heard good things about her from her colleagues. The Queen Mum bag had overheard a conversation between the directors of Periculum. The Countess had been away from her desk at the time and the directors happened to be chatting nearby, unaware that the Queen Mum bag, placed just under the desk, was listening to everything.

She reported back to the other accessories that evening what she had heard. "They said that providing the Countess did well at the conference, she would be promoted."

"That's good," said Pussy With Balls.

The Queen Mum bag continued, "One of them said, 'That's almost certainly going to happen. She's done a great job sorting out that mess in Frankfurt.' And the other replied, 'She really knew her stuff when we were in that bid meeting last week. The clients love her.' Then they went on to say that they had better get on and earmark an office for her."

"How fabulous," replied Mongolian Sheep Pussy. "If she's going to get her own office, then she must be doing really well."

Towards the end of the month, feedback also came directly from Aidan. It was a Sunday, and the Countess had decided to go into the office to start doing some work on her conference presentation. She enjoyed the peace and quiet of the empty office at the weekend, and it allowed her to focus on the presentation rather than her normal work. She spent a couple of hours going through the Periculum software packages, deciding which aspects of it she would highlight and was just about to pop out for a coffee when Aidan turned up.

"Hi there," she said. "How are you?"

"Not bad," he replied. "What are you doing here?"

"I decided it was time to start thinking about my presentation at the Risk conference. What's your excuse?" said the Countess.

"I'm impressed," he said. "I just came in to pick up my laptop. I left it here on Friday night, but I need to work at home tomorrow because I'm expecting a delivery."

"Anything exciting?" asked the Countess.

"Not really," said Aidan. "New dishwasher. It was supposed to arrive yesterday, but it didn't show up. Luckily, I managed to get someone on the phone, and they have promised me that it will come tomorrow morning."

"How annoying," said the Countess. "I was just about to pop out and get a coffee. Do you want to join me?"

"That would be lovely," said Aidan.

They stepped out of the office onto Berkeley Square. Even though it was cold, it was a bright day and blue sky was visible through the bare trees that stood in the tiny park in the middle of the square.

The Countess turned up the collar of Persian Dolly to keep her neck warm. "I think the Genoa is closed on a Sunday," she said, referring to the small family café around the back of the office in Bruton Street.

"Let's walk down to Piccadilly," said Aidan. "One of those new coffee chain places has opened up by the tube."

They walked down Berkeley Street towards Piccadilly. The street was very quiet, as the galleries, car showrooms and hairdresser businesses were all closed on a Sunday. Only the Persian rug shop, which had a perpetual closing-down sale, had its doors open.

They turned right onto Piccadilly and found the coffee-come-sandwich shop.

"To have here or take away?" asked the person at the till as they ordered their cappuccinos.

"Shall we go and sit in the park?" said the Countess. "It's a beautiful day."

"Good idea," said Aidan. "I spend far too much time indoors, especially in the winter. We'll take them away, please."

Having picked up their coffees, they walked out onto the street and waited for a gap in the traffic before crossing the road. Then they went into Green Park and found an empty bench.

As she sat down, the Countess noticed Aidan looking at Mongolian Sheep Pussy.

"This one's fairly new," she said. "I call her Mongolian Sheep

Pussy."

"Interesting name," said Aidan, removing the lid of his coffee, tipping in sugar and giving it a stir with a plastic spoon. "So, is this something to do with the pussy bag stuff that the SC Radcliffe people talked about. You never did tell me about it."

"Sort of," said the Countess as she took a sip of her coffee. "Mmm. That's a good coffee. I have a bag called Pussy Original, and I used to get up to a lot of mischief with it."

"Well, don't stop there," said Aidan. "Spill!"

"It's a small leopard-print furry bag," said the Countess. "My best friend, Marie, bought it for me one Christmas. I'd had a bit to drink and within about three nanoseconds of opening it, I connected its feline nature to something more naughty and declared that I could offer it to people and ask them if they wanted to stroke my pussy."

Aidan laughed. "And you did this?"

"Still do," said the Countess. "Though not as much. The pussy stroking heyday was definitely during my time at SC Radcliffe. We had a riot there."

A brown cocker spaniel ran up to them and sniffed at the Countess's boots. She patted its head.

"You really ask people if they want to stroke your pussy?" said Aidan.

The dog's owner whistled and it ran off back across the grass.

The Countess nodded. "Only when I'm out and I've had a few! Most of the time, people do give the bag a quick stroke. It's only backfired once."

"This I have to know." Aidan took a sip of his coffee.

"It was at a wedding," said the Countess. "I asked the groom's father if he wanted to stroke my pussy – not my finest hour."

121

Aidan laughed and coughed as he swallowed his coffee. "I can imagine." He coughed again then asked, "So, do you ask people if they want to stroke this one?"

"Not in the same way," said the Countess. "Although it's very nice. You can have a feel if you like." She held Mongolian Sheep Pussy out to him.

"No, you're okay," said Aidan.

"Go on. It doesn't bite," said the Countess.

Aidan took his glove off and touched the bag. "Oh, it's quite nice," he said and put his glove back on. He smiled at her. "Despite your obvious craziness, you've settled well into Periculum. I'm really impressed that you're working on the presentation already. I normally leave those things until the absolute last minute."

"I just wanted to make a start on it," replied the Countess. She swished her coffee cup around a couple of times then took another sip. "I've just thrown a few ideas down. They don't need the slides until the end of February, so there's lots of time still. Once I'm happy with it, I'll run it by you, and that will leave us plenty of time to decide on a final version."

"Perfect," said Aidan. "I knew you were the right person for this job. You'll have them eating out of your hand."

"And hopefully lots of new clients signing on the dotted line," said the Countess. "Did you pick up much business last year?"

"Yes," replied Aidan. "That's how we got Deutsche Landesbank, and we also did some work for a Swiss bank in Basel. It's a fun few days. You'll enjoy it."

"I hope so," said the Countess. "Do you know what day I'm on yet?"

"No," replied Aidan. "They haven't finalised the programme.

We've requested the second day. No one remembers anything from the first day, and on the third day, everyone is hungover from the gala ball the night before. The last day is crap because people are more interested in heading home than paying attention to anything they might learn."

"That's a good plan. Let's hope we get what we ask for," said the Countess. "How is work for you?"

"Not bad," said Aidan. "I've been trying to convince the guys in the States that they should let us do more of the development here."

"I bet they don't want to let go of it, do they?" said the Countess.

"No," said Aidan. "That's the problem. I'm going to arrange for some of them to come over here and visit. We can take them around some of our clients so they can see, at the coalface, that we face different issues here in Europe. I might need your help when we do that."

"No problem," said the Countess. "It'll be good to meet them." She took one more sip of her cappuccino then took the lid off and scraped the remaining foam from the inside of the cup with a spoon. "That was lovely," she said. "But I need the loo now. Shall we head back to the office?"

Good Things Come To Those Who Wait

It was the last Monday in February. By the end of the week, the Countess would have to submit her conference presentation. Even though she had submitted a draft presentation to the directors of Periculum the previous week, they had left it until the last minute to review her suggestions.

"I can see where you're coming from," said Aidan in the meeting where they were discussing her ideas, "but I want the emphasis to be that we provide a solution to any size of bank, especially the bigger ones. Keep all the integration stuff that you've got, but you need to highlight that we can implement on a large scale."

"We haven't done that yet in Europe," said the Countess.

"But we have in the US," said one of the other directors. "And that's the type of client we need to win over here. The banks we have in Basel and Frankfurt are okay, but they are just chicken feed compared to what we could have."

"Okay," said the Countess. "Who can I contact in the US who has worked on this type of project?"

They gave her contact names from their US office, and the Countess spent the afternoon on the phone to them. Towards the end of the day, Aidan stopped by her desk to check in with her.

"Are you okay with those changes?" he asked.

"Yes," said the Countess. "They're all good ideas, and I had a really good chat this afternoon with those guys in the States. I've got so much on this week though. We've got that big meeting tomorrow, I'm in Frankfurt on Wednesday, which only leaves me tonight and Thursday to get it all finished."

"That's the way it goes, isn't it?" said Aidan.

"Uh-huh," said the Countess. "Good job I hadn't planned on having a social life this week."

The Countess worked late that evening. Despite her exhaustion, she was in a buoyant mood when she arrived home at Kennington Mansions at around ten thirty. Although she had another busy day the next day, she procrastinated about going to bed and sat on her sofa as she half-watched a late-night news programme and half-flicked through a magazine. Eventually, just after midnight, she decided that it was about time she went to bed. She went through her usual routine of removing her make-up, having a quick shower and cleaning her teeth. By the time she climbed into bed and turned the light out, it was well past midnight.

No sooner had she got off to sleep when the phone rang. Not knowing whether she had been asleep for hours or had just dropped off, she groped for the telephone by her bed.

"Hello," she said, feeling slightly annoyed that someone was calling her in the middle of the night.

As she spoke, she heard a click and then silence. "Hello," she said again while fumbling to turn on her bedside lamp. She was about to tell the caller where to go when an American voice said, "Hi. Is that my favourite countess in London?"

For a second, with her head still full of sleep, she did not register the identity of the caller. Then the penny dropped. It was the MSL.

"Oh, my God, it's you," she said. "Hang on a minute." She put the receiver down then sat up in bed, looked at the time on her alarm clock and rearranged her pillows so she could sink back into them and talk more comfortably. She picked up the receiver and said, "I'm back with you now. How are you?"

"Good, thanks. And you?"

"Great."

"Did I wake you?"

"Yes. But don't worry. I'd only just gone to bed."

"Sorry," said the MSL. "I knew it was kinda late there, but I just wanted to hear your voice."

"Well, here it is," she laughed. "You're listening to it. Do you want me to talk about anything in particular?"

"Mmm, let's see," he said. "What's your view on the millennium. Is the world going to grind to a halt and come crashing down around us in a few months?"

"Gosh, I hope not. If it did, would you come over here and rescue me from annihilation?" asked the Countess.

"Sure," said the MSL.

"Really?" she said, surprised.

"Anything for my Countess," he replied.

"That's very sweet. But if the world was falling apart, how would you get here?"

"Good point. In that case, I'd better buy a ticket in advance and come to your side of the pond before it all happens."

"You're most welcome over here any time you choose."

"Thanks. I'll just check out the next flight," he said.

"Okay. Not that soon," said the Countess. "I need my eight

hours of sleep first."

"That's okay," said the MSL. "It'll take me an hour to get to the airport, an hour check-in, six hours' flying time and about an hour to get to central London. Let's see. That's nine hours. Perfect. You'll even have time to take a shower and have breakfast."

The Countess laughed. She could not believe he was talking like this. "Oh, I need a bit longer than that. If I'm going to meet you, I need to pop out, get a new outfit and perhaps get my hair done too!"

"No. I bet you look perfect just as you are. I can imagine you now. Lying in your bed looking like a goddess. Do you have silk sheets?"

"Of course," fibbed the Countess. She never understood the fascination men had with silk sheets. Her high-thread-count Egyptian cotton bedding was so much nicer.

"Mmm," he replied. "So, what have you been up to recently?"

The Countess chatted to him about work and a couple of recent social events. She asked him similar questions and then she spoke of the work she was putting in on her presentation. "Are you coming to Berlin?" she asked.

"Yes. I can't wait," he replied. "I've never been there before. I'm going to book my ticket in the next couple of days."

"Are you going to attend my presentation?"

"Only if you promise to autograph my conference booklet afterwards," he said.

"I think that can be arranged," she said. "Actually, there's something you can help me with."

"What is it?" he asked.

"We did some work recently for AmeriBank on inflation swaps. My directors say that I should include this in my presentation, but I don't really understand them. Do you have any literature that explains how they all work?"

"Sure," replied the MSL. "SC Radcliffe has loads of training documents. I'll dig one out and send it to you. You mustn't use it publicly though, or I'll be shot."

"No, of course I won't. I just need to understand them myself," said the Countess. Then she started to laugh.

"What's so funny?" he asked.

"It's almost one in the morning, and all of a sudden, I'm sitting in bed talking to you about the latest developments in derivatives. It just seems a bit bizarre."

"Oh. Excuse me. I forgot it's the middle of the night for you," he said. "I'll email you some stuff. Perhaps I'd better let you get your beauty sleep... Oh no... Not that you need beauty sleep. Shit! You know what I mean."

"That's okay. I suppose I better had get some sleep," she answered. "It's been really lovely talking to you. I can't wait to see you in Berlin."

"Me too," he said. "Which hotel are you staying in?"

"Kempinski. We booked everything last week," she said. "What about you?"

"Don't know yet. I haven't fixed anything. I'll see if I can get into the same place. Okay. Let's say goodnight. I'll email that stuff for you now, so it'll be there in the morning."

"Thanks. That's brilliant. I have to get it all finalised by the end of this week, so that's perfect. Goodnight. Thanks for calling."

"You're welcome. Goodnight. Sweet dreams."

"Thanks. Night."

"Night." Then the MSL hung up.

The Countess took the phone away from her ear and kissed

it before holding it against her heart. As she hung up, a smile spread across her face which beamed enough to illuminate the night sky.

"Was that him Madame?" said a voice from the wardrobe. It was Mongolian Sheep Pussy.

"Yes, yes, yes it was him," replied the Countess as she got out of bed. She opened the wardrobe doors and took out Mongolian Sheep Pussy and started dancing around the bedroom with her. "Isn't it exciting? He likes me! He phoned me! He flirted with me!"

Some of the other bags had been asleep and were awoken from their slumber.

"What, Madame?" said Pussy Deluxe. "Has something happened?"

"Has something happened?" exclaimed the Countess. "Yes! Something's happened. The MSL has phoned me! That's what happened. And we chatted for ages."

"That's lovely, Madame. Well done," he replied and went straight back to sleep.

Pussy Original was more attentive. "The MSL?" he said. "Great. What did he say?"

"Oh, we talked about life in general, Berlin, and he said he'd come over here and save me if the world falls apart at the millennium."

Pussy With Balls stretched and said, "That's great news, Madame. So, it sounds like you'll be seeing him soon. Is he going to come here before going on to Berlin?"

"Actually no. He didn't say that. Apart from joking, of course, that he'll be on the next plane over. No. We'll see each other in Berlin. He's going to try and stay at the same hotel. It's fantastic isn't it?"

"Yes, Madame, it's great. Just when you were least expecting to get anything from him, there he is," said Pussy With Balls.

"Did he sound keen on you?" asked Mongolian Sheep Pussy.

The Countess thought for a moment. "Actually, yes. He was very flirty. His voice sounded really warm and friendly. Like he really wanted to talk to me."

"See. I knew that we shouldn't give up on him," said Mongolian Sheep Pussy. "I'm really pleased for you, Madame. How were things left between you?"

"I don't really know," said the Countess. "He's going to email me some stuff to do with work. I suppose I can reply and maybe keep some contact going that way. But if he books it all up for Berlin, then I'll definitely see him there."

"Will you get time to spend with them there?" asked Mongolian Sheep Pussy.

"Oh yes," replied the Countess. "I'm presenting on the second day, but the whole thing lasts four days, so once my presentation is done, I'll have much less pressure and a bit more free time."

"So, you could go out with him after your presentation?" said Mongolian Sheep Pussy.

"Yes. That would be a triumphant end to my day, wouldn't it? Take the conference by storm during the day and…"

"…take him by storm at night, Madame." Mongolian Sheep Pussy could not help but finish off the sentence. She was dying to get more information from the Countess, but just as she was about to ask another question, a voice came from the bed. It was American Ted.

"Madame, it's past one o'clock. Don't you think it's time you went to sleep?"

"Sleep? How could I possibly sleep? That was the MSL,"

said the Countess.

"I know, Madame. I am very pleased that he has called, but you have another long day tomorrow. I don't know about you, but I'm tired," said American Ted, yawning.

The Countess laughed and went and picked him up. "Oh, Ted. You're funny. You never stop caring about me." She kissed him on his head then hugged him. "Well, folks," she said to the bags. "Looks like I'm being told to go back to bed. Teddy knows best, and the Countess must always do what Teddy says!"

"He's right, Madame," said Pussy Original. "It's great news that the MSL has called, but between now and Berlin, life goes on as normal. Try not to be too excited, though I know that's hard. Just take things as they come. The most important thing is that you are happy and that you do a great job when you are in Berlin. You're there to work. The MSL is secondary."

"I know," said the Countess. "You are so wise. I'd be lost without all of you. Thank you."

"You're welcome," said Pussy Original.

The Countess went back to her bed.

All went quiet for a short while until out of the darkness, Pussy Original suddenly called out, "Hey, Madame!"

"Yes?" she replied.

"We'd be lost without you too!"

The Countess smiled. "Thanks," she said. Then she turned off her bedside lamp, tucked herself up under the covers and tried to go back to sleep.

* * *

When she first awoke that morning, the Countess thought

immediately of the phone call from the MSL.

"Did it really happen? Did the MSL really call?" she asked American Ted. "Or did I dream it?"

"He called, Madame," said American Ted. "You had a lovely conversation with him."

"Great," said the Countess. "Wouldn't it be absolutely awful if it turned out to be only a dream?"

The Countess sang in the shower and then turned up the radio and danced and sang along to the music as she got dressed. When she arrived at the office, it was with much trepidation that she logged onto her computer and accessed her email. Would there be anything from the MSL? At first, she couldn't see anything, but then she scrolled down, and there it was. She clicked on the email and read it quickly.

He talked about the information that he had sent her and then said:

> *I really enjoyed talking to you earlier. You sound as wonderful as ever, and I'm looking forward to Berlin. Hopefully, I'll be able to stay at the same hotel. I've got my travel agent on the case. Tell me, are you going to bring your pussy purse with you? I remember how it used to cause a riot when you were here with it in New York. Anyway, gotta go now. Take care.*

Underneath that was a single capital 'X'.

She smiled. The note was a good mix of professional-but-friendly with a touch of flirtation. She especially liked the kiss at the end.

How am I going to reply to that? she thought. She hit the reply button and started typing a thank-you for the information.

Then she typed:

If I bring my pussy, will you stroke it?

She immediately deleted this text, thinking it too forward and overt. She typed a second attempt:

Of course I'm bringing my pussy purse. I don't go anywhere without it.

She decided this was boring so deleted it and made a third attempt:

I was going to leave my pussy bag at home, but seeing as you have been so helpful, I might bring it.

Then she added, in the manner of the first attempt:

If I do, will you stroke it?

Can I send this? she thought to herself. She signed her name at the end and put two kisses there. She hovered with her mouse over the Send button. *Shall I?* she thought. Then she thought, *Oh, fuck it. Why not? He raised the pussy thing in the first place. Might as well continue it.* Without further hesitation, she clicked the Send button.

Just after lunchtime, she received a reply from him:

Pretty please bring your pussy purse. Yes, I'll stroke it. So long as it doesn't bite me.

She wrote back:

Will feed it first. You should be safe.

A few minutes later:

What does it like to eat? Will bring supplies.

The Countess sniggered to herself as she typed:

Champagne and caviar.

He responded:

Consider it done.

* * *

Back at Kennington Mansions, Mongolian Sheep Pussy was in a mood with Pussy Original.

"What's up with you," he said.

"Nothing," she replied and went back to staring out of the window.

"Rubbish!" said Pussy Original. "I know you too well. You've got the hump about something."

"No, I haven't," she replied.

"Could have fooled me," he said. He sat silently next to her. Then he started whistling to himself.

"Do you want something?" she asked him.

"No. I'm just sitting here, whistling my happy tune. That

was exciting last night wasn't it?"

"Well, *I* thought it was exciting," said Mongolian Sheep Pussy. "You guys just treated it as if some boring nobody had called in the middle of the night."

"Ahh. Could that be what you're pissed off about?" he asked. "You're fed up that we packed her off to bed, aren't you?"

"Actually, yes I am," she replied. "You guys have not one ounce of romance in you. It was the MSL, for God's sake! Here is this man that she's so terribly in love with. She's cried and cried and cried over him. She's fallen apart and we've put her back together. She's now in good shape and then, out of the blue, this amazing thing happens. He phones up. He flirts with her. He offers her help and then says he'll stay at the same hotel at the conference. All I wanted to do was celebrate this with her, get all the gossip and make plans. You and American Ted cut straight across me and stopped us just when we were getting to the good bit."

"American Ted was wise to cut in then," said Pussy Original. "You two would have gossiped for ages and she would have been up half the night."

"No, we wouldn't. I was excited for her. She was excited too. I just wanted to know how it was for her."

"I'm sorry, Mongolian Sheep Pussy," said Pussy Original. "It's hard for us – we're just men. We don't understand you women."

"Too right you don't," said Mongolian Sheep Pussy. "I'm the only one here she can do girly gossip with. I just wanted to share her joy and get to the nitty-gritty. That's all."

Pussy Original smiled. He, like the other males in the house, adored Mongolian Sheep Pussy. She was the sweetest, cutest bag one could ever come across.

"I'm glad you're not like us," he said. "The house would be too boring and straight if you weren't here. Why don't you chat with the Countess when she comes home from work tonight? I'm sure she'll be bursting to talk about the phone call. And she'll hopefully have had an email from the MSL."

"Are you sure? I don't want to overexcite her," said Mongolian Sheep Pussy.

"Hey, don't be like that," said Pussy Original. "I tell you what. I'll get everyone out of the way tonight. Then, when she gets home and comes up here to take her suit off, you can ask her all about it."

"Okay then," said Mongolian Sheep Pussy. "I don't know about you, but I'm dying to know more. I'll find out all the details, then we can all figure out a strategy for her."

"That's a brilliant idea," said Pussy Original. "You'll find out stuff that she'd never tell me. Sounds like a team effort to me. Are we friends again now?"

Mongolian Sheep Pussy smiled. "Yes, I suppose so." She smiled again and nudged Pussy Original. "Yes, of course we are."

* * *

The Countess couldn't wait to get home and share her news with the accessories. When she arrived at Kennington Mansions, she went upstairs to change. In her bedroom she found just Mongolian Sheep Pussy on her bed. The other accessories were nowhere to be seen.

"Hi, Madame," said Mongolian Sheep Pussy. "Do you have any more news for me?"

"What about?" teased the Countess.

"You know. The MSL. Did you get an email from him?"

The Countess was beaming. "Yes," she said. "A few, actually. We were making pussy jokes. He's going to provide us with champagne and caviar because he's scared that you lot might bite him if you were hungry."

"What else?" said Mongolian Sheep Pussy. "Come on. I want to know everything about your conversation with him last night. I can't believe that American Ted made us all go to bed when there was so much to talk about."

"I know," replied the Countess. "I never thought I'd be able to settle and sleep, but actually, it was a good job he did that. I've had such a busy day today, I'd be even more exhausted than I am if he hadn't."

"So? Details, please," said Mongolian Sheep Pussy.

"Where shall I start?" said the Countess.

"How about at the beginning. The phone went last night. What did he say when you picked it up?"

"It was weird at first because I was half asleep and then it took a couple of seconds to connect. Then I heard this voice saying, 'Hi. Is that my favourite countess in London?'"

Mongolian Sheep Pussy squealed with delight. "Ooh, that sounds promising. What happened next?" The Countess sat on the bed and picked up Mongolian Sheep Pussy. She put her on her lap and stroked her as she spoke. She recounted every detail of the phone conversation and then told Mongolian Sheep Pussy of the email exchange. Apart from a few *oohs* and *aahs,* Mongolian Sheep Pussy just let the Countess talk.

When the Countess had finished speaking, Mongolian Sheep Pussy said, "Madame. It sounds ever so promising. He is being pretty flirty."

"Do you really think so?" said the Countess. "I'm too scared to get overexcited. He might just be being friendly."

"Maybe," said Mongolian Sheep Pussy. "But why would he phone weeks before Berlin, late at night and say stuff like he'd come to the end of the earth to save you. If he just wanted to find out if you were going to the conference and which hotel you were staying in then he could have emailed you. It sounds like a very playful conversation, Madame. This is very promising."

"Yes, it was very flirty. Just like we always used to be when we worked together. That's why a lot of people thought we were up to something. If he pulls out the 'let's just be friends' line again, I think I might have to kill him."

"Perhaps he never quite knew where he stood with you, Madame," said Mongolian Sheep Pussy.

"What do you mean?" asked the Countess.

"Perhaps he wasn't sure whether you liked him. A guy doesn't like to put himself in a place of rejection unless he's pretty sure that he is not going to be rejected."

"No, I don't think it is that," said the Countess. "He knows I like him. I told him last time we were in New York."

"Maybe it's a timing thing then," said Mongolian Sheep Pussy. "Perhaps it hasn't been right for him."

"Yes, that's kind of what he was saying in New York last time," said the Countess. "He was concerned that a relationship might cause problems if we ever worked together again. It's so exasperating."

"So, has anything ever happened with him?" asked Mongolian Sheep Pussy. "Have you ever, you know…"

"You know, what?" asked the Countess.

"Well, have you ever kissed him or, you know, gone further than that," asked Mongolian Sheep Pussy.

"Sadly, no," replied the Countess. "Though there were a couple of times when it might have gone further, but I didn't know what to do."

"Really? You've never mentioned this before," said Mongolian Sheep Pussy.

"Oh, they're almost nothing," said the Countess. "It's embarrassing really."

"Don't worry about that. Just tell me," said Mongolian Sheep Pussy.

The Countess giggled and blushed. "We held hands once," she said. "It was totally magic but really amounts to very little. We had been out after work to a happy hour and then to a nice restaurant. After dinner, we walked around and found a bar. As we sat at the bar, I noticed that our knees were touching. I love that type of body language when you don't shift away from the person, and they don't shift from you. I can't really remember what we were talking about. I think we were quite drunk. We were very touchy-feely with our hands too. You know, I'd brush my hand across his forearm, and he touched my upper arm a couple of times. It was fun, but it was also strange because we worked together, and it wasn't really a good idea to be getting up to any mischief. So, despite everything looking promising, I think we were both exercising restraint."

"What happened?" said Mongolian Sheep Pussy.

"Nothing much," replied the Countess. "Until we left the bar. It was late, and I was quite tipsy. As we were leaving, we just started holding hands. I think it was me who reached for his, and he didn't seem to mind. So, as we made our way out into the street, we were holding hands. Then he hailed me a cab, put me in it and that was it. I told you it was nothing."

"It sounds very romantic," said Mongolian Sheep Pussy. "How did you feel?"

The Countess smiled. "Like a queen," she said. "I felt magnificent, like the luckiest lady on earth. For a minuscule period, I was walking along, hand in hand with my man. It felt so right, so amazing…" She paused and then added, "…so perfect."

"What happened when he put you in the taxi? Did he kiss you?" asked Mongolian Sheep Pussy.

"No. It suddenly felt a bit awkward, as if we should have kissed but we didn't. Despite this, I went off feeling on top of the world."

"That's so sweet," said Mongolian Sheep Pussy. "Quite promising really and very romantic. So… what was the other thing?"

"It was around the same time," began the Countess. "Again, nothing really. There was a whole bunch of us heading out after work one day, and it started to rain. I had an umbrella, so I shared it with him. He put his arm around me and held my shoulder as we all walked along together. I was thinking, 'Does he have his arm around me, or is he just trying to get closer so that more of him is under the umbrella?' It was a bugger though because we weren't alone. I couldn't fully enjoy the experience or snuggle up to him that much because our colleagues were there."

"Madame, it sounds as though he really liked you. So that's it then – that's all that's happened between you?" asked Mongolian Sheep Pussy.

"Well… kind of," replied the Countess.

"Kind of?" said Mongolian Sheep Pussy. "That sounds like there's more. Do tell!"

The Countess smiled at Mongolian Sheep Pussy, "Well, it was later on that evening…"

"What? What happened later on that evening?" Mongolian Sheep Pussy asked excitedly.

The Countess laughed and patted Mongolian Sheep Pussy. "Something… and nothing, really."

"What do you mean?" asked Mongolian Sheep Pussy.

"Nothing really. We were close and touchy again all night. He kept looking at me and smiling. Even though there were quite a few of us out that night, he kept talking just to me, even when he and the other guys played pool. He always seemed to be around me, watching and touching."

"Madame, you never told us this. Why didn't you get together with him? It sounds like he was really into you," said Mongolian Sheep Pussy.

"I don't know. I didn't know what to do. We were with work people. One by one, the others left because they had to catch their trains back home to New Jersey. It got down to the two of us, but I didn't stay too much longer. I just had this feeling that I might have been imposing. It was a Monday night, not exactly a get-your-rocks-off night of the week. I couldn't figure out what was happening. He didn't pounce on me as soon as the others left, and I didn't want to hang around forever waiting, so after a while, I left too. And that was the end of that."

"Oh, Madame. That's such a shame. It sounded like he really wanted you," said Mongolian Sheep Pussy.

"So, why didn't he make a move when he finally had the chance?" said the Countess.

"Because those times when he did try, he didn't know if you wanted more," said Mongolian Sheep Pussy. "Perhaps he thought that you were worried about work and the consequences of you getting together. And then he started being all sensible about it."

"Bugger," said the Countess. "So, you mean that all the 'let's be friends' stuff is because he thought *I* was worried about it?"

"I don't know," said Mongolian Sheep Pussy. "It sounds as though there was a time when he wanted to go for it. Something was holding him back."

The Countess sighed. "I hope I haven't blown it."

"Don't worry," said Mongolian Sheep Pussy. "Maybe this is a new beginning. He phoned you out of the blue, and he was very flirty."

"Yes, but I can't build my hopes up only to be disappointed again," said the Countess. "It was fantastic to have a flirty conversation with him last night and by email today. But in doing so we have just ramped up the stakes."

"Let's see where this goes," said Mongolian Sheep Pussy. "You have nothing to lose. Focus on your work, and put on a good show at the conference. Let's just see what he does."

"I like that," said the Countess.

"Play it cool. But this time, if he does get touchy-feely with you, act on it," said Mongolian Sheep Pussy. "You can't give him any more mixed signals. Let him do the running though. You don't want to scare him off."

"I know. What you say makes sense. But it isn't easy to leave the ball in his court," said the Countess. "I just want to know where I stand."

"You will know by the end of this conference, Madame," said Mongolian Sheep Pussy. "He'll have either made a proper move or he won't."

"Argh," said the Countess. "I don't know how I'll cope if he doesn't."

"Don't worry," said Mongolian Sheep Pussy. "You'll have us to support you. We'll win together."

"Ah, thank you," said the Countess. She held Mongolian Sheep Pussy up to her face, snuggled against her fur and gave her a kiss.

* * *

When the Countess had left the room and gone downstairs, the wardrobe doors opened. There, inside, stood Pussy With Balls, Pussy Original and American Ted, cheering.

"Well done," said Pussy Original.

"I'm not just a pretty face, you know," said Mongolian Sheep Pussy, beaming. "It was good to talk to her woman to woman."

"You were brilliant," said Pussy With Balls. He bounced down to the floor and then up to the bed and gave her a playful push with his pom-poms.

"You gave her excellent advice," said American Ted. "She sounds in a much better place than she was."

"Let's hope she can stay there," said Pussy Original.

"And let's hope he comes up with the goods," said Pussy With Balls. "If it turns out that he's just leading her on, then I'm going to be very angry with him. He needs to come through now or get the hell out of her life."

* * *

The Countess, as planned, spent the following day in meetings and then flew out to Frankfurt in the evening. She got back late on Wednesday night and had been hoping to spend time during the day on Thursday to put the finishing touches to her presentation. Unfortunately, there was a software problem at one of her other clients, and she was called in to placate them and help sort out the mess. It was four in the afternoon before she got back to the Periculum offices. She was already exhausted from the Frankfurt trip, and figuring out what had gone wrong with the system had sapped her of creative headspace. When she sat down and tried to work on the presentation, she didn't know where to begin. She opted to take a break and go and get a coffee. Knowing that she was in for a late night, she also picked up some food for later and returned to the office just after five.

Aidan had already left. She decided to commandeer his office so that she could pace about and pretend to be giving the presentation. One of the sections didn't flow correctly, so she had to figure out how to rework it. Then she printed out all of the slides to check them. By the time she had rehearsed a couple more times, it was almost midnight.

She went home and flopped into bed at just after one o'clock.

American Ted was sitting on the other pillow to where she lay.

"You're very late, Madame. Is everything done now?" he asked.

"Yes," she replied. "All I have to do is proofread it tomorrow, make corrections and then email it off. Then I can relax. I'll have to refocus again before the gig, but basically, I'm done."

"Goodnight, Madame. Sleep well," said American Ted.

"Night night. Thanks for your support these last few days."

Despite her late night, the Countess only slept for a few hours. She set her alarm for six thirty and struggled out of bed when it buzzed. She showered, dressed quickly and ate a slice of toast as she walked out the door of Kennington Mansions. She wanted to be in the office by seven thirty to get an early start and have her work despatched by the midday deadline. As soon as she arrived at the office, she printed out the whole presentation again. Then, enjoying the empty office at such an early hour, she was able to have a clear and objective look at everything. She decided on a couple of very minor tweaks which she executed quickly.

By this time, it was nine thirty, and Aidan had just arrived in the office. He noticed her working away.

"How is it going?" he asked her.

"Control S – save," she said. "I'm done. Hallelujah."

"You look exhausted," he said. "Have you worked all night?"

"No, but it was a late one," said the Countess. "And I wanted to get a final look at it early this morning."

"Do you fancy going out for some breakfast?" he asked. "Coffee and chocolate croissant?"

"Oh yes. That sounds perfect," replied the Countess. "A big fat cappuccino. That's exactly what I need. When we come back, will you proofread it all for me? I don't think I can see straight anymore."

"Of course, my dear. But first, food. Let's go," said Aidan.

The Countess was very grateful for a break from her work. She liked her chats with Aidan, whether they were over breakfast at a café near the office or after work in a cocktail bar.

They walked around the corner to the Genoa café.

"Take a seat," said Aidan. "I'll get these. The usual?"

"That'll be lovely," said the Countess. "Can I have an orange juice as well, please? I need the vitamins."

"Coming right up," said Aidan.

The Countess sat down at one of the Formica tables in the corner. While Aidan was at the counter, she looked at the old pictures on the wall. Her favourite was one of all the staff lined up outside, standing in front of the café. Judging by the picture quality and what they were wearing, it must have easily dated back to the 1920s or even before.

After a couple of minutes, Aidan returned with the Countess's juice and a pain au chocolat each.

"They're going to bring the coffees over," he said as he sat down. Then he added, "You've really been burning the midnight oil, haven't you?"

"Yes. It's been a tough week," she took a bite of her pain au chocolat, "but I want the presentation to be good. I don't want to stand in front of all those people if what I'm saying isn't spot on."

"It will be fine, don't worry. You're good at this kind of thing," said Aidan. He took the first bite of his croissant. "So, is your American friend going to be there?"

"Yep," said the Countess. All of a sudden, she felt as if she was going to cry. It had been a hard week, and she was very tired.

"Are you okay?" he asked.

"Yes," she replied and mustered up a smile. "I'm just really tired. Exhausted, actually."

Their coffees arrived. Aidan picked up the old-fashioned sugar pourer and shook it vigorously over his cup.

"Have you heard from him recently?" he asked as he stirred his drink.

"Yes. He called me out of the blue this week. And we've emailed a bit in the last few days. He's been very helpful actually. But I don't know where I am with him, and I don't want to make an arse of myself like I have in the past."

"You won't," said Aidan. "There's going to be lots to keep us busy there. Every time I see you looking wistfully at him, I'll thrust someone in front of you whom you ought to be talking to. Stick with me. You'll be fine."

The Countess smiled. "Thanks."

"You're welcome," replied Aidan. "It's all teamwork."

They chatted for a few more minutes, then Aidan announced it was time to leave. "Right then. Back to the grindstone. Do you want to email your stuff to me?"

"No need, I've already got it all printed out. If you find any silly errors, could you please mark them up for me, and I'll make the corrections."

Back in the office, the Countess made a few phone calls while Aidan reviewed her work. But she couldn't really concentrate on anything else until the presentation had been dispatched.

Aidan came back half an hour later with a couple of small mistakes but nothing serious.

"Do you think it is okay?" she asked him.

"It is indeed brilliant, my dear – bloody brilliant! You're quite a star, aren't you? You'll have them all eating out of your hand, never mind about that one in particular. Hey, maybe, when you see him, you'll think he's pig ugly and wonder what you ever saw in him in the first place. Either that, or you'll charm the pants off the guy, and he'll be sitting through your presentation with a hard-on the size of Mount Fuji!"

The Countess slapped his arm playfully. "Stop it," she said. "You're so rude."

She got everything completed by midday and emailed her files off to the conference organisers. "Done," she said to herself. Then she thought of the MSL. Should she send him an email before leaving the office? *Yes, I think I will*, she decided.

She sent him a very quick note saying that she had completed the work, thanked him for his help and told him that her presentation would be the event of the century, so he must sign up for it when he registered for the conference. Then she logged out of her computer and locked it in her office drawer as she had absolutely no intention of doing any more work between then and Monday morning. She left the office at about twelve thirty, stopped for a sandwich then headed back to Kennington Mansions with only the thought of getting into bed and sleeping on her mind.

"You're home early," said American Ted as the Countess went straight to her bedroom, stripped off all her clothes and leapt under the duvet.

"It's been a long week," she said.

"Did you get everything finished?" asked American Ted.

"Yep," said the Countess. "Signed, sealed and delivered. I got Aidan to have a final look at it just in case I'd screwed up in any way. All is well, and it's done. I'm going to have a very relaxing weekend now. My laptop is at work, so it's a complete weekend off."

"That's good, Madame," said American Ted. "You've had a busy time."

Flight 984

A few weeks later, it was with a sense of trepidation that the Countess boarded flight BA984 to Berlin. It seemed that both her professional and personal life hung in the balance on this trip. If she was successful with her presentation and subsequent networking, then she would almost certainly be made a director of Periculum Software Solutions. As well as the satisfaction of having been promoted so quickly, directorship would give her an equity stake in the firm and a profit share. The following day she would lead a conference session in front of a large audience, but the attention of only one of them would matter most.

The previous day had been hectic. Despite it being a Saturday, she had met Aidan at the office, along with the other staff who were attending the conference, so that they could go through the final checks. Everyone except the Countess had flown out to Berlin that evening to set up the stand and be ready for the start of the conference the next afternoon. The Countess, being a speaker, was relieved of this duty and did not have to leave until Sunday morning.

She was finished at the office by about midday on Saturday and then met up for lunch with Marie at a café in Islington.

"Are you ready for it?" asked Marie as they perused the

menu.

"Ready as I'll ever be," replied the Countess and then sat very quietly.

"Are you all right?"

"No. I'm quite scared, to be honest."

"About the speaking or the MSL?"

"I'm not at all worried about the presentation. I know I can do that. I'll enjoy doing that, and hopefully, it will go well. But I'm absolutely terrified about the MSL."

"Why?" asked Marie.

"I don't know," said the Countess. "I'm so confused as to how I should act around him. I'm nervous that I will make a complete idiot of myself. Then I panic that I won't like him anymore and will think myself stupid for being heartbroken for so long. But most of the time, I worry that I'll like him even more than ever before, but he won't want to spend any time with me. Basically, there is all this rubbish going through my head, and I feel like it's going to explode."

"Okay. Just calm down," said Marie and she put her menu down on the table. "Don't have preconceptions either way. When you see him, just say hello, and see where it goes. Remember that he will probably be feeling a bit strange too. He's been flirting with you by phone and email recently, but he hasn't *seen* you in ages. And both of you have to do business while you're there. Neither of you can focus solely on each other."

The Countess nodded.

A waiter came and took their drinks order.

"Diet coke, please," said the Countess, then, turning to Marie, "I can't drink today. I need to keep my wits about me later and get everything packed."

"White wine spritzer please," said Marie to the waiter. She continued talking to the Countess. "Take each thing as it comes. The most important event is your presentation. Don't let anything, not even him, interfere with that. In fact, your presentation will give you the perfect excuse not to get too wrapped up with him when you first bump into him. He'll understand that you have a big task in front of you and give you the space to do that."

The Countess smiled. "I know. Everything that you are saying makes sense, and I suppose, at the end of the day, I'll be fine. But it is just such an unknown quantity and I've invested too much heartache in it previously. I don't want to be hurt and feel let down again."

"You won't be," said Marie. "It's either going to work or it won't this time. He's either going to be all over you, and you will enjoy it, or it's not going to happen, but for a good reason – which you will be completely okay with. I've got quite a good feeling about it. I think you've worked through a lot of stuff these last few months and you're much more grounded and focused. I think you'll be able to handle it, whatever happens."

"Thank you," replied the Countess. "I hope you are right."

"So, what's the plan for the next few days?" asked Marie.

"The whole thing kicks off at midday tomorrow," said the Countess. "The exhibition hall opens at that time, and there is a keynote address at about two thirty. Then there are a couple of sessions which run to around five, the exhibition goes on for a while after that, and that's the first day."

"Wow," said Marie. "Big schedule. Funny how it starts on a Sunday. You lose the weekend."

"Yeah, it's a bummer," said the Countess. "Aidan and the rest of them are flying out this afternoon so they can get there and set up ready for opening the exhibition tomorrow. My flight doesn't get in until nine fifty-five, so it's going to be tight on time. I have to go straight to the hotel, where I hope I can check in so I can quickly dump my stuff, race over to the conference hall and start shaking hands and being nice to all our clients and potential clients. When I've been to conferences in the past, I usually skip the first couple of sessions, but I can't this time because I need to be aware of what's being said so I can tie it into my presentation."

"What day are you presenting?" asked Marie.

"Monday," replied the Countess. "There are several other sessions going on at the same time. I rang the organisers yesterday and they said that nearly three hundred people had registered for mine. Usually, everyone gets hammered on the first night, but I won't be able to because I have to be in good shape for the next morning. I'll probably have one drink to be sociable, then dinner in my room and do my last-minute preparations. That bit is going to be very boring."

"At least you get it over and done with though," said Marie.

"Yes, then the worst is over. Later that evening is the gala ball where I would like to get lucky with the MSL. I shall be wearing my new silk frock, and I am absolutely certain he will look very yummy in black tie. Then there are other sessions on Tuesday, followed by more parties that night, half a day on Wednesday and then we are done. It's going to be exhausting but hopefully, on all fronts, worth it."

"That's good," said Marie. "You're going to be free in time for the big gala ball. Imagine having to stay sober and go to bed early on the night of the main party."

"That's why Aidan requested the second day," replied the Countess. "I figured that it would give me time to get settled in but then get it all over and done with so that I am free to spend the rest of the time socialising and networking and not having to think any more about presenting. And this way, hopefully, I get two nights with the MSL. Even if he prostrates himself naked at my hotel room door tomorrow night, I'll have to say no, not now, because of my preparation."

"If that happens, at least he'll be gagging for you by the time of the ball," said Marie. "Do him good to have to wait for you. Bloody hell, you've had to wait long enough for him to get his act together!"

"Exactly," said the Countess.

Their drinks arrived.

"Are you ready to order?" asked the waiter.

"No, we haven't even looked at the menus yet," said the Countess. "Can we have another couple of minutes, please."

"The seafood risotto is excellent," said Marie. "I have it every time I come here."

The Countess scanned the menu. "I think I'm going to have pasta. Something with a creamy sauce. It's my comfort food."

"What time do you have to leave in the morning?" asked Marie.

"I have a cab booked for ten to six."

"Ouch! On a Sunday morning. Why don't you just go out all night and then go straight to the airport?"

"Tempting, but I've got to be functioning one hundred per cent the whole time in Berlin, and somehow, I don't think I'd be in very good shape later in the day tomorrow if I did that. It's not just the MSL. I've got a big promotion riding on this conference. If I speak well and pull in lots of business, then they will make me a director. It feels like my whole bloody life is resting on the next four days."

"What about the MSL?" asked Marie. "Will you sleep with him if you get the chance?"

"Hmm, don't know. I'll have to wait and see what happens," said the Countess. "I've spent years thinking about nothing else, but on the other hand, it might be better to wait. I don't want him to think I'm easy. Who knows? I'm just going to see how it all pans out."

"Make sure you don't get drunk and give in to him too soon," said Marie.

"Yes, I need to be careful about that," said the Countess. "I've drunk a lot less recently, but this conference is known to be a very boozy affair. It's going to be a challenge not to get plastered."

"Don't be embarrassed to switch to soft drinks," said Marie. "If you drink tonic water, then it looks like a G&T anyway. It can be quite an advantage to be sober when everyone else is drunk because you find out all their secrets."

"Yes, I've noticed that in the last few weeks," said the Countess. "Shit! Now you've made me all nervous again."

"Don't panic," said Marie. "Use your wisdom, do what comes naturally and savour every moment."

The waiter returned.

"Tortellini, please," said the Countess. "And a green salad on the side."

* * *

By the time the Countess had finished lunch with Marie, made a quick trip to the shops to buy a few bits for her trip and returned to Kennington Mansions, it was just after four thirty. She decided to pack there and then. Usually, she left her packing until bedtime and subsequently had a late night. However, this time, she really wanted to be on form, so as soon as she walked through the door of Kennington Mansions, she began to round up the accessories.

Mongolian Sheep Pussy was on the sofa where the Countess had left her from her previous night out.

"Hello, my darling Mongolian Sheep Pussy," said the Countess. "Are you ready for our trip tomorrow?"

"Yes, Madame," she replied. "I'm really looking forward to it."

"Okay, let's go and sort everyone out."

The Countess picked up Mongolian Sheep Pussy and went upstairs to her bedroom. She took her weekend suitcase from her wardrobe and began to put her things in it. She placed her evening dress and her suit in a garment bag. Everything else went into the case. She put her work papers and other paraphernalia she needed for the conference in her laptop bag.

"Okay, chaps," she said as she grabbed Pussy Original, Pussy With Balls and Mongolian Sheep Pussy and took them to the case. "Is everyone ready for our trip?"

"This feels like the old days," said Pussy Original. "I haven't been away for ages. When you worked at SC Radcliffe, I think I pretty much travelled right around the world with you."

"Yes, you probably did," replied the Countess. "Gosh, those days seem such a long time ago now."

Pussy With Balls was very excited about going to the conference with the Countess. This was his first time out of London. He had never even been on an aeroplane. "Do I need my own passport, Madame?" he asked.

"No," laughed the Countess. "You'll be fine. However real

you all are to me, bags, coats and even teddy bears don't need a passport."

He had spruced himself up especially for the trip. Earlier, he had gone downstairs to where Mongolian Sheep Pussy had been and asked her to give him a brush with one of the Countess's hairbrushes.

"I want to look my best for Berlin," he said to Mongolian Sheep Pussy. "I don't want everyone thinking us Brits don't know how to present ourselves."

Mongolian Sheep Pussy was impressed with Pussy With Balls' attitude and had him brush her as well.

"There you go," said Pussy With Balls. "You look lovely. I'm a lucky bloke to be going away with you."

Mongolian Sheep Pussy adored Pussy With Balls. He was such a sweetheart. "Thank you," she said. "I'm looking forward to going away with you too. Perhaps we can have a day of sightseeing together."

"That would be great," he replied. "I'll take you anywhere you want to go."

"I'd like that," said Mongolian Sheep Pussy. "I know that I'd feel safe in a strange city if I were with you."

"You would be," he said. "I'd lay my life down for you."

* * *

When packing, the Countess was suddenly undecided about whether to use Pussy Deluxe or the Queen Mum bag for the journey. She was reluctant to pack Queen Mum bag lest she was crushed, but in the end, as she would be travelling on a Sunday and the first day of the conference was informal, she decided to stick with Pussy Deluxe. In order to save the

Queen Mum bag from being too squashed, she rolled up her underwear and packed them into the bag before placing her in the case.

"Thank you for that kind consideration, Madame," said the Queen Mum bag as the Countess placed her in the case.

"You're welcome," said the Countess. "You're going to be my right-hand bag on Monday. It's my big day, and I know that you'll give me the perfect image for my presentation."

"That's right," said the Queen Mum bag. "Actually, you already have the perfect image. Never underestimate that, Madame. You are exceptionally talented and doing very well in your career. I have no doubts that you will give an exemplary performance on Monday and win as much business as you need to secure your promotion to director. As far as I can see, Madame, your success is already assured."

"Thank you," said the Countess. "Coming from you, that is quite a compliment."

The Countess, with so much practice over the last few years, was quick at packing and had completed the task within an hour. All she had to do was throw in her toiletries after her morning shower and the job was done.

She spent the rest of the day and evening relaxing. At around seven o'clock, the phone rang. The Countess had a feeling that it was going to be the MSL, and she was correct. "Hey, you," he said as she picked up. "Are you all ready for your big moment?"

"As I'll ever be," she replied. "Are you in the US or are you already in Berlin?"

"I'm still in New York," he said. "I'm leaving in a few hours and get into Berlin tomorrow mid-morning. I take it you're going there tomorrow too?"

"Yes," she said. "I'm leaving really early. I have to be up at five."

"Ouch!" said the MSL echoing Marie's reaction. "Well, we'll both be tired. I'll be flying the red-eye, so it won't be a pretty day."

"You can always skip the keynote stuff and have a sleep. I have to go in case anyone asks me awkward questions about it on Monday. Are you still planning to attend my presentation?"

"Of course. I wouldn't miss it for the world," he replied. "I'm going to be at the back, claiming credit by telling anyone who'll listen that I taught you everything you know."

"Bloody cheek," said the Countess. "Although, that's probably not far wrong. I suppose I have followed in your footsteps but in my own unique, European-influenced way."

"In a unique, Countess-influenced way more like," said the MSL, laughing softly.

"Did you get into the Kempinski?" asked the Countess.

"Yes. Is it anywhere near the conference hall?" he asked.

"Sort of. It's not right next door, but it's a short cab ride or a few stops on the U-Bahn," said the Countess.

"The what?"

"Subway in your language," said the Countess. "There are a couple of stations near the hotel, and one of them is on the same line as the conference centre. A lot of the parties and entertaining will be at the Kempinski anyway. It's the main hotel for the conference. The gala ball on Monday will be there and I think a couple of the events of Tuesday night too."

"So, we will be in exactly the right place," said the MSL.

"Of course. I'm always in the right place. Do you not trust me?"

"Countess, I trust you implicitly. I can't imagine there'll ever be a time when you're in the wrong place."

"Thank you. Do you have your tux all ready for Monday night?" asked the Countess.

"Yes. Hopefully the wrinkles will have dropped out by then."

"Hang it in the bathroom when you are showering. The steam makes all the creases drop out." The Countess could not help but think about the MSL in the shower as she said this.

"I never knew you were so practical. Don't you have an entourage to take care of that kind of thing?"

The Countess joked in her reply. "I usually hire someone locally on arrival to take care of the practicalities. I'll hire you if you like. You can sort out my evening dress at the same time."

"I'm not sure I'd know how to take care of an evening dress," said the MSL. "I wouldn't want to ruin it for you."

"I'm sure a smart man like you would figure it out," she replied.

"Well, I guess I'll bump into you at some point tomorrow then, either at the Conference Hall or back at the Kempinski," said the MSL.

"I'll be looking out for you. I'm afraid I won't be able to be that sociable tomorrow night because I have to be on the ball and not hung-over for Monday," she said. "But if you ask me nicely, I'm sure I could have one drink with you."

"You'd better. I would be disappointed if you didn't. But I do understand that you have to be well behaved tomorrow. That will make a change for you, party girl that you are!"

"I'm going to be the picture of good behaviour, especially on Monday. You won't recognise me," said the Countess.

"Yes, I will. You'll be the tall gorgeous one standing at the front of the hall."

The Countess felt a bolt of excitement run through her. *He called me gorgeous!* This temporarily threw her, and she could not think of anything to say in reply, so a brief embarrassed silence ensued. Then the MSL started to talk again. "Yes. Anyway, I should let you finish your packing, and I'll see you tomorrow."

"Okay then. Have a good flight."

"You too," he replied.

"Bye." The Countess hung up then slapped herself on her forehead. "That was so lame," she said aloud. "He gives you one compliment, and you completely lose it. You're going to have to do better than that in Berlin."

* * *

Despite her good intentions, the Countess did not go to bed until just after midnight. When her alarm rang at four forty-five, it came as quite a shock. She snoozed for about ten minutes then knew that she had no choice but to get out of bed. "Come on Ted, time to wake up," she said to American Ted as she threw back the bed covers.

American Ted yawned and rubbed his eyes with his paws. "Morning, Madame," he said. "It's just too early, isn't it?"

"You can say that again," said the Countess. Straightaway, she took American Ted and placed him in her suitcase. She had been undecided whether to take her teddy with her as if she did end up in hotel room with the MSL, she certainly did not want him to know that she still slept with a teddy. However, it seemed unfair not to take American Ted when she was taking all the other accessories, and anyway, she could do

160

her usual trick of hiding him if things were looking promising.

She showered and breakfasted quickly and was relieved that she had packed everything the night before. She had written a list of the most important things she needed for her presentation and the gala ball. After completing a final check against this list, she placed her toiletries and make-up in her luggage and, surprisingly, had five minutes to spare before her taxi arrived.

"This is a very efficient departure, Madame," said Pussy Deluxe.

"Thank you," said the Countess. "I just hope my cab arrives on time now. I don't want to miss the flight."

"You have plenty of time, Madame," he said. "It will only take twenty or thirty minutes at the most to get to Heathrow at this hour on a Sunday morning."

"Yes, I suppose you are right. I'm used to catching the early plane on a Monday morning, when even before seven o'clock, the traffic is a nightmare. I don't suppose there are many people mad enough to travel at this ungodly hour on a Sunday morning."

"Will you be using me all day, Madame?" asked Pussy Deluxe.

"Probably," replied the Countess. "As soon as we get to the hotel, we'll have to head off to the conference centre. In a way, I ought to have Pussy Original with me, as if we do bump into the MSL, he would be the best one to meet him, but unfortunately, he doesn't quite reflect the right image for our exhibition stand."

"Of course not, Madame," said Pussy Deluxe. "Don't worry – I will do my best to make you look business-like but with a Sunday-casual feeling."

The Countess's taxi arrived, so she grabbed Persian Dolly. She had debated whether or not to take him, but the weather forecast for London was chilly for the time of year. She figured that Berlin would be similar, and therefore, she might be glad of a warmer coat. If it was too warm, she could always wear him around her shoulders.

While the driver loaded her bags into the boot, she stood outside and looked up at the pre-dawn sky. She wondered if her life would be the same when she returned or whether a significant event would occur with the MSL that would change things forever.

* * *

Normally, on a flight, the Countess would tuck into any food that was on offer. However, when the breakfast was served, she found that she only nibbled on the croissant, didn't fancy any of the scrambled egg and just drank coffee. All the time, she kept wondering at which point she would bump into the MSL and how that would go. *Please don't let me make an idiot of myself*, she kept thinking. *I must be cool, calm and relaxed. Remember, the business you are doing here is more important than him. He is just a bonus. Remember, remember, remember this.*

The Countess was on tenterhooks from the minute she disembarked the plane at Berlin's Tegel airport. What if she bumped into him here? Did she look good, or did she look as though she had been up since four forty-five that morning? In the end, she reasoned that he had been flying all night, and if they did meet up there, he would also not be looking or feeling his best. Additionally, she was panicking about timing. The plane had been delayed by half an hour, so it was already ten thirty, and she was supposed to be at the conference hall by midday.

The MSL was nowhere to be seen, and the Countess quickly passed through immigration, collected her luggage and made her way to the taxi rank. "Hotel Bristol Kempinski, bitte," she said as she handed the taxi driver her bags. As always seemed to be the norm when travelling in Europe, the driver immediately realised she was British and spoke to her in excellent English all the way to the hotel.

The Countess enjoyed the journey. As the taxi made its way up the Kürfürstendamn, West Berlin's main shopping street, she smiled as she saw her favourite shops. Names such as Max Mara, Bruno Magli and Versace flashed by and momentarily helped her to forget all her fears. Then the taxi turned off the Kürfürstendamn and took a couple of side roads before pulling up outside the main door of the Kempinski, where a smartly dressed member of staff opened the door of the taxi for her. She paid the driver, left her luggage with the doorman and walked into the hotel.

The lobby was huge, with very comfy-looking couches everywhere, marble floors, high ceilings and an air of class and luxury wherever one looked. On the walls were expressionist style paintings depicting 1920s Berlin which had the same green, brown and red tones as the other décor. Again, she immediately scanned around for a sighting of the MSL, but none was forthcoming.

The check-in desk was straight ahead. There were two people ahead of her in the queue. *Bugger,* she thought. She looked at her watch. It was eleven twenty-five. She really needed to be on her way.

As the first person finished their check-in, the Countess

looked around the reception. There was another woman typing something into a computer at the far end of the desk, and now, two more people had arrived and were standing behind her. Why couldn't they have more reception staff on? This was going to be a busy conference, and everyone was arriving now.

The woman who had been typing looked up and saw the queue. She walked a few paces towards the centre of the reception desk then called out, "Kann ich Ihnen helfen?"

"Ya, danke," said the Countess as she pulled out her booking documents from Pussy Deluxe.

"Come this way, please, madam," said the receptionist.

The Countess gave her name and conference details, and the receptionist tapped away at her computer. "Ah, this is good," she said. "I can see that you are a speaker for Periculum. We've just had a suite become unexpectedly available. I could let you have it for a small surcharge over the conference rate."

"Oh, that sounds tempting," said the Countess. "How much extra would it be?"

"Fifty Deutsch Marks per night," replied the receptionist.

The Countess thought for a moment. It wasn't too much money, and she could always offer to pay the difference herself if Aidan had a problem with it. Should anything happen with the MSL, it might be nice to have a lounge area as a buffer before moving on to the bedroom.

"I'll take it," she said. "Thank you."

"Good," said the receptionist. "It's a beautiful suite. I hope you'll be very comfortable there."

"I'm sure I will," said the Countess, as an image of the MSL lounging on a sofa flashed through her mind.

The receptionist finished registering the Countess and then

gave her the key. "It's on the sixth floor. Take the corridor directly ahead from the lift, and your suite, the Nollendorf, is the second door on the right. Have a wonderful stay."

The Countess followed the receptionist's directions to her room. The suite had its own small entrance hall with a coat stand and hall mirror. Ahead was a reasonably sized lounge area with a sofa and two armchairs around a wooden coffee table, and a large wooden TV cabinet opposite the sofa. Between one of the armchairs and the sofa was a standard lamp. In the corner was a square table against the wall with two chairs positioned at it. The soft furnishings were in an elegant gold and red pattern, all of the wood looked as if it were cherry and the walls were in a neutral pale, sandy gold colour. Pale gold drapes with a fleur-de-lys design hung at the windows.

In the furthest left corner of the lounge was a door that led through to the bedroom. Again, this was of a good size; a huge double bed with a big wooden headboard was flanked by full-length mirrors either side. There was another television and then two doors on the left as one stood at the entrance to the bedroom. The Countess walked up to one and squealed with delight when she opened it. It was a walk-in closet. At the back of the closet was another door which opened onto the bathroom making the bathroom en suite to both the bedroom and the closet. The bathroom contained a huge corner bath as well as a separate shower cubicle.

"This is an excellent room, Madame," said Pussy Deluxe.

"I'll say," said the Countess. "I could live here. It's fantastic. We're so lucky to have this."

She went back into the living room and noticed that there were two doors in the entrance hall. The first was a lavatory, and the second was another shower room.

"Fantastic," said the Countess. "I have two toilets and two shower rooms. Do you think that will be sufficient for the next three days?"

"Probably, Madame," replied Pussy Deluxe. "Just think, if you do get lucky with the MSL, he can have his own shower room."

"Honey," said the Countess. "If I *do* get lucky with the MSL, we're going to spend the whole time in that bath. We definitely won't need two showers!"

There was a knock at the door. It was the porter with the Countess's baggage. This jolted her back to reality, and she suddenly remembered that she had to get to the conference hall. She quickly opened up one of the bags and pulled out her computer and some papers. Then she opened up her suitcase and found Mongolian Sheep Pussy, Pussy Original, Pussy With Balls and American Ted.

"Here you go, guys," she said. "Check this out. Have a good time here, but keep the place tidy. Who knows when I'll be coming back? Bye."

Without stopping to talk to the other accessories, she picked up Persian Dolly and Pussy Deluxe and rushed out of the door, back down to the lobby and out onto the street where she took a taxi to the conference hall.

* * *

On arrival, she had to register and then search for the Periculum stand. She spotted it towards the back, in a corner, and rushed towards it.

"Where the hell have you been?" said Aidan. It was already

166

getting busy, and he desperately needed the Countess to get to work.

"Sorry, the flight was delayed by half an hour, and it was busy once I arrived at the hotel. They gave me a suite though. It's really amazing."

She was about to broach the topic of the cost of the room but Aidan snapped back at her, "I'm glad everything is to your liking. Some of us have been working. Now put this on, and get talking to people." He threw her a short-sleeved burgundy polo shirt with the company logo on it.

The Countess pulled a face. She'd had a horrible suspicion that she would have to wear such an awful thing, but she knew that this was not the time to have a discussion with Aidan over her sartorial standards. She took the shirt and went off to find somewhere to change before returning to the stand. She was glad that she had worn black jeans, as at least they were neutral with the shirt.

"Lock your stuff into this cupboard," said Aidan when she returned. He gave her a key and pointed at the cupboard.

No sooner had she done this than people started coming up to her, and she launched into her spiel about how marvellous Periculum was and the wonders they could do for everyone's risk strategy.

The Countess enjoyed such events, as she was good at talking the talk. In between chatting to prospective customers, handing out brochures and other gimmicks, such as pens and key rings, she discreetly scanned the hall for a glimpse of the MSL. At just after two o'clock, the crowd in the hall started to thin out as people made their way to the main auditorium for the keynote address.

Aidan relaxed a little, and the Countess took the opportunity to mention her room upgrade. "I'm very happy to pay the extra myself," she said.

"How much more is it?" asked Aidan.

"Fifty Deutsche Marks a night," she replied.

"That's very noble of you," said Aidan. "But don't worry about it. Periculum can pick up the tab. It's a fraction of what the company will spend in the bar just for tonight."

"Thanks very much," said the Countess. "I appreciate that."

"You're welcome," said Aidan. "Make sure you keep it tidy though. If push comes to shove, we can use it for entertaining. So, if your hot American is already in residence there, make sure he stays in the bedroom. And don't leave a trail of underwear lying around!"

"I wish," said the Countess.

"Have you seen him yet?" asked Aidan.

"No," replied the Countess. "But he called last night before he left New York. I guess I'll bump into him soon."

After chatting for a couple of minutes, they both decided to leave the stand and make their way to the keynote address. After this, they returned to the exhibition stand where the Countess spent almost an hour chatting to some delegates from a Dutch-owned bank called ACS Smith Gladstone.

At just before six thirty they started to pack up. "Thanks for chatting to the ACS bunch," said Aidan as he tidied some brochures. "They're on my hit list. I've been trying to get an opportunity to talk to them for over a year."

"You're welcome," said the Countess. She gathered up some pens, turned them the same way up and put them back into a company mug. "They're attending my session tomorrow, so hopefully I'll wow them into signing on the dotted line."

"Good. That's why you are here. Right, I think that's

everything done. Let's head back to the hotel. It's been a long day, and I'm dying for a drink."

They locked the cupboards on the exhibition stand then made their way to the lobby of the conference centre. A few delegates were still there, but all of the refreshment stands were closed up. Dusk was starting to fall when they went outside.

"Bugger, no taxis," said Aidan as they started walking across the square in front of the building.

"You'd think for a massive event like this, there would be a constant flow of them," said the Countess. "I've got the card of the guy who took me from the airport to the hotel earlier."

"Don't worry," said Aidan. "The U-Bahn is just a couple of minutes' walk. The fresh air will do us good. Did you use it earlier?"

"No, I didn't," replied the Countess. "As you know, I was already running late, so I just jumped into another cab."

Aidan smiled. He had been annoyed with the Countess earlier, especially as she had ended up with a better room than him, but she was always so good at her work that he couldn't really complain.

When they got back to the hotel, they quickly went back to their rooms to dump their belongings and then the intention was to go straight to the bar.

"Can I take this shirt off now?" asked the Countess as they were in the lift.

"No," said Aidan. "We've got a lot of bums to lick while we are drinking tonight, and we still need to stand out as a team."

"Terrific," replied the Countess, who now seriously hoped that she did not bump into the MSL.

* * *

Despite the arrangement to go straight back to the bar, the Countess decided it was much more important to unpack and organise her things. She hated having to run straight out earlier. Anyway, Aidan had told her to keep the suite tidy, so she reasoned it was hardly tidy with her bags plonked in the middle of the lounge and her accessories running riot.

As soon as she walked into the lounge area of the suite, Mongolian Sheep Pussy asked her, "Have you seen him yet?"

"No," replied the Countess. "I'm sure I'll bump into him later, though I can't stay downstairs too long because I need to get ready for tomorrow."

"Good luck when you do, and stay calm," said Mongolian Sheep Pussy.

"Thanks," said the Countess.

"That's a nice shirt, Madame," said Pussy With Balls.

"Don't take the piss," she said with an awkward smile. "I have to wear it."

"I know. I was just teasing," he replied. "Anyway, Persian Dolly will have been far more mortified about it than you."

The Countess laughed. "That is so true," she replied. "I could feel him cringing with embarrassment when I put him on as we were about to leave the conference centre. It's almost worth wearing him downstairs later just to wind him up a bit more."

The Countess wheeled her suitcase into the bedroom and quickly unpacked her other belongings. She took care to ensure that her evening dress was hung up properly. The accessories had spent the afternoon exploring the suite, and they all came into the bedroom to chat to her as she unpacked.

"This suite is fantastic, isn't it, Madame?" said American Ted.

"Yes, it's lovely," said the Countess. "But Aidan may commandeer it for company entertaining, so in the evenings I have to ask you not to hang out in the lounge, just in case we suddenly come in here with some clients. As much as I love you all, my clients from the corporate world probably wouldn't appreciate your presence in the same way."

"That's no problem at all, Madame," said Pussy Original. "I'll see to it that no one knows we are here. Do you need us to stay in the bedroom now?"

"Hmmm… to be honest, tonight is probably okay. I'm just going to go downstairs for one drink, then I have to come back up here and work."

"Whatever you think best, Madame," said Pussy Original. "Now, stop fussing around with us here and get yourself down to that bar. You never know who might be waiting down there for you. You look great. Don't worry about a thing. Just go down there and do your job."

"Thanks," said the Countess. Then she picked up Pussy Deluxe and left the suite.

Her sense of trepidation returned, as it was now very likely that she would run into the MSL. On the one hand, she was nervous about it, but no matter what happened, she had a very fixed agenda for the evening because she needed to return to her room and do her final preparations for the following day's presentation. That way, nothing could go wrong.

She got into the lift and went down to the lobby floor. It stopped three times on the way, and other conference delegates got in. Her heart thumped on each of these occasions, as she anticipated the MSL stepping in. On arrival at the ground floor, she exited the lift and made her way across the opulent green marble floor of the lobby, through a packed lounge and into the hotel bar. She knew that she would find Aidan at the bar, organising drinks for everybody. From her confident stride, no one would have guessed that her eyes were flickering around in search of a certain American gentleman.

"Glad you could join us, your ladyship," said Aidan. "What's your poison?" The Countess considered whether to go for gin, vodka or Jack Daniels. She decided on the latter, with coke.

Having been in the industry for a few years, the Countess knew half the people in the bar and immediately was waving, navigating around people to get across the room to those she had not talked to for a year or two. It was a very social occasion, and she had soon finished her drink. She was chatting to someone she had worked with in Frankfurt who was trying to persuade her to have another drink. She explained her predicament and was about to refuse the drink when into the bar walked the MSL. Of course, now, there was no way she was leaving. "Oh, go on then, just one more," she replied, hardly looking at the person who had offered her a drink, her gaze instead on the MSL.

He was wearing a casual off-white coloured suit with the jacket slung over one shoulder and a light blue cotton shirt. He looked just as the Countess had remembered him – utterly devastating – and any doubts that she might not be attracted to him anymore evaporated into the ether. Her heart had lurched when she saw him, and now, a few moments later, she found herself rooted to the spot, willing him to look her way. She was standing alone, as her companion was already en route to the bar. She wished that she was still talking to someone so that she could have casually looked up from her conversation as if it were no big deal to see him, but it had not worked out like that and she didn't know what to do. He remained in the doorway of the bar. Was he looking for people that he knew, or was he looking specifically for her?

When the MSL finally noticed the Countess, his eyes lit up. He smiled, and the Countess waved at him. He waved back and made his way through the crowd towards her.

He gave her a big hug as he said hello and then kissed her on the cheek. The Countess said hello back but didn't know what else to say. After the hug, the MSL stood back from her, and there was a brief embarrassed silence. Pussy Deluxe banged himself against her side, which succeeded in jolting her into action.

"How was your trip?" she asked.

"Pretty awful," he replied. "The flight left two hours late, there was a storm and we had the worst turbulence ever coming out of New York."

"Oh no," she said. "I hate it when that happens. My flight was a bit late today as well but not as bad as yours. Anyway, welcome to Europe and to Berlin."

"Thanks," he replied. "I am a bit bamboozled by it all at the moment. I'm used to being in London, so I forgot that this is Germany and everyone speaks a different language. It was so weird this morning, going through the airport and getting a taxi here."

"Do you know any German?" she asked.

"None at all," he replied. "I learned French and Spanish at school, but they're not much use here. You've worked here a lot. You must be fluent."

"No," she laughed. "I know a bit, but I'm really bad at it. I can do bars, restaurants and taxis, but that's about it. Everyone

173

speaks good English though. Especially in big hotels like this. You won't have any problems."

"I know," he replied. "Even the taxi driver chatted to me in perfect English. I can't imagine that happening in New York."

"It puts us to shame doesn't it?" said the Countess. "Have you managed to get any sleep at all? You must be feeling exhausted."

"I slept about an hour on the plane," he replied. "The turbulence was so bad that they had to wait two hours before they could serve up dinner, so there wasn't much of a window for getting rest. Before you knew it, they were bringing out the breakfast stuff."

"Nightmare," said the Countess. "What time did you get here?"

"Around eleven thirty," said the MSL. "I showered then went straight out to the conference place. I was so tired this afternoon. I kept nodding off in that keynote address, so I came back here later on and took a nap. I'm feeling almost human now."

The Countess laughed. "I'm not surprised that you fell asleep in that speech. It wasn't very exciting, was it? The standard stuff you hear at this kind of thing. However, tomorrow, I hear that there is an extremely exciting and interesting speaker, so you'd better not fall asleep in that one!"

"No, ma'am," said the MSL. "I wouldn't dare. If I do, you'll be hurling that pussy purse at me to wake me up. Where is it, anyway?"

"Upstairs in my room. I didn't think he was quite corporate enough for tonight's gathering. But I have many new pussies since we last met. This is Pussy Deluxe. I bought him last time I was in New York."

The Countess offered Pussy Deluxe up to the MSL who immediately stroked him. "Gee, he looks real. What did they have to kill to make this one?"

"Nothing. He's fake. Good fake. I bought him in Bloomingdales."

The person who had been buying her a drink returned.

"Still drinking your favourite then?" said the MSL, referring to the Jack Daniels and coke.

"Of course," replied the Countess. "Thanks very much. Let me introduce you two." The Countess switched to work mode and introduced the MSL to the Frankfurt person. It turned out that they knew each other from phone contact years earlier, but they had never actually met. Then, as is the norm at such occasions, someone else recognised the MSL and began to engage him in conversation.

The Countess also continued her business conversations, pretending to be completely unphased that she had just seen the MSL for the first time in ages and he had instantly hugged and kissed her. Eventually, she drifted over to Aidan.

"He looked pleased to see you," said Aidan.

"Yes, so far so good," said the Countess.

"He's wearing a nice suit. I bet you can't wait to rip it off him," said Aidan.

"That all depends," said the Countess. "Anyway, it won't be tonight. I need to go back up to my room and run through the presentation again. Can I be excused, please, boss?" The Countess drained her glass.

"Yes, you may," said Aidan. "Although, I think there's someone behind you who would prefer you to stay."

While they had been talking, the MSL had moved closer to the Countess. On hearing Aidan's comment, she turned

175

around and saw him.

"Hello again," she said to him. "You've met Aidan before in New York."

"Hi Aidan, how are you doing?" said the MSL. "I'm Ed Crawford."

"I'm good, thanks. Nice to see you again," replied Aidan.

"That glass is looking very empty. Would you allow me to refill it with Jack Daniels?" said the MSL to the Countess.

"I think you'll have a hard job persuading her," said Aidan. "She was just telling me she was about to go back to her room and do some work. She has a busy day tomorrow."

The Countess smiled and was grateful for Aidan's interjection. "He's right, I'm afraid. I only came down for one drink and I've already had two. I really do have to do my final preparations for tomorrow. Sorry."

"No problem," said the MSL. "I completely understand. I don't want to do anything to distract tomorrow's star attraction. Perhaps you would allow me to walk you over to the elevator?"

"That would be lovely," said the Countess. Then to Aidan, she said, "What time shall we meet in the morning? I'd like to get down there at eight to check out the equipment."

"That works for me too," replied Aidan. "Do you want to meet for breakfast?"

"No, I'll probably take it in my room. We can share a cab though. Seven forty-five in the lobby?" said the Countess.

"Done," said Aidan. Then he turned to the MSL and said, "Lovely to meet you again, Ed. The Countess has told me a lot about you. When you've deposited her at the lift and made sure that she doesn't escape from doing her preparation, come back over and let me get you a drink."

"That's a deal," said the MSL. "I'll be with you in a couple of minutes."

The MSL and the Countess walked back through the lounge and into the lobby. The whole area was thronging with conference delegates, all doing business and networking while enjoying a drink. Many, like the Countess, were dressed in a company uniform.

"Do you like my shirt?" she joked with the MSL.

"Oh, yes," he replied. "It's very fetching. The colours really match…" he then struggled to find a comparison. "…your complexion."

The Countess playfully slapped his arm. "Thanks," she said. "Have those two JDs made my skin red then?"

"No. I wish you'd have one more, but I understand that you have things to do," he said.

"It's very tempting to stay, but I really do have to get busy now," said the Countess.

By now, they had reached the lifts. They paused and looked at each other. Neither of them had pressed the button to call the lift.

The MSL smiled. "It's really wonderful to see you. You look terrific."

"What, even in this shirt?"

He laughed, "Even in that shirt. Life has obviously been good for you of late."

The Countess smiled back. If only he knew of her recent traumas and how it had taken four fur bags, one posh handbag and a teddy to put her back together again. Not to mention some tough love from a coat.

"Thanks," she replied. "Yes. Life is pretty good."

They paused again. This time, the Countess broke the

silence. "I suppose I'd better get the lift then." She pressed the button and one of the lift doors opened immediately. "I guess I'll see you tomorrow," she said.

"Yes. I'll be there, cheering you on. Good luck – not that you'll need it."

"Thanks. Good night," said the Countess as she walked into the lift. The MSL waved at her as the doors closed.

Inside the lift, the Countess leaned back against the wall and smiled. Stage one complete. She had met the MSL and had not made a fool of herself. More importantly, he had been very attentive to her.

The Presentation

As soon as she got back into her room, the Countess got straight on with her work. She was excited about the MSL, but she did her best not to dwell on it too much. She had other things to do. As promised by Pussy Original, the accessories were nowhere to be seen in the lounge area of the suite but had retired to the bedroom where they were all sitting on the bed, chatting.

The Countess started up her computer, arranged her papers and then ordered dinner from the room service menu. After a couple of minutes, Pussy Deluxe spoke, "If it is all right with you, Madame, I'll go and join the others. I presume they are in the bedroom."

"Yes, whatever you want to do," she replied, staring at her computer. Then she turned to face him and added, "Thanks for your help tonight. I was about to make a fool of myself, but you saved me just in time. Tell me, did you like the MSL?"

"He comes across as a decent man, Madame," said Pussy Deluxe. "He seems very keen on you."

"Yes, it's looking good isn't it? Anyway, I'm determined not to get too excited about it now." She saw him struggling to get down from the sofa. "Here, let me take you into the bedroom."

"Thank you, Madame," replied Pussy Deluxe as the Countess

got up from her chair and picked him up. Then she turned to Persian Dolly whom she had earlier thrown over the back of the sofa and said, "What about you, Persian Dolly? Do you want to go in the bedroom with the others?"

Persian Dolly had deliberately not chosen this option earlier but had remained in the lounge when Pussy Original had told everyone else that they must return to the bedroom. At that time, Pussy Original had said to him, "You too, sheep. You look untidy, thrown over the back of that couch."

"I'm fine here, thank you," he had replied. "If she brings anyone up here, they won't think it odd to have a coat left lying around. It's just you freaks that she needs to hide away."

Pussy Original could not be bothered to argue. Persian Dolly was a law unto himself, and Pussy Original did not want any aggravation that would later upset the Countess, so he left him alone.

"Is Persian Dolly not coming in?" Mongolian Sheep Pussy had asked.

"No," Pussy Original had replied. "He considers that it's only us lot that need to be hidden away and that it is okay for one of the Countess's business associates to find him lolling around on the sofa. He's got a point in a way. It won't matter if anyone sees a coat in that room. I just left him to it."

"Good," Pussy With Balls had said. "I don't want him in with us anyway."

Now that the Countess had asked him where he wanted to be, Persian Dolly figured that he had better play along and pretend to be one of the gang. "Okay, then," he replied. "Sure, take me into the bedroom. Whatever suits you, Madame."

"I've been very good this evening to come away from the drinks party when it was only just getting going, to say nothing of dragging myself away from the MSL," said the Countess as she picked up Persian Dolly and Pussy Deluxe.

"Well done, Madame," said Persian Dolly. "Just stay as well controlled as that for the rest of the conference, and you'll be fine."

The Countess carried them both into the bedroom where she put them down on the bed with the other accessories.

"Hello, everyone," she said. "I hope you've settled in okay. I'm busy now, but I'm sure that Pussy Deluxe will be delighted to fill you in on the news so far." She left the room immediately and went back to her work.

"What happened?" asked American Ted. "Did she see the MSL?"

"Did he ask her out?" said Mongolian Sheep Pussy straight away.

"Was she okay?" asked Pussy Original.

"Patience," said Pussy Deluxe. "Give me time, and I will tell all." He enjoyed this position of power. It was not often that he was privy to the Countess's business, as it always seemed to be the others she spent the most time with or confided in. He intended to milk this for all it was worth.

"Come on, hurry up," said Pussy With Balls. "This is important."

"Did she see him?" asked Mongolian Sheep Pussy.

"Yes. He was there," replied Pussy Deluxe.

"Fantastic," said Mongolian Sheep Pussy. "What was he wearing? What did he say? Did he kiss her? When is she going to see him again?"

Pussy With Balls smiled at Mongolian Sheep Pussy. She was such a fantastic girlie bag. He loved how women needed to know all the fine details, whereas men are generally interested in answers to more earthy questions like, "When will they shag?" or "I wonder what she looks like *under* that dress."

Pussy Deluxe related the events in a quick, unembellished style. "He was wearing a light-coloured suit and a blue open-neck shirt. He hugged her and kissed her on the cheek the minute he saw her, but other than that, there were no other exchanges of bodily fluid. He wanted to buy her another drink, but she insisted, with a bit of prompting from Aidan, that she needed to come up here and work. She will see him again tomorrow when she does her presentation."

"What did they talk about?" asked Mongolian Sheep Pussy.

"Nothing of a sexually explicit nature. Boring stuff like their respective journeys and how everyone here can speak English. Oh, and yes… he asked after you, Pussy Original, but the Countess told him how she had decided to use me today, and he stroked and admired me. Did he used to admire you?"

Persian Dolly sniggered.

Pussy Original heard the snigger and said, first to Persian Dolly, "Oh, so you've decided to join us now, have you? We weren't good enough for you earlier, but any chance to suck up to the Countess and you'll stoop to our level. I heard you… *whatever suits you, Madame,*" he said, mocking Persian Dolly's voice.

Then he replied to Pussy Deluxe. "I'm a legend with the New York crew. Are you?"

Pussy Deluxe didn't answer, so American Ted asked him, "How was the Countess? Did she cope okay when she saw him? And how is she now?"

"She nearly lost it," said Pussy Deluxe. "When she saw him, she didn't move or say anything but just stared at him while he made his way towards her. He came straight up and hugged her, but still, she didn't say much. So, I saved the day and nudged her into action. Then she was fine, and they started chatting normally. He was very keen to spend more time with her."

"Thank you," said American Ted. "It is vital that we all keep working as a team throughout the next few days. We must all remain vigilant when we are in her company to ensure that she doesn't do anything that she will regret later. That way, we can keep distress levels to a minimum."

"No problem," replied Mongolian Sheep Pussy.

"Sounds good to me," said Pussy With Balls.

"All of us," repeated American Ted. "That includes you, Persian Dolly. Will you promise to look after her? You will probably spend the most time with her over the next few days. I know that you think we are all strange, but we really need you to be of the same mind, just this once."

"Yes, of course I'm going to look after her," snapped Persian Dolly. "Just because I don't mollycoddle her doesn't mean that I don't care. Anything to avoid another one of her emotional outbursts."

"Thank you," said American Ted. "What about you, Queen Mum? Are you listening?"

The Queen Mum bag had already tidied herself away into the closet. "Yes, I can hear you," she replied. "Of course you can count on me. I shall be with her tomorrow, and I will make sure that she conducts herself like a lady at all times. There'll be no emotional mishaps when *I'm* with her."

The others smiled. Although the Queen Mum bag rarely mixed and chatted with them, they all admired her old-fashioned sense of duty. Her manner was from another age, and they all respected that. Her separateness from the group was entirely different to the snobbish, self-interested mode of Pussy Deluxe or Persian Dolly.

* * *

After a couple of hours of sitting at her computer alternated with walking around the lounge, rehearsing sections of her presentation, the Countess finally decided that there was nothing more she could do and that it was time for bed. She was very tempted to go back downstairs, especially to see if the MSL was still there, but she decided not to as she was extremely tired. If she went for one more drink it could well end up being one of those times where one finds oneself still there at four in the morning. That would not be good.

As she undressed, she walked around the bedroom, still practising her opening speech. Then she hung the clothes up. She loved the walk-in closet and wished that her apartment in Kennington Mansions was big enough to have one. She saw the Queen Mum bag neatly positioned on one of the shelves.

"Hello, Queen Mum bag," she said. "Isn't this closet fabulous? One day, I'm going to have to find a way of building one for all you accessories. Would you like that?"

"It would be very nice, Madame," said the Queen Mum bag. "But not completely necessary. Even if you did have a special room for us, I think everyone would still go out and chat on your bed."

The Countess laughed. "Yes, that's true, isn't it? I must have the most sociable collection of handbags in the world. You very rarely join them though. Don't you get lonely on your own?"

"No, Madame," said the Queen Mum bag. "Lazing around

informally is just not for me. I like to be on the shelf, ready and waiting for you. Your bedroom at Kennington Mansions is smaller than this, so when we are at home, I can hear everything that is being said. Don't worry, I'm not really left out."

"That's good," said the Countess. "I want you all to be happy. Tomorrow is the big day, and you'll be with me. I hope you enjoy it."

"I always enjoy sitting in on your business, Madame. You always do an excellent job, and I'm sure that tomorrow will be no exception. Now, Madame, perhaps it is time you went to bed. I'd like to say an hour before midnight is worth two after but you've already passed that."

The Countess looked at her watch. "Well, I can still manage it if we pretend that we're on London time."

"That'll have to do," said the Queen Mum bag. "You want to look and perform your best in the morning."

"Yes," said the Countess. "That's exactly what I have in mind. Goodnight."

"Goodnight, Madame," said the Queen Mum bag.

The Countess got ready for bed. "Where do you guys want to be?" she said to the gathering of accessories on the bed. "Shall I take you through to the sofa, or do you want to go in the closet?"

"Let's do the closet," said Mongolian Sheep Pussy. "We haven't done that room yet."

The Countess scooped up the bags in her hands and took them into the walk-in wardrobe where she set them neatly on the shelves next to the Queen Mum bag. Then she hung up Persian Dolly on the rail.

She ate the chocolate left on the pillow from housekeeping

before going into the bathroom to clean her teeth and cleanse her face. Finally, she climbed into bed, set her alarm clock and fiddled with the light switches to figure out which one controlled which light until she finally managed to get the room into darkness.

American Ted was sitting on the pillow on the other side of the bed from where the Countess lay.

She pulled him towards her. "Good night, Ted."

"Goodnight, Madame," he replied. "Sleep well, and don't worry about tomorrow. Everything will be fine."

"Thanks," she replied.

"Madame. Just one more thing. We've heard all about your meeting with the MSL. Are you okay?"

"Yes, I am," she said. "It was a good start. I almost made an arse of myself, but Pussy Deluxe gave me a shove just at the right moment. The MSL seemed pretty keen, and he even kissed and hugged me a couple of times. He looked gorgeous. A picture of perfection. So far, so good."

"I'm pleased, Madame," said American Ted. "Let's hope everything goes okay and he behaves appropriately with you."

"I hope so," replied the Countess. "I don't want any more mixed signals from him. I want him to either go for me or go away. And tomorrow night is the big one. I bet he's going to look amazing in black tie."

"You're going to look stunning too, Madame. Your dress is beautiful, and he won't be able to resist you in it. Anyway. I don't want to disturb you anymore. Let's get some sleep."

"Yes. Let's. Goodnight."

* * *

The Countess's alarm clock went off at six thirty. She hit the snooze button for an extra ten minutes and then got out of bed and staggered into the bathroom. She wished that she had time to enjoy a luxurious bath in the enormous corner bathtub, but like most business trips, there was very rarely any time to take full advantage of all the wonderful facilities offered by a top hotel. "Maybe at some point, I'll make it in there," she concluded as she showered.

After her shower, she ordered her breakfast and then got dressed and dried her hair. After breakfast, and while still drinking her coffee, she applied her make-up and finished her hair. She did a final clean of her teeth and then walked into the closet to get the Queen Mum bag.

"It's time," she said to her. "Let's go."

"Good luck, Madame," said Pussy Original. "I hope everything goes okay today. We'll see you later. I guess you'll be coming back here to change for this evening?"

"Yes. I'm going to wear this lovely dress," she said as she felt the fabric of the dress.

"I'll be all ready for you later, Madame," said Mongolian Sheep Pussy. "You're going to do really well today. Don't worry about a thing."

The Countess smiled at them all, gave them a wave, picked up the Queen Mum bag and transferred her wallet, phone and lipstick from Pussy Deluxe. Before leaving the bedroom, she popped her head back in the closet and said, "Thanks for everything you guys have done for me in the last few months. Today is the day. Let's see how it all turns out."

"You're gonna be great," said Pussy With Balls. "Get out there and knock 'em dead."

"Remember not to chase after the MSL," said Mongolian

Sheep Pussy. "He's got to come to you."

"I know," said the Countess. "Thanks."

The Countess picked up American Ted and gave him a kiss on his forehead. "Thanks, Ted. I'm going to do my best. Have a good day here. You guys can run around the suite all you like during the day, but make sure that everyone is tidied away from about five, just in case I have to bring any clients back."

"Of course, Madame. Goodbye," he replied.

The Countess did a final check on her lipstick, gathered up her work materials and the Queen Mum bag and made her way to the hotel lobby. It was just before seven forty-five. When she arrived in the lobby, she scanned the room for Aidan but could not see him. She decided to take a seat on one of the sumptuous velvet couches that were arranged in front of the reception desk. Five minutes went by, and Aidan had still not arrived. The Countess was feeling twitchy because she desperately needed to get down to the conference centre and set everything up. She decided to go and phone his room from reception. There was no reply, which meant that he must be en route to the lobby. A minute later, he appeared from the direction of the lifts.

"Jesus, you look awful," said the Countess. "What time did you get to bed last night?"

"I think it was close to five," croaked Aidan.

"Bloody hell! Definitely a High Priestess morning then. Good job I left the bar when I did. Come on. I need to get to the conference centre."

They chatted in the taxi.

"You look really pale. I haven't seen you like this for ages. Were you in the bar here until five?" asked the Countess.

"No. We were in some club somewhere. It seemed like a

good idea at the time. Now, I feel absolutely awful. I don't know how I'm going to survive the day. Are you all ready?" he asked.

"As I'll ever be," replied the Countess. "I just need to get there and make sure all the equipment works."

"Stop panicking. You'll be fine. You always are. I'm so glad that it is you doing this today and not me."

The Countess smiled at him. "You can creep off somewhere and have coffee while I sort things out with the sound guy."

"Yes, they had some fabulous pastries at one of the coffee stands. I hope they're open when we get there," said Aidan. "I had more of a chat with your man last night. I think he's on the lookout for some work in Europe."

"Really?" said the Countess. "That sounds promising. Now, don't you go offering him a job. That's the last thing I need right now."

"Yes, ma'am," said Aidan. "Shame though. He's a pretty clever bloke, isn't he?"

"Yes. I learned a lot from him when we worked together. Did he say anything about me?" she asked.

"Maybe."

She punched him lightly on the arm, "Don't tease me. What did he say?"

"He asked about the work you were doing now and where you were heading," replied Aidan. "He told me about some of the times you worked together. I think he really likes you. His face was beaming every time he mentioned you. He brought the conversation back to you a couple of times."

"I hope you said nice things about me," said the Countess.

"Of course, darling," said Aidan. "I told him that you were a class A tart, you were useless at work, and we only gave you the opportunity to present today because you have the best legs in the company and they're great for getting business!"

The Countess punched him again, a little harder this time, "You better not have. Although talking about my legs to him is no bad thing. He needs to know what he has missed out on all his life and need never miss out on again if he plays his cards right."

The Countess's suit skirt was fractionally above knee length, so as she sat in the back of the roomy Mercedes taxi, legs crossed, it rode up her thigh a little.

Aidan patted her knee and said, "That's a good strategy. Sit like that with him and he'll soon be licking your ankles and working his way up. You look very good today, dear. Very wise not to stay up drinking last night. I wish I had followed your example."

The taxi arrived at the conference hall, and the Countess snapped into business mode. The previous day, she had already discovered the room she would be using and introduced herself to the conference technician who would be looking after the equipment for her. He was waiting in the room when they arrived. Aidan slunk off for a coffee as the Countess and the technician set to work.

She wanted to ensure that her laptop would plug into the equipment and work correctly with it. She only had fifteen minutes to do this before she had to vacate the room, as the person who was presenting at nine o'clock also wanted preparation time. Luckily, on the second attempt, everything worked. There was nothing more she could do to prepare. She decided not to return to the exhibition stand but to have a quiet coffee and be ready to go straight back into the room as soon as the earlier presentation had finished.

At ten thirty, she made her way back to the conference room and paced around at the front of the auditorium, wondering when people would start to arrive. What if her opening fell flat? How would she recover? What if someone asked awkward questions? What if she had got the subject matter completely wrong and no one was interested in what she had to say? She remembered that she had left her mobile phone on, so she opened up the Queen Mum bag, took out her trusty Nokia and switched it off. This was a good move as the Queen Mum bag was able to whisper to her some last-minute reassurance.

At ten forty-five, a few people started arriving in the room, and Aidan made his way back in. He had a little more colour in his face, thanks to the coffee and breakfast, but his eyes were still bloodshot. He recognised a couple of members of the audience as the people he had been pitching business to in the exhibition hall the previous day. He shook their hands and then introduced the Countess to them. As the four of them were chatting, the Countess noticed the MSL arrive. Her stomach lurched as she waved at him. He waved back and took a seat in the front row on the opposite bank of chairs. Two other people came and sat next to him, and he started talking with them.

At ten fifty-five, the room suddenly started to fill up. It seemed as though two or three hundred people turned up within the space of two minutes. The Countess walked over to where Aidan was sitting.

"How are you feeling?" he asked.

"Fine. Nothing that a shot of Valium wouldn't cure," she replied. "There are lots of people here."

"That's good," said Aidan. "The more people who hear about

us, the better. The material you have is fantastic. Use your slides as a prop to get going and then it will just look after itself. You talk to people all the time at work, and you're very good at it."

The Countess went back to hovering around the front of the auditorium. She caught the eye of the MSL. He gave her a thumbs-up signal. She thought about going over to say a quick hello to him but decided against it as she didn't need any additional stress, and she didn't want him to see how nervous she actually was.

Before she knew it, the clock at the back of the room had reached eleven o'clock. The Countess looked up at the technician's box on the back wall of the auditorium. He gave her a sign that meant one minute to go. She could see the helpers at the back of the auditorium. They closed one set of the main doors, leaving only one door open for latecomers. The technician indicated to her to start. It was showtime. The Countess looked first at Aidan, then at the MSL and then she began to speak.

She nailed the start, giving her the confidence to move through her material in an easy, everyday style. She began by giving her own background and credentials and then went straight into telling a story of how Periculum had helped one of the biggest banks in the USA, AmeriBank, with their risk systems. She demoed other areas of the Periculum software, particularly those relevant to investment banks, peppering her speech with details from her own experience as well as the stories from other Periculum clients. A couple of times, she had noticed the MSL making notes and smiling appreciatively at what she was saying. Several hands shot up when she got to the end of the formal presentation and asked if people had any questions. She answered each question with competence, spending time on those of a more complex nature.

There were still a couple of questions left, but she could see the technician signalling to her, by waving his fingers across his throat, that she needed to finish.

"That's all we've got time for," she said. "Thank you very much for listening today. Please come and see me by the Periculum stand in the exhibition hall if you have any further questions. Enjoy the rest of the conference."

She received an enthusiastic round of applause and then the delegates stood up and started moving out of the hall. The MSL got straight out of his seat and came up and hugged her.

"Was it okay?" she asked as she held his arms.

"It was fantastic," he said. "Honey, you're a natural. It was interesting, easy to follow, funny, animated... do you want me to go on?"

A few of the delegates had also come to the front to ask her further questions.

"I'd better get out of your way," said the MSL. "I'll see you later." As he released her from the hug, he gave her a quick kiss on the cheek and then moved away.

Flustered from this, but needing to get on and talk to the people in front of her, the Countess, ran her fingers through her hair, pushed it back from her face and said, "Okay, who's first?"

Aidan also came to the front and started taking questions. He spoke to the representatives of ACS Smith Gladstone who had been speaking to the Countess in the exhibition hall the previous day. After answering their questions, he invited them to dine that evening and made arrangements to meet them in the bar at seven o'clock.

Happy with the arrangement, they left the auditorium.

"Yes!" said Aidan and punched the air in front of him with his fist. The Countess, who had also just finished speaking to the last person said, "What's that about?"

"We're having dinner with ACS tonight," he replied. "This is brilliant. You were brilliant. It's all brilliant!"

"That's good. Will they eat at our table at the gala thing then?" asked the Countess.

"No, the gala ball is just drinks and dancing. We have work to do before that. I've already got a table at a restaurant down the road from the hotel. We'll take these guys out, schmooze them and have them eating out of our hand by the end of the night. They loved your presentation. Well done!"

The Countess, being focused for so long on her presentation, had not paid attention to the logistics of the rest of the day. "Oh, so we go out for dinner. I hadn't realised that." Even though she knew that the conference was all about business and that her promotion depended on her winning new clients, she had seen the gala ball as a relaxing reward for working so hard. She had also been looking forward to seeing the MSL there, with both of them dressed up in their finery.

"Okay, whatever you say," she added as she shut down her computer.

* * *

It was a relief to have done the presentation. The Countess was very pleased with herself. She had given many before and been the lead facilitator in many situations, but she had not done anything on the scale of this conference. Now, having completed the task, she wished that she could have a moment to relax. After the presentation, she took her computer back to the exhibition stand and had hoped to sneak off and have some lunch. However, she was again in demand to talk about the services and software that Periculum offered and was soon embroiled in conversation with some conference delegates. Eventually, just after two o'clock, she was able to grab a quick sandwich.

When she returned to the stand, Aidan said, "Ah, thank God you're back. We've been so busy. Here, take these cards and start handing them out. I've got some other things to go and do."

He didn't return until twenty to six when they were starting to pack up.

"Where have you been? I've been trying to phone you," said the Countess. "It's been manic this afternoon."

"Oh, here and there," replied Aidan.

"You look much better than you did earlier," said the Countess. She peered at his face and studied him closely. "Did you take off for a nap this afternoon? Is that why you didn't answer my calls?"

Aidan ran his right hand through his hair and turned away from her as he answered, "We have a very important evening ahead. A gentleman has to refresh himself."

The Countess moved to her left, so she was in front of him again. "You did, didn't you? You buggered off for a sleep."

"Well, I was feeling so awful from last night. And there's a lot riding on dinner tonight."

"Hmm," said the Countess. "So, what time is dinner?"

"We're meeting them in the bar at seven. Our dinner reservation is seven forty-five."

The Countess looked at her watch. "Shit! By the time we

get back to the hotel, I'll have practically no time to get ready."

"Why don't you head off now?" said Aidan. "I'll finish packing up here. Thanks for everything. You have done extremely well today."

"Okay. I'll see you in an hour or so," she said and thrust a pile of brochures she was holding into his hands.

* * *

As she wandered out of the exhibition hall into the foyer, the Countess suddenly felt light-headed and in a daze. She had worked for months towards the presentation and had just expended huge amounts of energy on it. All she wanted was to have a nap, then get into her evening dress, make herself look glamorous and fall into the arms of the MSL. Instead, she would have to rush back, have a quick shower and be ready to talk business again.

She decided that a taxi would be the best option back to the hotel. However, when she got outside, she found that everyone else had the same idea. There was a queue with at least ten people and not a taxi in sight. Then she spied the MSL who was second in the queue. *Perfect*, she thought.

Remembering everything that had been drummed into her by the accessories, she took a deep breath and prepared to appear cool, calm and collected.

She casually strode up to him and said, "Hi. You still around here? I'd have thought you'd be back at the hotel by now, putting your tux on."

"Ahh, Countess," he said, his face suddenly coming alive. "The star of the show. You were so good today. I wanted to chat with you longer, but there were so many people wanting to talk to you, I thought it best that you deal with your fans."

"Are you not one of my fans then?" she asked.

"How could you say that? I'm your biggest fan. Do you want to share a taxi with me?"

"Yes, I'd love to," said the Countess. "It's lucky that you're near the front of this queue. I need to get back to the hotel and get ready for tonight."

"Oh, so you only want to talk with me to get to the head of the line?" replied the MSL.

"Well, yes," said the Countess. "That was part of my motive."

"No problem," said the MSL. "At least I know where I stand. Ed Crawford, Risk Technology Consultant, good at getting taxis."

A taxi arrived for the lady in front of them, so they were now next in the queue.

"I'm sure you're good at other things too," said the Countess who suddenly imagined him being very adept in the bedroom.

"Yes, I can put up shelves, change the oil in a car, and I know never to look in a lady's purse."

The Countess laughed.

"Are you going to the gala ball tonight?" he asked.

"Yes," she said. "Well, hopefully. I have to go out to dinner with some people from ACS first. I wish I didn't. I'm exhausted, and I just want to relax. I thought the gala thing included dinner and we would all be there together."

"Yes, I know what you mean," said the MSL. "I've also got some wining and dining to do. It's time for me to move on from SC Radcliffe. I got chatting to some really interesting people last night, so we'll see how tonight goes."

A taxi arrived.

The MSL opened the door for the Countess. "Your chariot

ma'am," he said.

"Thank you, my dear sir," she replied.

They settled themselves in the taxi, and the MSL instructed it to go back to the Kempinski hotel.

"So, who are you meeting up with tonight?" asked the Countess. "Anyone I know?"

"A few people from Deutsche Bankverein. Do you know Walter Oppenheimer? He knows you," replied the MSL.

"Yes, that name is familiar. Where do I know it from?" said the Countess. "Oh, I know, I worked with him about six or seven years ago. He left soon after I started on the project."

"He spoke very highly of you," said the MSL. "You'll probably bump into him at the gala event. I suppose everyone will converge there later. I can't wait to see you in your evening dress. I'm sure you're going to look stunning."

The Countess blushed. She could not believe that the MSL, after rejecting her when they were in New York, was being so flirty.

"I'll try my best," she replied.

"Do you think you'll be able to spare a dance for a poor lowly American?" he asked.

"I might be able to," she replied. "However, my time is not my own tonight. You'll have to book an appointment with me via my boss. He controls my every move at the moment."

"It's taken care of. I've already given him a very hefty bribe. Hopefully, it will be worth at least two dances with you."

"Okay, that's great," said the Countess. "I'll mark you on my dance card. I'll save the better ones for you."

"I am most honoured," he replied and bowed his head to her.

They chatted about the day just gone at the conference and then the Countess asked, "How's the gang at SC Radcliffe?"

"Same as ever. Dan likes to give me a hard time whenever he can. Mary's got a boyfriend now," replied the MSL.

"Really?" said the Countess. "What's he like?"

"He's a good guy. He works in fixed income at AmeriBank. They seem really in love with each other."

"That's brilliant," said the Countess. "I'll have to send her an email when I get back to London. Are you seeing anyone at the moment?" She was not sure whether this was a good thing to ask him, but the words had slipped straight out of her mouth before she'd had a chance to think about it.

Unlike previous conversations, the MSL was not flustered by the topic. "Nope, I'm all on my lonesome," he replied.

"Me too," said the Countess.

"So, you haven't been snapped up by a handsome British guy?" he asked.

"No, not yet," she replied and looked him straight in the eye.

He nodded, smiled at her and said, "I'm pleased to hear that."

The taxi arrived at the hotel. As they were walking into the lobby, the MSL again made references to meeting up later.

"Well, I guess I'll see you in the ballroom later," he said.

"Yes," said the Countess. "I have no idea what time. I think it goes on until two in the morning, so we are bound to have finished our dinners and be back here by then. See you later."

"I hope so," he replied.

The Countess headed off to her room to get changed, and the MSL went off to find someone in the bar. Two or three seconds after they had gone their separate ways, the MSL called across the lobby, "Hey Countess!"

The Countess heard him, stopped and turned around.

"Don't forget those two dances," he shouted.

The Countess smiled, half waved and then continued her

journey to the lift.

* * *

The Countess was alone in the lift.

"Wow!" she said to the Queen Mum bag once the doors had closed. "Is he, or is he not interested in me?!" She pressed the button for the sixth floor.

"He certainly was pleased to hear you are still single," said the Queen Mum bag.

"Yes, he was," said the Countess. "I'm not mistaken, am I? He seems really into me now."

"Yes, Madame. He does appear keen to make sure he dances with you later on," replied the Queen Mum bag, "but it is important that you keep focused on your business. I know you don't want to have dinner with that Dutch bank, but you must. If he is serious, then he will be there for you later on."

They went straight to the sixth floor without stopping. The Countess entered her suite. She knew the accessories would all be lurking in the bedroom, so she opened the door and said, "Hello chaps."

As usual, they were all on the bed.

"How did it go?" they asked.

"She was a triumph," said the Queen Mum bag before the Countess had a chance to answer. "She had the whole auditorium eating out of her hand. Our mistress is an incredibly talented lady. Now, she has little over half an hour to get ready for tonight, so let's not detain her."

The accessories were dying to talk to the Countess to catch up on the latest developments with the MSL, but they knew that they had to respect the time constraints. Instead,

Mongolian Sheep Pussy quizzed the Queen Mum bag.

"Did she see the MSL today?" she asked.

"Yes. He sat in the front row at the presentation and they have just shared a taxi together to get back here," replied the Queen Mum bag.

"Wow," said Mongolian Sheep Pussy. "That sound's good. How is it going between them? Has he asked her out yet or professed undying love?"

"No," replied the Queen Mum bag, "but he does seem very pleased to be around her. She has promised to save him two dances tonight. First, they both have to entertain over dinner."

"So, they don't get to dine in the same place?" said Mongolian Sheep Pussy. "I bet she is disappointed about that. She had visions of spending the whole evening with him."

"Yes," said the Queen Mum bag. "But she must do her work. That is why she is here. She has a very important engagement tonight where she will help her employer clinch a huge business deal."

"But what if they miss each other?" said Mongolian Sheep Pussy. "This is supposed to be their night. She's going to be looking gorgeous in her dress, and he will be in his dinner jacket and bow tie. They are supposed to dance together, have a perfect time, fall in love and then live happily ever after."

Pussy Original sighed while Pussy With Balls smiled. It was just impossible to suppress Mongolian Sheep Pussy's sense of romance.

The Queen Mum bag answered brusquely, "Don't get too carried away with that thought, my dear. That man has done nothing but leave her disappointed from the day she ever fell in love with him. Now, if he does turn out to be worth his salt, then he will find her and pursue her and just…" she hesitated. The Queen Mum bag never swore but now, out of exasperation, she said, "…just bloody well be there for her."

"Oh, let's hope so," said Mongolian Sheep Pussy. "It would be so wonderful to see them happy together."

The Countess was also dying to talk with the accessories about her taxi journey back to the hotel, but she did not have much time. She had a quick shower and then embarked on her beauty routine for the evening. Wearing the sumptuous hotel bathrobe, she used a heated curling brush to give her hair more volume and took a section from each side at the front and pinned it back with a pearl-covered hair slide. Then she did her make-up.

She went into the closet, picked up her dress and came back into the bedroom.

"Are you enjoying it here?" she asked the accessories.

"We've had a lovely day, Madame," replied Mongolian Sheep Pussy.

"The Queen Mum bag told us about your wonderful presentation, Madame. We are all so proud of you," said American Ted. "We hope that this evening is as successful."

"Yes, today could not have gone better. I was really pleased with it. No major cock-ups and no one asked me any questions that I couldn't answer. Lots of people congratulated me afterwards, and we're going to get loads of business out of it. The Dutch bank is a real coup. All I have to do is sweet-talk them tonight and then we can get down to proper negotiations within a few days. And the MSL, at last, is dying to dance with me. He's been saying all the right stuff to me since we got here. Tonight, my dear furry friends, is going to be my night in all ways. This is my moment. My perfect moment."

"We're all rooting for you, Madame," said American Ted.

"I hope everything goes okay. We don't like it when you get upset. But, if things don't go as you hope, you know we are here for you. You can pop up here any time during the evening if you need bolstering."

"Thanks, Ted," replied the Countess. "As always. Where would I be without you all? You know something? I think I'm finally beginning to get the hang of letting the MSL pursue me. Today, I wasn't even trying with him, but he was there for me. He has said and done all the right things. He seems to be after me in a way that he never has been before. Tonight, in the taxi coming back here, it was so magic, and I loved it. For the first time ever, I have such a good feeling about him. I've never had this before. Tonight is going to be easy. I don't have to do anything. I can see it now. He's just going to be there. I don't have to panic anymore."

"Oh, Madame, that's wonderful," said Mongolian Sheep Pussy. "I'm so glad that I'm going to be there with you."

"Congratulations, Madame," said Pussy Original. "We always knew you'd come through in the end."

Mongolian Sheep Pussy shot him a look. *Liar*, she thought. *You'd given up on her ages ago, and you've spent the last few months doing damage limitation*. She never said anything though. She, Mongolian Sheep Pussy, had never given up on the MSL situation and she couldn't wait for the Countess to get it together with him at the gala ball. Then she would be able to crow over the other bags that she had been right all along. That would be *her* perfect moment!

"Well done, Madame," said American Ted. "Now, don't stand here talking to us any longer. You have to get that dress on and get out to dinner."

The Countess put on her carefully selected La Perla underwear and then climbed into the dress. She went back into the bathroom to play with her hair again and touch up her make-up a bit more.

"Well, what do you think?" she asked the accessories as she emerged.

"Oh, Madame, you look so lovely. If that MSL doesn't go for you, and if those clients don't want your business, well, then they need their heads testing," said Pussy With Balls.

The Countess laughed. "Thank you. I hope you're right. I've been dying for an opportunity to wear this dress. It's fantastic isn't it?"

"You look a million dollars and more," said American Ted. "I wish I could be seen with you tonight."

"Ted, dearest. I wish I could take you. But somehow, I don't think our Dutch friends will want to do business with me if I show up with a teddy bear."

"Of course, Madame. And I think the MSL will find it a bit strange too," said American Ted.

"Yes, I think he would," she replied.

"Will you need us to be tidy again tonight, Madame?" asked Pussy Original.

"Yes, I suppose so," said the Countess. "Though I don't know whether I should invite the MSL back here."

"A lady wouldn't," said the Queen Mum bag. "He needs to prove himself as an honourable gentleman and worthy of you before you even consider it. One flirtatious conversation in a taxi does not a potential suitor make!"

In the past, the Countess had always ignored the Queen Mum bag's old-fashioned opinions and just humoured her as one would if being nagged by one's mother. However, since her disastrous one-night stand at New Year and subsequent conversation with Persian Dolly, she had come around to the fact that she needed to treat herself, and sex, in a more respectful manner.

"Let's see what he does," she said. "Actually, we do need to keep the suite tidy because Aidan might want to entertain up here. You can lounge around for a couple of hours, then you better had be in the bedroom or the closet after that."

"Of course, Madame," said Pussy Original. "Leave it to me. I'll round everyone up later."

"Thank you," said the Countess. "Right. It's nearly time to go."

She transferred her things from Queen Mum bag to Mongolian Sheep Pussy and also grabbed her mascara and blusher.

"Best of luck, Madame," said the Queen Mum bag.

"Thank you," said the Countess.

She picked up Mongolian Sheep Pussy and did a final twirl for the accessories. They cheered and wished her luck. She grabbed Persian Dolly by his hook, slung him over her shoulder and left the suite.

As she walked down the hall to the lift, Persian Dolly whispered in her ear, "Stay cool, Madame, and go easy on the booze. That's all you have to do."

Double Dutch

The MSL was dining with delegates from Deutsche Bankverein and another boutique bank that was based in Frankfurt. The restaurant was a long-established, traditional Berlin dining institution. Like Randolph's in New York, it had an old-money feel to it, and one could imagine generations of affluent Berliner ladies with their fur coats lunching there by day and gentlemen conducting business in a very civilised manner over dinner in the evening. Many of the conference delegates had the same idea, as the place was full of people in evening dress, who later on were going to return to the gala event in the grand ballroom at the Kempinski hotel.

He was having a conversation about the differences between American and British ways of speaking English when something caused him to look up. There she was, the Countess, with Aidan and the rest of her party following the waiter to their table. He hadn't known that they would be dining in the same place.

She looked like an A-list film star on Oscar night. Her hair was different. It was swept back off her face at the front and looked more bouncy. Her dress was out of this world. It was floor length and shimmered between a dark blue and black. He liked the split which showed off her wonderful legs to perfection. She wore long black gloves which he thought were very sexy. She carried a small furry bag which was the same colour as the dress. It must be one of the new pussy bags which she had mentioned. As she walked across the restaurant, she looked very self-assured, as though formal dining was something she did every night of the week. In short, he found her completely and utterly ravishing.

Without thinking or rounding off his conversation, he just stood up and walked towards her. At that moment, she glanced around and saw him. She paused and looked at him, smiling. She took a couple of steps towards him and then stood still, while the rest of her party continued to their table.

He went straight towards her, held her arms and kissed her on both cheeks. He could not let go of her. They stood looking at each other.

"My God, you look so beautiful! Glamorous! Completely divine! A true countess!" he said as he let go of her arms and took hold of one of her hands. As he held it, he stepped back and admired her again. "I love your dress."

"What, this old thing?" said the Countess, laughing. "You look fantastic too. I love a man in black tie."

"I wish I could have dinner with you tonight," he said.

"So do I," she replied.

He noticed how bright her eyes were as she said this. He let go of her hand, stood back and looked at her again. "It's a shame that we're here on business," he said. Over her shoulder, he could see Aidan and the rest of her party standing by their chairs, waiting for her before they sat down. "I think you'd better go. They're waiting for you. I don't want to get in the way of your dinner."

She turned and looked over her shoulder. "I guess so," she

said. "I suppose I'll see you later then."

"Don't worry, you'll see me. Two dances, remember," said the MSL.

"Two dances," said the Countess. "See you then."

He stood and watched as she returned to her table. Her back looked very sexy in the dress. Only when she was seated and had given him another brief smile did he remember that he had his own guests.

He returned to his table. "Sorry about that," he said as he sat down. "We used to work together."

* * *

"Nice of you to join us," said Aidan as she returned to her table. "I'm sorry, folks. Occupational hazard of having the conference star attraction on the team."

"Sorry about that," said the Countess as she stepped around her chair to sit down. "We used to work together."

"Just work?" said the older gentleman from ACS Smith Gladstone. His name was Dirk Ritter, and he had worked at the original Amsterdam Centrale Spaarbank before it bought out the old English bank, Smith Gladstone, just a few years previously. "He seems very taken with you."

Aidan raised an eyebrow.

"Definitely, just work," said the Countess, ignoring Aidan as she tried to gather herself and focus on her guests and not the MSL.

The Periculum team were joined by three delegates from ACS Smith Gladstone, the older gentleman, Dirk, and a younger man and woman who worked in their technology division. Even though she wished she could immediately run off with the MSL and dance the night away, the Countess forced herself to concentrate on business matters.

She decided that the best bet was to talk mainly to the older guy and win him over. She did this easily. By the end of the meal, he was pouring her drinks, suggesting dessert wines she might like, and as they left the restaurant, he helped her with her coat, opened the door for her and generally fell over himself in the hope that such a beautiful young lady would maybe give him the time of day. He then suggested that they went for a drink first.

"I'm not really keen to get back to the racket of that party," he said. "How about you allow us to buy you a couple of drinks? There is a lovely old bar near here. It's just around the corner from the hotel."

"Sure," replied Aidan. "It's a bit early for the party yet anyway."

The Countess remained silent and just smiled in agreement. She was desperate to get back to the hotel and be in sight of the MSL, whose party had left earlier. She realised that it was not appropriate to smooch with him for the whole night, but she did at least want to be in the same place where she could look at him and he could look at her, just as he had earlier, on her arrival.

The Countess was also conscious of making sure she didn't get drunk, which was so easy to do at events like this. She had made sure that she had drunk lots of mineral water over dinner, but the waiters had been so attentive in their service, that they seemed to come around and top up the wine glasses every few minutes, so she had no idea how much Chablis she had actually consumed. Although she did not feel too drunk, she decided that it would be best to switch to soft drinks so that she was properly sober when they reached the gala ball. Her Dutch friend had other ideas though.

"Nonsense," said Dirk. "You can't drink tonic water in a place like this. I used to come to Berlin regularly many years ago, and I know for a fact that this place serves the finest cognac in town. Please join me in one."

"Okay," she replied. "But just a small one."

The Countess then excused herself to go to the ladies room. Once safely away from the others, Mongolian Sheep Pussy spoke. That evening had been the first time she had seen the MSL.

"Madame, the MSL is just so lovely. He's crazy about you. Look at the way he jumped up to greet you when we arrived."

"I know," said the Countess. "Everything seems to be going so well. We'll have a couple of drinks here and then we can go on to the party. Hopefully, I won't need to stay with these guys all evening, so I'll be free to dance with him."

"It's a shame we can't go straight there now. Do you have to do all this business stuff?" asked Mongolian Sheep Pussy.

"Sadly, yes," replied the Countess. "It's my job. It's going well though. With a bit of luck, we'll get this client. It will be my first major win for Periculum."

"You're very good at it, Madame. I've never seen you in a work situation."

"It's all bullshit really," replied the Countess. "Everyone talks the talk and does the deals. And that, at the end of the day, is how we all get paid. But I do enjoy it. And someone has to pull in the cash so we can all enjoy a countess lifestyle."

"One day, you won't have to," said Mongolian Sheep Pussy. "You'll marry the MSL, and he will keep you in the manner to which we've all become accustomed."

"Hey, I don't want him for his money," said the Countess. "I'm pretty good at making my own. Anyway, let's not get too excited about that. I need to score with him first."

"You will easily," said Mongolian Sheep Pussy. Then she added, "If you don't, that old guy out there loves you. You could have him as a sugar daddy and still find a younger man for excitement!"

"Shh," said the Countess giggling. "You'll get me into trouble. Be quiet. I think someone else has come in here."

* * *

The Countess's party stayed for two drinks in the bar and then made their way back to the hotel. When they arrived, they paused in the lobby. Aidan said, "What does everyone want to do now? We can go into the ballroom, but if you have any other business that you'd like to discuss or questions to ask, then we have a suite available, and we could go and have a drink there first."

The younger ACS man and the Countess were not keen on disappearing for another drink, but Aidan, Dirk and the woman from ACS favoured going to the suite, so they were outnumbered.

As they walked through the lobby, the Countess looked around to see if she could spot the MSL. She could see that there were a lot of people in the bar, but it was too crowded to pick him out. As an insurance policy, she drew level with Dirk and said, "Follow me. Our suite is on the sixth floor. Let's make this a quick one and then perhaps we can have a dance together in the ballroom." His face lit up at this prospect.

* * *

The accessories were sitting on the bed when they heard the main door of the suite open.

"Okay," said Pussy Original. "Action stations. Here she is. We'd better get into the closet quickly."

"No. Wait," said Pussy Deluxe. "There are lots of voices. She's doing business, it's not the MSL. We're okay here."

"Maybe we should move anyway," said Pussy Original. "What if she shows her guests around the suite or they want to use the bathroom or something?"

"She won't. There's only one person she is going to show this room to, and she hasn't got around to him yet. There's a toilet out there anyway. Stop panicking," replied Pussy Deluxe.

Pussy Deluxe was wrong, for Aidan came straight into the bedroom to use the bathroom while the Countess organised drinks for everybody. He saw all the fur lying on the bed and smiled at them. He thought that the Countess was strange for bringing all her bags to Berlin, but since she was very successfully charming the Dutch bank into doing business with Periculum, he didn't care. However, when one of their guests wanted to use the main bathroom, he gave an excuse about how messy the Countess must have been when she was getting ready to go out and suggested that they use the other toilet.

* * *

The Countess was relieved that they only had one drink before heading back downstairs to the ballroom. Since it was her suite, she was in charge of serving the drinks and could, therefore, have just tonic water without being pressured into having any more alcohol.

Periculum's objectives for the evening had been successfully reached. Aidan and the Countess would arrange to visit the bank in Amsterdam and London on a fact-finding trip. This would give them enough information to prepare a formal proposal of service and hopefully, then go on to negotiate a deal and come up with some risk technology solutions for the bank.

Downstairs, Dirk immediately asked the Countess for a dance. Meanwhile, Aidan had found them all a table and had arranged drinks. The Countess had insisted on a mineral water. When she returned from the dance floor, she took a few sips of it and then excused herself to visit the bathroom. This was an escape ploy so she could have a look around and locate the MSL. She took the long route, which was a casual walk all around the edge of the ballroom. She quite enjoyed this promenade as it gave her a chance to show herself off in her dress, and for the first time that evening, or that day for that matter, she was no longer in work mode. Some people recognised her from the day's presentation and said hello to her, but she was careful to keep moving and not get stuck in a business-related conversation. Unfortunately, her stroll to the bathroom did not yield its primary purpose – there was no sign of the MSL.

She tried not to panic, reasoning that he was probably out in the bar. She walked that way and looked for him, but he wasn't there either. After visiting the ladies room, she made her way back to the ballroom and to the table that Aidan had procured. Still no MSL. There had been so many signs that day that the MSL was desperate to spend some time with her that she was confident he would soon appear. She felt rather pleased with herself at how calm she was being about the whole thing.

She went back to her table and chatted, drank and danced with Aidan and the ACS people. She also bumped into some ex-colleagues from Creditbank Zurich and had an enjoyable time chatting with them. Then she happened to look at her watch. It was almost one o'clock. She had not realised it was so late.

It was then that she felt a sense of foreboding in her gut. The evening had flown by. With dinner, going to the bar, time spent in her suite, she realised that they had not got into the ballroom until nearly midnight. Now, there was only an hour left of the party and still no MSL.

Panic set in. She knew that she should not go looking for him or try too hard to attract him, but she couldn't help herself. She left the dance floor and did another round of the ballroom, just as she had done earlier. There was no sign of him. Then she decided to wander out to the lobby as if she was going to the ladies' room. Again, she checked the hotel lounge and bar. Both these places were full of people in their evening wear, but still, the MSL was not there. By now, she was starting to unravel inside. She wanted to cry, but she had to keep up her business-like façade, as all the way around, she kept bumping into people she knew who wanted to chat with her.

She'd had such high hopes for this evening – she'd dreamt of dancing together, looking gorgeous and glamorous in their formal attire. She'd dreamt of the MSL realising that he could no longer live without her, kissing her, telling her how much he loved her and asking if there was any way that they could be together. She had hoped that by now, he would have been romancing her and had imagined how special that would have made her feel. Since their arrival in Berlin, everything had seemed so promising. He had given out such positive signals. This should have been the climax of their evening, dancing in one another's arms, oblivious to everyone. But he was nowhere to be seen.

She made her way into the toilets, ran into a cubicle and slammed the door behind her. A couple of tears fell on her shaking fingers as she slid the lock across. She tried not to cry, as she did not want to ruin her make-up and make her face look awful, but it was too late. She couldn't stop the tears from flowing.

She stood with her back to the door and leaned against it. Then she bowed her head and put one hand over her eyes, Mongolian Sheep Pussy hanging from her wrist. She slid down the door until she was crouched down, bent forward, crying into her hands.

"I can't do this anymore," she said, holding herself under her breastbone. "I just can't do it. It hurts too much. I really thought he'd be here. It was all looking so hopeful."

"He'll show up, Madame," said Mongolian Sheep Pussy who was squashed in her lap. "He was here earlier. He'll be back. There's no way that he'll miss those dances with you. He was so excited to see you earlier."

"No," said the Countess, shaking her head. She held Mongolian Sheep Pussy in front of her. "It's all gone wrong. I bet he thinks I'm not interested, so he's gone somewhere else."

"Why would he think that, Madame?" asked Mongolian Sheep Pussy. "It sounds to me like you've responded positively to everything he has said to you in the last couple of days. He is chomping at the bit for you. When you guys met in the restaurant, he could barely contain himself. If it had been a movie, there would have been fireworks going off as your eyes met and you moved towards each other. He's going to be here, and you're going to get those dances he promised you."

"We didn't get here till late," said the Countess. She put the toilet lid down and sat on it, still bent forward, Mongolian Sheep Pussy in her hand.

Between sobs, she continued, "We went to that stupid bar and talked about stupid business to those stupid ACS people. And then Aidan suggesting that we had another drink in my suite. I wish I hadn't upgraded my room now, then we couldn't have gone there. All that time he would have been waiting for me, and I didn't show up. Now he's gone. Everything is ruined, and I can't cope anymore."

"Yes, you can, Madame," said Mongolian Sheep Pussy. "He's got to be here. There has to be an explanation."

"No," sobbed the Countess. "This is just like every other time. It never goes right. Something always happens, or rather, it doesn't happen." She took a tissue out of Mongolian Sheep Pussy and blew her nose. "Perhaps he wasn't interested after all. Perhaps I read the signs wrong, again! Perhaps the flirting was just part of friendship, like it always was. The whole thing has slipped through my fingers again. Just when it was all looking so good."

The Countess kept crying. Mongolian Sheep Pussy was at a loss, as she too was mystified as to the whereabouts of the MSL. He had seemed so enthusiastic earlier – where could he be?

"It's going to be okay, Madame. He'll show up at the last minute and sweep you off your feet, just as you've always dreamt."

"No, he won't. He's gone," said the Countess. "It's over. It'll never happen. Never."

"It will. I know it will," said Mongolian Sheep Pussy.

"No, it won't. Please stop saying that it will," said the Countess. "We don't know anything. I just feel so let down. So disappointed… so fucking disappointed. I really thought this was the moment. I thought that the waiting was finally over. I thought that I'd be dancing with him by now." She dissolved into tears again. "And I'm not."

"Please, Madame," said Mongolian Sheep Pussy. "Don't give up now. He could show up at any minute. He's probably in there right now, frantically looking for you. Dry your eyes, patch up your make-up, and let's get back out there. The evening hasn't finished yet, but it will soon if you don't get a move on. Come on. Look at your watch. What time is it?"

"One fifteen," said the Countess, as wiped away another tear.

"That's forty-five minutes of dancing left," said Mongolian Sheep Pussy. "He will show up. I promise you. Please believe me."

"I can't," said the Countess. "I look a mess. If he sees me now, looking like this, then he'll just walk the other way. Let's give up and go back to my room. I'm exhausted. Let's just go to bed. It's over."

"No!" said Mongolian Sheep Pussy.

"Yes!" said the Countess, and she stood up.

"Madame, no," said Mongolian Sheep Pussy. "You're going to have to do something with your face anyway. You can't walk across the lobby to the lifts with tears running down it. So, you might as well go back to the ballroom."

"I can't. I'll just cry and look ridiculous. I'm wiped. I've done really well on the business front today and that's the only success that I have. I don't want to ruin that."

"Madame, you can do it," said Mongolian Sheep Pussy. "I'm with you. We can do it together. All you have to do is go back in there, sit at our table, chit chat with anyone who is around and wait for him. He will be there."

The Countess was silent. She reached to open the lock of the toilet door. Mongolian Sheep Pussy spoke again. "Please Madame... what have you got to lose? You can go to bed now, or you can go to bed in an hour. Just think though, what a difference that hour might make."

The Countess's hand paused on the lock as she listened to this last plea from Mongolian Sheep Pussy. The handbag continued, "One hour, Madame. I promise you. It really will make all the difference. You can give yourself the chance of going back to your room in one hour's time completely triumphant, or you can go there now a broken woman. One hour."

The Countess took her hand off the lock. "Oh, fucking hell. Okay – I hope you're right. I can't take any more of this."

"You won't regret it, Madame," said Mongolian Sheep Pussy. "I just know he'll show up. Now, fish your make-up out of me and get yourself sorted out."

The Countess did as she was told. She retrieved her make-up from Mongolian Sheep Pussy, but she needed to splash some water on her face first. Tentatively, she opened the door to see if anyone else was in the room. Luckily, she was alone, so she was able to quickly wash and dry her face and then repair her make-up.

She took a deep breath, put her make-up back into Mongolian Sheep Pussy and looked at herself in the mirror. "That'll have to do."

She made her way back across the lobby, feeling as though

she could cry again but forced back the tears in an attempt to look normal. She stopped off at the bar and ordered a double Jack Daniels and coke. Then she went back to the table and made a reasonable show of being cheerful.

"Where's that man of yours?" asked Aidan. "I thought tonight was the night. He looked like he was ready to sweep you off your feet there and then when we were in the restaurant."

"He's not here," said the Countess. "I've just walked around the lobby, the lounge and the bar, but it looks like I've missed him."

Aidan looked at her. "Are you all right?" he asked.

"Not really," said the Countess. "But when it comes to him, I'm well practised at disappointment."

"He's probably tied up somewhere," said Aidan. "I bet he's sucking up to the top brass of some bank and getting himself a better job. These conferences can be like that."

"Yes, I suppose so," said the Countess. "We've been busy too. Hopefully, it will be worth it. The ACS lot are eating out of our hands."

"He'll probably be here any minute. And if not, then I'm sure he'll have a very good excuse tomorrow," said Aidan. He put his arm around her and gave her a hug. "Sweetie, if it's meant to happen, then it will."

"Hm, I guess," said the Countess. She had heard this so many times from so many well-meaning friends as well as the accessories, she couldn't bear hearing it again.

Time passed quickly. At one forty-five, the Countess was sitting alone at the table, pretending to enjoy watching everyone else dance. Mongolian Sheep Pussy was on the table in front of her. The Countess looked at her watch and stood up to leave. She picked up Mongolian Sheep Pussy.

"Don't, Madame," said Mongolian Sheep Pussy. "He'll be here. There is still time for your two dances. He's not going to miss out on that. Stay put."

"He's not going to be here," whispered back the Countess, sitting down again.

Two minutes later, Aidan came up to her. The music had just changed to slow records.

"Hi there," said Aidan. "Now, I know I'm not your dream-boat, but would you do me the honour of dancing with me? It will stop you sitting here looking bloody miserable, and it will make me look more straight and respectable in the eyes of our Dutch friends."

"God, are they still here?" asked the Countess as she got up.

"Over there. I reckon the old boy wants to dance with you again. He's talked about you a lot tonight, you know. Perhaps you should give up on your American chap and have him instead. He's here, and he is willing and able! Actually, I'm not so sure about 'able', but he's definitely willing!"

The Countess playfully slapped his shoulder. "Stop it," she said. "I think I'd rather have you, given a choice."

"Ah, but we work together," said Aidan.

"And he's about to be a client. So, no can do either way. Anyway, I'm a sad and lonely spinster, and it's looking like that's how it is going to stay."

The song came to an end. "Go on," said Aidan. "Go and ask him to dance. You'll make his day."

"Okay then," said the Countess, and sure enough, the old man's face lit up as she approached him.

* * *

At the end of that dance, the Countess excused herself. She could not wait to escape back to her room. This time, Mongolian Sheep Pussy didn't try to stop her. She felt terrible. She had been so certain that the MSL was going to turn up.

The Countess got the lift up to the sixth floor. She ran down the corridor to her door. Tears poured down her cheeks as she fiddled with the electronic key.

"I'm so sorry, Madame," said Mongolian Sheep Pussy. "I really thought he would be there."

"So did I," said the Countess as she opened the door and went into the suite. She slumped down on the sofa holding Mongolian Sheep Pussy in her lap and bent forward as she cried. "That was the worst night of my life. I wish we hadn't stayed until the bitter end. I must have looked like a desperate fool."

"I'm sorry. That was my idea," said Mongolian Sheep Pussy. "But no one would have thought you desperate – you did a brilliant cover-up, dancing with that old guy and Aidan. You only think that because you're hurting, no one else does."

"I wish I didn't feel this way," said the Countess. "I wish we hadn't met up in the restaurant. I wish he hadn't looked at me the way that he did. And I wish he hadn't even come to the conference. I could have been over him by now. But I'm not! I'm so not! And it just hurts so fucking much."

She stood suddenly, Mongolian Sheep Pussy falling from her lap, and went into the bedroom and threw herself down on the bed. The bedroom was clear of the other accessories. On hearing her sobbing, they pushed opened the closet door. She was alone, lying face down, crying into a pillow.

"Oh, shit!" said Pussy With Balls. "Not another snot-and-tears moment!"

American Ted made the first move. He left the closet and climbed up on the bed. He walked over to where the Countess lay and stroked her face.

"Madame, what happened?" he asked.

The Countess did not reply but kept crying, her body heaving with her sobs.

He stroked her again. "Madame. Please talk to me. What happened?"

She turned her head and looked at him. "Nothing," she sobbed and buried her face back in the pillow. American Ted sat down on the next pillow. Over the last few months, he had learned that she would talk to him eventually. They would find out what had happened, and then they would all come up with a solution for her.

The other accessories, still sitting in the closet, looked at each other and shrugged.

"Mongolian Sheep Pussy will know," said Pussy With Balls. "I'll go and find her."

He left the closet and headed out of the bedroom into the living room of the suite. Mongolian Sheep Pussy saw him and made towards him.

"Mongolian Sheep Pussy! What happened?" he asked her.

"Nothing happened, that's what," said Mongolian Sheep Pussy. "It was a disaster. I feel so bad about it. I made her stay till the end. She wanted to give up, but I wouldn't let her. I promised her he'd show up, but he didn't."

"What? She didn't see him all night?" asked Pussy With Balls.

"No… well, yes – they saw each other in the restaurant," said Mongolian Sheep Pussy. "You should have seen them. He couldn't take his eyes off her. And then they had this arrangement to meet up later, but somehow, it all went wrong."

"What do you mean, it all went wrong?" asked Pussy With Balls.

"She was expecting to go to the gala ball straight after dinner at the restaurant. But then she had to go to a bar and then had to come back here for drinks, so it was really late by the time we got there," said Mongolian Sheep Pussy. "And he just wasn't there. I felt so sure that he would show up. But he didn't, and now she's a mess again. I wish there was something we could do."

"We're going to have to wait till she calms down," said Pussy With Balls. "And then figure out what the hell is going on. I wonder what happened to him."

* * *

After a while, the Countess told American Ted about the evening. He tried to persuade her to get ready for bed properly. He wanted to prevent her from waking up with her eyes resembling a panda from her mascara and pimples already forming because she had not cleansed her face.

While the Countess was in the bathroom, he talked with Pussy Original and the Queen Mum bag.

"I wish Mongolian Sheep Pussy hadn't encouraged her so much," said Pussy Original. "She's too much of a starry-eyed romantic. She couldn't get her head out of the clouds and see the reality. Now look at the mess we're in. Madame has got to be fit to go to the exhibition tomorrow and keep working. Judging by how she looks now, that's going to be a tall order."

"Where is Mongolian Sheep Pussy?" asked American Ted.

"In the living room somewhere," replied Pussy Original.

"Pussy With Balls is with her. I don't want to see her at the moment, I might say something she won't like hearing."

"Are you going to be able to handle this, American Ted?" asked the Queen Mum bag. "Is there anything I can do?"

"I don't know," replied American Ted. "There's probably not much you can do right now, but tomorrow, you'll be with her again at the conference hall. Just say whatever you think best to help her perform her duties and avoid further heartache. That's if we make it to tomorrow. What are we going to do with her?"

"The best we can," said Pussy Original. "Let's take it one step at a time. Tonight, we just need to get her to go to sleep. Tomorrow, we'll have to drag her out of bed in time to make it to the conference. We'll have to see how she is when she wakes up and take it from there."

The Queen Mum bag tried to comfort American Ted. "He's right, Ted," she said. "There's nothing more we can do other than deal with each thing as it happens. We're a team – a damn good team," she said, choosing, for a second time that night, to use strong language.

"Thank you," said American Ted.

"You'd better get back on the bed, Ted," said Pussy Original. "She'll be out of the bathroom any time soon. Do you want me to join you up there? It's going to be a tough night."

"Will you?" said American Ted. "You seem to be the one with all the ideas right now. I don't think I can do this without you."

"No problem," said Pussy Original.

Meanwhile, the Queen Mum bag went into the bathroom. She found the Countess sitting on the edge of the bath, crying. Her face was clean of make-up, and she held her toothbrush in her hand.

"Come on, Madame," said the Queen Mum bag. "Finish your teeth and then go to bed. American Ted and Pussy Original are waiting for you, and they're going to make you feel better."

"Nothing can make me feel better," replied the Countess. "Nothing at all."

She stood up, put her toothbrush down by the sink and ripped off some toilet paper. Sitting back on the bath, she blew her nose, screwed up the paper and threw it towards the toilet. It landed on the floor.

"There, there, Madame," said the Queen Mum bag. "I know you won't believe me, but after a while, this isn't going to hurt quite as much. If you go to bed right now, then this awful day is over, and tomorrow, you can have a fresh start."

"Tomorrow, I can have more rejection," said the Countess, still sniffing.

"I don't think so," said the Queen Mum bag. "You feel rejected right now, but apart from the MSL, you've had a very successful day. Your presentation was excellent – I was so proud of you. Think about how many people you won over – that means things can only get better."

The Countess smiled at the Queen Mum bag. "Thanks," she said. "But what's the point of being a successful business-woman if I end up my days as an old spinster? Work-wise it did go well today. ACS will sign with us. Periculum will make me into a director... and I'll be even more of a single woman career girl than I am already."

"It'll work out somehow, Madame," said the Queen Mum bag. "Perhaps there was a good reason that the MSL didn't show up. Maybe *he* had to spend time talking to the right people, just like you did. He could well be feeling just as upset as you right now because he missed you. You looked so beautiful in your dress tonight. His loss is much greater than yours."

"Do you think so?" asked the Countess as she wiped her eyes again.

"Yes, Madame," replied the Queen Mum bag. "And I also know that we are not going to find any more answers tonight. Please finish off in here, and go to bed."

"Okay," sighed the Countess. She got up from the bath, went to the sink and continued cleaning her teeth.

The Queen Mum bag left her and went back to the bedroom. "She's coming out in a minute," she said.

"How is she?" asked American Ted.

"Upset," said the Queen Mum bag.

"What shall we do?" asked Pussy Original.

"What we always do," replied the Queen Mum bag. "We'll comfort her and try and make it all better."

American Ted and Pussy Original had never seen this soft side to such a strict bag. It was amazing how a crisis often revealed the hidden side of a person.

Crossover

Mongolian Sheep Pussy had been right. The MSL had indeed reappeared in the ballroom while the Countess was sobbing in the toilets. Like the Countess, he had also been wrapped up in business affairs and was having to be at the beck and call of his dinner companions. Following the dinner, he and his party had gone straight to the gala ball and had spent a couple of hours there. All the time, he had desperately wanted the Countess to show up. She had looked so stunning when she had arrived in the restaurant earlier that he could have eaten her alive on the spot. Now, he could not wait to dance with her. He wanted to touch her, hold her hand, stroke her arm and kiss her.

From the beginning, the MSL had had enormous respect for the Countess. He thought she was the most astonishing woman he had ever met. She was beautiful, sexy, funny and hugely capable. Yes, he fancied her, and he had fantasised about being with her.

Equally, as much as he wanted her, he was also daunted by her. She was one of those modern, accomplished, fiercely independent, scary women. She was also a countess, and he was not sure what that really meant. Was she part of the British royal family? Was she destined to marry a prince? A British prince? Did that mean that no one else was else good enough for her, especially an American? He didn't understand her background or how she came to be a countess. He knew it was something to do with her father when he had died a few years ago, but that was all.

He wanted her, but for those reasons, he believed he could not have her. He thought it would be too difficult and that he would not be able to satisfy her life. Then there was the question of work. They were colleagues. If something happened between them and subsequently went wrong it could be a disaster.

So, he dated other women, but nothing ever lasted beyond three or four months. At that point, two things happened. Firstly, they ceased to engage his attention and he just lost interest. Secondly, they wished for the relationship to be more serious and attempted to dominate his life too much. This always became the death knell for the relationship because as much as he liked female company, he also liked his freedom.

He remembered one girlfriend telling him he was always mentioning this "woman at work" and "why don't you just go out with her?" He knew that the Countess too was dating and having encounters, but it always seemed that, although she liked to be around men, she did not appear to need one as a long-term fixture in her life.

It was only after the Countess had left SC Radcliffe to work at Periculum that he realised how much she had illuminated his life. He missed her, not only at work but also in the social life that they had shared. She had been a huge ray of sunshine, a dynamism, a bright light.

He was very excited to see her again last fall when she had been in New York on business. As usual, she had looked fabulous and was the perfect hostess as she took care of the drinks party. He was very pleased that her new job was going so well and was envious of her for having the courage to jump at such an interesting career opportunity. Though he was technically very competent and enjoyed managing people, he was not sure that he was as able at being so natural at client relationships as she was.

At the end of that night, when he watched her walk away down Fifty-Fourth Street, he had kicked himself. She had dropped a massive hint that she liked him, and he had brushed her off with some bullshit about how they might work together in the future. He felt wretched. The truth was he couldn't see how a relationship would work with the distance. And she was still that fiercely independent, scary woman.

What did he do after that? He did what guys always do. He filed her away in a pigeonhole marked "*Emotional Dynamite. Do Not Revisit!*" He had fun with his friends, went out on a few dates and continued his work-hard, play-hard lifestyle. Anything to erase the memory of that pigeonhole!

Even though he had mentioned the Risk conference to her when she was in New York, he had no idea if she would be there or whether he would actually make the effort to go to Europe. One Friday afternoon, the conference programme landed on his desk. As he'd browsed through, his heart had stopped when he saw she was presenting. He realised just how much he had missed her and that he wanted to see her again. That weekend, he was out for a drink with one of his friends, Ryan, and he mentioned her.

"The British one?" asked Ryan. "The Duchess?"

"She's the Countess," said the MSL.

"Oh yes. That's it. I knew she had some kind of title. The

one you used to talk about all the time and then you suddenly never spoke of again?"

The MSL smiled. "Yes. That one. She's going to be at a conference in Europe in April. I was thinking of going there anyway."

"You really like her, don't you?" said Ryan.

"Yes, I do," said the MSL. "She's gorgeous, and she's clever. She challenges me. We have the most amazing conversations. She's funny too, and she always lights up a party. We used to laugh so much in the office. Everyone liked her. It's not been the same since she left. I miss hanging out with her."

"And she's definitely going to be at this conference?" asked Ryan.

"Yes. She's presenting one of the slots. I saw it in the programme yesterday."

The reply was straight and direct: "There's only so many times you can let the woman of your dreams slip through your fingers. Eventually, you have to take the opportunity and go for it."

"But what about the distance. Work and all of that?" said the MSL.

"Don't give me that," said Ryan. "You've talked about working in Europe for ages, and you're bored at SC Radcliffe. You could get a job in a bank there, right?"

"Yes, easily," replied the MSL. "The conference will be a good place to look for one."

"Then get yourself over there, and go get her."

As soon as he arrived at work on the Monday morning, he booked his place on the conference. Later that day, he called her. He wasn't sure if he had the right number or whether she still lived in the same place, so when she answered the phone, he was over the moon. It was an extra bonus that she needed his help as this gave him the excuse to keep communicating with her. It was so good to talk to her again, and he couldn't resist flirting.

* * *

It was with much apprehension that he arrived in Berlin. Would he still feel the same about her when he saw her? His flight had been awful and he was very tired. He called her room when he arrived at the hotel, but there was no answer. At the conference hall, he tried to spot her. He found the Periculum stand but she wasn't there. In the end, he gave up. He was feeling so jaded from the flight, that in the afternoon, he returned to the hotel and slept for a couple of hours. He ordered room service, took a refreshing shower and prepared himself for an evening in the bar.

When he came down from his room that evening, he stood at the edge of the lounge and scanned the area, looking for her. He couldn't see her, so he made his way straight into the bar. He surveyed the scene before going to get a drink. Then, he saw her. Her hair was slightly longer than it had been last time he saw her, and he noted she had a huge fur bag over her shoulders. He smiled as he saw that she was wearing one of her company's shirts. He knew how much she would hate having to wear such a thing. It didn't matter to him though. She was as beautiful as ever and, as far as he was concerned, she would look sexy in a sack.

Throughout the conference proceedings, he had enjoyed every minute in her company. There was something different about her that he couldn't quite put his finger on. Physically she looked slightly different – curvier, more womanly. She seemed to be self-assured and was acting in a more mature, settled way, rather than being the slightly chaotic party queen that she often was in New York. She was softer somehow, and he liked it.

He had actually felt a little intimidated by her as he watched her give her presentation. She was very confident speaking in public and came across as natural, chatty and interesting. She was still a little scary to him, but he had made up his mind that she was going to be *his* scary woman and no one else's. The time had come. He had to have her, no matter what.

He couldn't believe that she had not shown up at the gala ball. He had danced with other people now and then but had kept a vigilant eye out, waiting for her to arrive. He went out into the bar and lounge area several times and expected to see her holding court there, the life and soul of the party, a sight he had witnessed so many times before. But every time, she was nowhere to be seen. Then something terrible happened. One of the Europeans from his party announced that everybody was going to head off to a bar, away from the hotel, and insisted that he join them. He desperately wanted to stay and wait for the Countess, but he didn't have much choice but go. He felt under pressure to join them, and he needed to talk with them about work opportunities. He looked at his watch. It was almost midnight. *Where was she?*

He went along with the group, drinking and chatting with them, but all the time, his mind was on the Countess. He was desperate to get back to the Kempinski and the gala ball. Ironically, he was in the same bar that the Countess had been to after dinner, but she had long since left. Then someone suggested going to a nightclub. Again, they wanted the MSL to join them, but this time, he thought of an excellent excuse. He told them he was expecting an urgent call from the US and that he needed to go and check his messages.

"I'll catch up with you," he said. "I only need to be in the hotel for ten minutes or so."

Free at last! He was walking so fast and with such excitement that he was almost running. When he arrived back at the hotel, he went first to the cloakrooms to check his appearance in the mirror then he strode confidently across the lobby and around to the ballroom. He expected to see her straight away, and he could at last claim his dances.

It was much later now, and the crowd had thinned out. He looked around, but still, she was not there. He saw Aidan dancing with two women at the same time, one of them was in the Countess's dinner party, so he knew that their group had returned and the Countess ought to be there. He walked around the ballroom, just in case the Countess was ensconced in conversation and was sitting down somewhere. Nothing. Having finished his circuit, he went back out of the lobby and tried the lounge and bar again. Still nothing. All the time he was thinking, *This can't be happening. Where is she? All those years, and I was too stupid to make a move. Now I want to, and she has vanished.* And then came the tortuous thoughts that perhaps she had gone off with someone else. She was, after all, a very attractive lady.

He went back to the ballroom and stood in the entrance. Aidan was still dancing. Had she given up and gone to bed? He considered calling her room but decided not to as perhaps she was exhausted after her very long and tiring day.

Never mind. His plan would have to wait another day. He would catch up with her in the morning and ask her out on a date. He figured that now her presentation was over and she had wined and dined her clients, she would have more time. He looked at his watch. It was one fifteen. He thought about going to bed himself but decided that he might as well keep his group happy and catch up with them after all. He wanted to impress them and not have them think he was a lightweight American. If he was going to have a chance of working in Europe, then he needed them.

At the same time that the Countess was patching herself up in the ladies bathroom and putting the finishing touches to her make-up, he was walking back through the lobby of the hotel and out to hail a taxi to the club. She missed him by seconds. If she had got herself moving just a fraction earlier, she would have bumped right into him.

The Morning After

"That's a miracle," said Pussy Original as soon as he heard the Countess put the television on in the lounge area of the suite. "I thought we'd be dragging her out of bed this morning and super-glueing a fresh coat of make-up to her face."

"Yes, it is quite astonishing," replied American Ted. "It's just a front though. I bet she's crumbling inside. I wish I could do more to help her."

"So do I," said Pussy Original. "But there is nothing more we can do right now."

"I guess I'll be with her again today," said the Queen Mum bag. "Don't worry. I'll keep her focused on the conference and we'll just have to hope for the best. I'm just a bit worried about will happen when she sees him down there. I don't want her getting upset and embarrassing herself in front of her colleagues."

"It's so frustrating. If only we could talk to the MSL and find out what the hell he's up to. It did seem so promising this time," said Pussy Original.

* * *

Mongolian Sheep Pussy and Pussy With Balls had spent the

night on the floor in the lounge near the sofa. The Countess wasn't ready to face the world in the dining room of the hotel so she ordered her breakfast in her suite again. When it arrived, she placed the tray on the coffee table, turned on the television and sat down on the sofa.

Mongolian Sheep Pussy bounced up and sat with her. "Are you OK, Madame?"

The Countess sighed. "I've had enough," she said. "I'm done with making myself vulnerable. From now on, I need to start protecting myself."

"But you're bound to see him today," said Mongolian Sheep Pussy. "And you'll find out what happened last night. And everything will be okay."

"No," said the Countess. "I'm done. I can't do this dance anymore. I wish I'd decided this before coming out here. It would have made everything so much easier. He was right all along – we should just be friends."

"But I thought you were in love with him, Madame," said Mongolian Sheep Pussy.

"I am. Or I think I am," said the Countess. "But maybe it's just the idea of love. Maybe it's all in my head. Maybe it's not real. Outside of work, I barely know him – we could be completely incompatible! No, it's just better to move on. I should have done it months ago. Then I wouldn't be feeling so bloody awful right now."

"But, Madame—"

"No," the Countess said. Mongolian Sheep Pussy's insistence was starting to annoy her. "It's better this way."

Mongolian Sheep Pussy sat quietly as the Countess ate her breakfast. When she had finished, she took the bag over to the table and shook the contents out so she could transfer her things to the Queen Mum bag.

When she was done, Mongolian Sheep Pussy said, "Can I go back on the floor with Pussy With Balls?" And then, looking at the Countess, she tried one more time, "Are you really sure about the MSL Madame?"

"Yes," said the Countess. "I am." She walked over to the sofa, bent down and placed Mongolian Sheep Pussy back on the floor. "This has been a wake-up call for me. It's time to start protecting my feelings and to get over him. I need to learn to be happy on my own. Then we won't have to go through anything like this again." She stood up. "Right, I need to get on. My face looks like shit from last night."

After trying her best in the bathroom to hide the red, puffy eyes and calm the blotchy skin, she came back into the bedroom to pick up the Queen Mum bag.

"Are you going to be all right, Madame?" said Pussy Original.

"Yes," replied the Countess. "I'm bloody determined to be. I just want to get through to the end of this conference and then we can all go back home."

"Good for you, Madame," replied Pussy Original. "You're a fighter. You'll make it."

"Thanks," replied the Countess. "You guys are incredible. I don't know how I'd survive without you."

"It's no problem, Madame," said Pussy Original. "We wouldn't get far without you either. We're a family, and we're going to make it through this."

She picked up Pussy Original and kissed him. "I know," she said. "See you later. I've really got to go now."

In the living room, she took her wallet and phone from the top of the table and placed them in the Queen Mum bag. Then she took Persian Dolly, who was hanging in the hallway of the suite, and made her way out to the lifts.

* * *

While Pussy With Balls lay next to her, still sleeping, Mongolian Sheep Pussy pondered the situation. It was a disaster. The Countess and the MSL had come so close to being together, but now, even the Countess had lost faith. Mongolian Sheep Pussy was livid with the MSL for letting the Countess down and at Aidan as well. She felt that Aidan had boxed the Countess into a business situation which had caused her to miss the MSL.

It just didn't stack up. She had seen the way that the MSL had looked at the Countess when they met in the restaurant. The chemistry between them had been undeniable.

She felt sure in her heart that the Countess and the MSL were destined to be together. But now, the only way that the Countess seemed to be able to cope was by shutting down and swearing off him completely. Pussy Original and Pussy With Balls had also been more cautious about the MSL and would have liked the Countess to move on. But what if she was right and they were all wrong? What if the Countess and the MSL really did love each other and there had been a big misunderstanding that had caused them to miss their chance of love? Mongolian Sheep Pussy wasn't having that!

She had to find the MSL. A few minutes later, a chance occurred. The housekeeping maids had just arrived to clean and service the suite. They came in and out a couple of times and then they propped the door open while they went about their work.

It's now or never, thought Mongolian Sheep Pussy. There

was no time to consult the other accessories and anyway, she knew that they would think she was crazy and had done enough damage already. While the door was still open and the maids were in the bedroom, she bounced along the floor of the lounge and out through the door. Initially, she just made her way down the corridor but then she realised that she at least needed a plan. She paused under a side table which was positioned near to the lifts. *It's breakfast time*, she reasoned. *I'll go and see if Aidan or the MSL are in the dining room.*

There were two men and a woman waiting for the lift. When it arrived, she slipped in with them. On reaching the ground floor, she darted behind by a huge plant pot. This gave her a very good view of the reception area. She surveyed this view, desperately trying to spot either Aidan or the MSL. Her luck was in. Within a couple of minutes, she saw Aidan go to the reception desk. She watched as he talked to the lady behind the counter. Then, as he was turning to leave, she moved towards him.

* * *

Aidan felt himself kick something as he moved away from the reception desk. He half-glanced down, saw nothing and kept walking. Then it happened again. He stopped and looked at his shoe. Next to it, he saw the Countess's handbag.

He bent down to pick it up. What was it she called this one? Mongolian something or other. He stood up and looked around for the Countess.

He guessed that maybe the Countess was close by and had dropped it. It was weird though, as when he peeked inside, it was empty apart from a tissue, but he definitely recognised it as the bag the Countess had used the previous evening. Oh well, he would be seeing her soon, and he could give it back to her. He stuffed the bag into his coat pocket and carried on.

When he got back to the exhibition stand, the Countess was already there, busy chatting to a couple of delegates. He stood and observed her for a moment. He could see that she looked a bit rough from the previous evening. Her eyes were heavy, and she had obviously tried to fix them with make-up.

It was a shame about Ed, that American chap. Everything had seemed like it was going so well between them. When they had met in the restaurant, it had been so romantic, as if Romeo had just clapped eyes on Juliet. The poor cow was covering it well though, yammering away about the delights of Periculum.

He felt inside his pocket and checked that the bag was still there. He wondered, should he get involved? Normally, he would stay out of the love lives of employees, but he liked the Countess and thought of her as a friend. He touched the bag again and stroked its fur.

His mind made up, he left the stand and started wandering around the exhibition. Then he went out into the foyer of the conference hall, and it was there that he bumped into the object of his quest – the MSL.

* * *

Earlier, the MSL had attempted to speak to the Countess. It had been a struggle for him to get up that morning, as the late boozy nights followed by early mornings were starting to take their toll. However, the urge to find the Countess and arrange to spend some time with her had propelled him up from his bed and out of the hotel to the conference hall.

Initially, he had felt confident that everything would be okay with her. He would apologise for not hooking up with her the previous evening, express his regret at this and then ask her out. He had expected that she would immediately and happily accept.

He was wrong. As he approached the Periculum exhibition stand, he saw her look at him but then turn to a woman who had been hovering nearby. She launched into her spiel about Periculum's risk solutions.

"Oh yes, the whole system is fully configurable," he heard the Countess say. She glanced over the lady's shoulder at him but then immediately turned her attention back to the prospective customer. "We've accommodated various pricing models over the years, whether from a European or North American perspective."

He hovered a bit longer. She was really good at her work. Before long, she was flipping through the company brochure, talking about capital adequacy, counterparty risk and interest rate derivatives. She didn't look up at him anymore. Damn!

He decided to wander off to a conference session and figure out what to do later. But he couldn't concentrate on anything that was being said, so after a few minutes, he quietly left.

He was in a world of his own, pondering the situation, when Aidan approached him.

"Ah," said Aidan. "Just the man I was looking for."

"Hello there. Me?" said the MSL.

"Yes, you. This is a bit embarrassing," said Aidan, "but I've got a bit of a tricky situation with one of my staff, and I think you might be able to help."

"If you're talking about the Countess, then she doesn't want to see me," said the MSL.

"Really?" asked Aidan. "Rumour has it she is distraught that she didn't get to meet up with you last night."

"Really? I kept looking for her, but she wasn't there."

"I have to admit it was partly my fault," said Aidan. "I kept her busy until at least midnight, by which time you weren't around."

"I popped back there sometime after one, but she was nowhere to be seen," said the MSL. "I figured she had gone to bed or something."

"No, she was there until the end," said Aidan. "She was trying not to show it, but she was waiting for you."

"Shit!" said the MSL. "That explains why she's just given me the cold shoulder."

"You've seen her?" asked Aidan.

"A while ago," replied the MSL. "She wouldn't speak to me."

"Bugger. That's not good," said Aidan. "Look, please excuse me for asking this. I don't normally get involved in other people's private affairs, but the Countess has become very special to me, and to the company."

"And me too," said the MSL.

"Then you won't mind me clarifying this. Do you like her or not?" asked Aidan. "Only, I think it would be easier if we all knew what the exact situation was."

"Like her?" said the MSL. "I'm crazy about her! She's the most amazing woman I've ever met. I've been very nervous about getting involved with her, but now I realise that I just can't let her go. I really want to be with her."

"Good. I'm glad we've established that fact," said Aidan. "Right. Well, you're going to have to find a way of getting back into her good books. This might help." He pulled out

Mongolian Sheep Pussy. "Tell her that you found this bag lying around somewhere and that you've rescued it."

"That was the bag she was using last night. It's one of her pussies. How come you've got it?" asked the MSL.

"I found it in the lobby of the hotel," said Aidan. "God knows how it got there."

The MSL took Mongolian Sheep Pussy. "Thanks for this. I hope you don't mind, but can I ask you a favour? I know you guys are busy here, and there's a lot of stuff going on. But do you think I could take her out this evening? You know, to make up for last night."

Aidan smiled. "Yes, go on. I don't think I can bear to get in the way of true love again."

"Thanks," said the MSL. "I really appreciate it. Now all I've got to do is to convince the Countess."

* * *

The MSL tucked Mongolian Sheep Pussy carefully inside his conference folder then made his way back towards the hotel where he had a chat with the concierge.

Following their instructions, he left the hotel, crossed the tree-lined Kurfürstendamm shopping street and then turned right until he found the street with the French cinema on the corner. A few hundred yards further, on the left, sandwiched between a chemist and a brasserie, he found what he was looking for – a florist.

On entering the tiny shop, it was with much relief that he discovered that the mature, grey-haired gentleman who worked there spoke English.

"For a special lady?" asked the florist as he counted out

twelve red roses.

"Yes," replied the MSL. "I've only just realised how special."

"Then she will love these," said the florist. He took the roses to the counter.

"I hope so," said the MSL as he followed behind, weaving his way back through all the buckets of flowers. "I've kind of screwed up."

"You'll have to talk to her," said the florist.

"I've tried. She won't speak to me."

The florist smiled. "Find a way. You have to tell her what's in your heart." He touched his chest as he spoke. "Do you know what is truly in your heart?"

"I do now," replied the MSL. "I suppose I've always known, but I was just too scared. And now I'm worried that I've ruined it. I think she's angry with me."

"That's a good sign," said the florist. "She likes you."

"I know she does. But I've hurt her," said the MSL. "I think I might have blown it."

Having wrapped the flowers in cellophane and gold paper, the florist turned to the shelf behind him and reached for a reel of thick gold ribbon. He cut a length and tied it around the stem of the roses. Then he took the scissors and cut into each end of the ribbon to create a fringe. Methodically, he ran the blade of the scissors along each piece of fringe to make them curl.

He paused, looked up at the MSL and said, "Do you love her?"

"Yes. Yes, I do," said the MSL. "I love her." He took a breath and then blew the air out through his lips. "Wow. It feels really good to say that. Yes, I love her. I've always loved her. She's the most amazing woman I've ever met. And I've been so dumb not to realise that until now."

The florist kept working away until he finished making the curls in the ribbon. He picked up the roses and held them in front of him to inspect his handiwork.

He put them down on the counter again and adjusted the bow. "Does she know that you love her?" he said without looking up.

"No," replied the MSL.

The florist stood up straight and handed the roses to the MSL. "Then go and tell her."

* * *

The MSL caught a taxi back to the conference centre. Having placed the roses carefully on the seat beside him, he took Mongolian Sheep Pussy out of his folder. He stroked her fur, remembering all the fun times they'd had in the New York office of SC Radcliffe with the Countess's leopard-skin bag.

He liked this bag. Its fur was soft, and it belonged to the woman he loved. Something made him hold it against his face and he caught a whiff of the Countess's perfume. He closed his eyes and sniffed the bag again, imagining that he was nuzzling the Countess's neck, not her handbag.

Opening his eyes, he looked down at the roses. "I hope this works," he said aloud. "It's time. She's the one."

As Teddy's Door Closes, Another Opens

Back in the Countess's suite, things had not been running smoothly. Everyone had snoozed for a while. Pussy With Balls woke up and realised that Mongolian Sheep Pussy was no longer sleeping next to him. He thought that perhaps she had moved because of the cleaners. He was worried about her and wanted to make sure she was all right. He had a look around the living room and then went into the bedroom as he called her name.

"Shh!" said Pussy Original. "American Ted's sleeping."

"Sorry, mate, but I'm looking for Mongolian Sheep Pussy. She was next to me earlier, but now she's disappeared. Is she in here?" asked Pussy With Balls.

"Haven't seen her," said Pussy Original.

"Shit," said Pussy With Balls. "Where the hell is she then?"

"No idea. Are you sure she's not in there?" said Pussy Original.

"Yes," said Pussy With Balls. "Are you sure she's not here?"

Their conversation woke up American Ted. "What's happening?" he said.

"Nothing," said Pussy Original. "We're not sure where Mongolian Sheep Pussy is, but she's bound to be here somewhere.

Don't worry. We'll sort it out. You can go back to sleep and keep resting."

"Mongolian Sheep Pussy is missing?" said American Ted. "Are you sure?"

"I've looked everywhere," replied Pussy With Balls. "And I've been calling out her name. There's neither sight nor sound of her."

"Okay – hang on a minute," said American Ted. He slid down the bed covers to join the bags on the floor. "Let's all have one more look and then we'll have to figure out what to do. Is she with the Countess?"

"No," said Pussy Original. "The Countess took the Queen Mum bag this morning."

"Oh God," said American Ted. "What's happening to us all?"

"Cracking up," said Pussy Deluxe who had been watching the exchange from the entrance to the closet. "You're all cracking up!"

"Why don't you just be quiet," said Pussy With Balls. "You're not helping."

"Truth hurts," said Pussy Deluxe. "You lot ought to be jumping up and down that the Countess didn't get the MSL."

"And why exactly is that?" asked Pussy Original.

"Because that man doing a runner last night has just extended your lifespan here. Especially yours." He pointed his strap at American Ted.

"What do you mean?" asked Pussy Original.

"He means that if the Countess had the MSL then she wouldn't need us," said American Ted. "He's right. Once she has a man properly in her life, she definitely won't need me."

"How dare you say such a thing?" Pussy Original shouted at Pussy Deluxe.

"You deserve a bloody good…" said Pussy With Balls as he swung is pom-poms at Pussy Deluxe.

"Stop!" said American Ted. "Don't hit him. He's not worth it. We've got far more important things to worry about right now than our future. Mongolian Sheep Pussy is unaccounted for, and we don't need anything else going wrong on this trip."

"Sorry, Ted," said Pussy With Balls. "I just don't like him saying things like that."

"Sorry, Ted," mimicked Pussy Deluxe. "He's a teddy bear, for God's sake. Why do you lot cow-tow to him so much?"

"We don't," said Pussy With Balls. "But unlike you, we look after one another. He's worth ten of us lot put together. He knows that things might change in his life, but he still puts the Countess and everyone else first. That's something you'll never understand the meaning of."

"What are we going to do about Mongolian Sheep Pussy? Let's have one more look around," said Pussy Original. "She's got to be hiding out here somewhere."

Pussy Deluxe laughed at them all and went back into the closet. Meanwhile, Pussy Original, Pussy With Balls and American Ted searched every inch of the suite. Of course, they found no trace of her.

"She's not here," said American Ted after they had looked in every possible space at least twice.

"Maybe she did go off with the Countess," said Pussy Original.

"No," said Pussy With Balls. "The Countess took the Queen Mum bag. Why would she take two bags? Anyway, the Countess put Mongolian Sheep Pussy back on the floor next to me when she left the room."

"So Mongolian Sheep Pussy was definitely here when the

Countess left?" said Pussy Original.

"Definitely," said Pussy With Balls.

"What happened next?" asked Pussy Original.

"I don't know," replied Pussy With Balls. "I went back to sleep. The cleaners came in and disturbed me. I slept again and then I woke up, noticed she wasn't there and came into the bedroom looking for her. That's when you saw me."

"Was Mongolian Sheep Pussy there when the cleaners came in?" asked American Ted.

"I can't remember," said Pussy With Balls.

"Think!" said Pussy Original.

"I am thinking," said Pussy With Balls. "She was to start with. I think they came in and out a couple of times. I dozed off again and then got woken by the vacuum cleaner. They shoved it right under me, you know."

"Was she there then?" asked American Ted.

"No," said Pussy With Balls. "Because I turned to talk to her at that point, to make some comment on the vacuum, and she wasn't there."

"Did you worry about her at that point?" asked Pussy Original.

"No, not really. I was half asleep, and I just assumed she had moved somewhere else. We are all used to doing our own thing in the Countess's space, so I didn't really think it odd at the time."

"But you did when you woke up the next time?" asked Pussy Original.

"Yes. Maybe," said Pussy With Balls. "Again, I assumed that she could have gone anywhere in the suite, but I just had that funny feeling that I needed to find her and make sure she was okay. She felt bad about making the Countess stay to the bitter end last night. But it wasn't her fault that the MSL let the Countess down."

"I know," said Pussy Original. "But she just would never let the thing drop. We have tried to get the Countess to move on from the MSL, but she kept encouraging her. And look where it ended up."

"She only wanted the Countess to be happy," said Pussy With Balls. "She's a girl. She wants the most perfect and romantic outcome for the Countess. Prince Charming on his white horse. All of that."

"Let's not get into this argument now," said American Ted. "The bottom line is that Mongolian Sheep Pussy is missing. We know she was here when the Countess left this morning, we think she might have been here when the cleaners arrived, but sometime after that, she disappeared."

"Perhaps the cleaners stole her," said Pussy With Balls. "She's an attractive bag."

"Please, no," said Pussy Original. "If that is what happened, then we'll never see her again."

"It's something we may have to face," said American Ted. "If that has happened, there is nothing we can do about it."

"What will we tell the Countess?" said Pussy Original. "She'll be mortified. And in her current emotional state…"

"She's coped with worse," said American Ted.

"The Countess may cope with losing Mongolian Sheep Pussy," said Pussy With Balls. "But I can't. We can't let this happen. I'm going to go and look for her."

"Don't," said Pussy Original. "We might lose you too. Then we'll have two missing handbags to report to the Countess. No… There has to be an explanation for this."

"Is it possible that Mongolian Sheep Pussy escaped?" said

American Ted. "She meant well in encouraging the Countess to stay on at the ball last night, but it didn't help and now, she's feeling ashamed and taken herself off somewhere."

"But where would she go?" said Pussy With Balls. "And why?"

"She could be anywhere," said Pussy Original. "I can't see her running away. She loves being part of the accessories, and she wouldn't survive without us."

"Imagine her lost in Berlin," said Pussy With Balls. "All bedraggled and dirty, begging on a street corner. She doesn't even know any German. We can't let this happen. I've got to go and look for her."

"No," said American Ted. "We don't know where to start. You don't know any German either, so you wouldn't get very far."

"I don't know," said Pussy Original. "Perhaps Pussy With Balls is right. Perhaps we should go after her. If we can find her, then the Countess need never know. Eventually, this whole episode will blow over and things will return to normal."

"No," said American Ted.

"Pussy With Balls and I could go together," said Pussy Original. "I've travelled lots with the Countess. I've been to Switzerland with her and they speak German there. I reckon I could get us around okay. You can hold the fort here."

"No one's going anywhere," said American Ted.

"Why?" said Pussy With Balls.

"For a start, you can't get out that door," said American Ted, pointing to the main door to the suite. "And secondly, the person who could conduct the most effective search for Mongolian Sheep Pussy is the Countess herself. We're going to have to wait until she gets back."

"But telling her about this is going to be just awful," said Pussy Original.

"Not as awful as it would be if you two are at large in Berlin as well," said American Ted.

"Oh dear, Ted," said Pussy Deluxe who had decided to join them. "This *is* a tough one. You've hung on in the Countess's life purely because she can't get a man, and now you've got to deliver really bad news to her."

"Why don't you shut up?" said Pussy With Balls. "I wish it was you who was missing because then not one of us would give a shit. I'd love to see you lying in a gutter, being trodden on by everyone."

"It'll never happen," said Pussy Deluxe. "They would see how fabulous I am and be racing to claim me for their own. I'd quite like to live here. It's a very opulent place and would suit me down to the ground."

"I'm sure it can be arranged," said Pussy Original. "We'll sell you to the cleaners tomorrow. At least you'd fetch a good price."

"A lot more than you would," said Pussy Deluxe. "I can't see a well-heeled Berliner picking you up from the street. I haven't noticed anyone wearing leopard skin when I've been out with the Countess during the conference."

"Stop it!" said American Ted. "Pussy Deluxe, if you've got nothing useful to say, then please go back into the closet. Some of us are at least trying to find a solution."

"What, go and hide away and miss your star performance as you fess up to the Countess that an accessory is missing?" said Pussy Deluxe. "Oh no. I'm staying right near you until that door opens and the Countess comes in. This is the best thing that has happened around here in ages."

"You don't have to tell her, Ted," said Pussy Original. "I'll do it if you like."

"No, I will," said American Ted. "As Pussy Deluxe has so gleefully pointed out, my days of responsibility for the Countess's life may be numbered, but until that time arrives, I will carry out my duty to the full. I'm still accountable for what happens with the accessories, and I will, therefore, inform her that we have a problem."

* * *

In the exhibition hall, the crowd had died down, and the Countess was leaning against one of the cupboards, leafing through the Periculum company brochure.

"How're you doing?" Aidan asked her.

"Fine. Just fine," she replied, still reading the brochure.

"Don't worry," he said. "Your American chap might yet get to stroke your pussy."

The Countess looked up at him. "You what? I can't believe you just said that."

Aidan stood with his hands in his pockets, smiling. "I just meant one of your furry bags."

"Oh, them," she said. "No, it's best left. I've got other things to focus on now."

"Are you sure of that?" asked Aidan. "Only, things are about to change. Look over there."

The Countess glanced over her shoulder. She saw the MSL approaching, carrying a bunch of roses. *Why is he doing this now?* It was too late. Her mind was made up.

She turned back to Aidan. "Yes," she said. "I'm sure."

She started to walk away, but the MSL caught up with her

and grabbed her arm.

"Don't go," he said. "Look, here – these are for you. I'm so sorry about last night. I really wanted to dance with you. I desperately wanted to be at the gala but kept being railroaded to other places. And when I did get there, I couldn't see you and thought you'd left. I'm sorry you were waiting for me and that you were upset."

"These are lovely," said the Countess. "But I can't take them."

"You can't?" said Aidan, his mouth dropping.

"Why?" asked the MSL. "Please. I want to make it up to you. Perhaps we can go out tonight?"

"That's really sweet of you," said the Countess. "But…" It was then that she noticed Mongolian Sheep Pussy. "How come you've got my bag?"

"Ah yes," said the MSL. "I found her. Here." He handed the bag to the Countess.

"Thank you," said the Countess, looking confused as she clutched hold of Mongolian Sheep Pussy. "I've no idea how you got this, but thank you for returning her."

The MSL offered her the flowers again. "Please, take them," he said.

They were beautiful. Part of her wanted to take them, smell their perfume and then fall at his feet, but the other part of her remembered her resolve, that it was time to get over him, no matter what.

"It's a lovely gesture, but no," she said. She could feel Mongolian Sheep Pussy quivering in her hand as she spoke. "Perhaps we're better off as friends. After all, as you said in New York last year, it's a small world and we might work together again in the future."

She could still feel Mongolian Sheep Pussy moving. It was

as if Mongolian Sheep Pussy was trying to wriggle free, so she gripped her tighter.

"I was wrong," said the MSL. "I'm crazy about you. Please, please come out with me tonight."

The Countess looked at him. The earnest look on his face that tugged at her heart, his eyes that she could get lost in, the little mark on his cheek that she had always wanted to touch. But no, it all hurt too much. Best to end it now, before anything went wrong again.

"I appreciate the sentiment. I really do." Her voice started to shake. "But I need to say no. Thanks for returning my bag. I have to go now."

She turned to Aidan. "Have you got the key for the cupboard? I need to put this in there." She held up Mongolian Sheep Pussy as she spoke.

Aidan rummaged in his trouser pocket and pulled out a leather keyring with a single key hanging from it. He gave it to the Countess.

The Countess looked once more at the MSL. "I'm sorry."

She walked briskly to the back of the stand and crouched down to the cupboard as she wiped away a tear. She struggled to get the key in the lock because her hands were shaking.

"Madame, are you crazy?" said Mongolian Sheep Pussy.

"No, it's for the best," said the Countess. "Like I said this morning, I need to move on."

"But he loves you," said Mongolian Sheep Pussy.

"No, I don't think so," said the Countess. "He would have acted before now if that were true."

"He does. I heard him say it."

"When?"

"To the florist earlier," said Mongolian Sheep Pussy. "He

said he loves you."

"He loves me?" said the Countess as she finally got the cupboard door open.

"Yes. And in the cab, he said that you're the one."

"What? You spoke to him?"

"No, of course I didn't," said Mongolian Sheep Pussy. "He was talking to himself. He loves you, Madame."

"Why didn't you tell me?" said the Countess.

"I was trying to," said Mongolian Sheep Pussy. "That's why I kept trying to move in your hand. I couldn't talk, could I? Not with Aidan there. He's crazy about you, Madame. So what are you playing at? Get back around there and say yes to him."

"You're sure of this?" asked the Countess. "I can't be hurt again."

"Madame. Yes. For God's sake, listen to me," said Mongolian Sheep Pussy. "He loves you. He says you're the one. Now go find him!"

The Countess stood up, leaving the cupboard open. Still clutching Mongolian Sheep Pussy, she went back around the front of the stand. The MSL wasn't there.

"Shit!" she said. "Where did he go?"

"Over there, towards the exit," said Aidan.

"Here, take this," said the Countess as she handed him Mongolian Sheep Pussy. "Can you put her in the cupboard, please. The key's in the lock."

She ran through the crowd. Thank goodness she was tall and could see over the top of people's heads. He couldn't have gone far, as it had been less than a minute.

She went around the corner of a stand and then she saw him. "Hey! Ed! Wait!"

She barged through the middle of a conversation between

three delegates. "Sorry," she said to them as she kept moving.

She called out again to the MSL. "Don't go! Wait! I'm sorry."

He turned. She caught up with him and touched his arm. She felt her heart lurch with longing as their gaze moved from her hand on his shirtsleeve to one another's eyes. For a long time, they stood there, staring at each other until at last she breathed, 'Yes, yes, Ed, I'll go out with you... if you still want to, that is."

"But you said..."

"Forget what I said. I was being monumentally stupid. A total idiot in fact. I'd love to go out with you. Dinner, drinks, anything."

"Really?" he asked, his face lighting up.

"Really," said the Countess. "But only if you still want to."

"Of course I want to. Of course I want to," he repeated, "And do you still not want these?" he waved the roses at her playfully.

The Countess laughed, "Ah, well – if you insist. They look beautiful, thank you."

She took the roses and sniffed them. "Mmm, they smell amazing. And I owe you an apology. I'd kind of reached the end of the line." She paused awkwardly, "You see... I feel silly saying this but... well, I've been a bit nuts about you for such a long time, and when it all went wrong last night, I lost the plot a bit."

"Don't worry. It's okay," said the MSL. "We'll go out tonight and have a really good time. I never want you to feel like that again. Nothing is going to get in our way this time. I'll pick you up from your room at seven thirty. Is that okay?"

"Yes," she said. "That's very okay. I'm in the Nollendorf suite. See you later."

* * *

Towards the end of the afternoon, Aidan and the Countess were in conversation with a delegate from a French bank.

When their discussion ended, Aidan turned to the Countess and said, "Why don't you take off now. You've got a big night ahead."

"Are you sure, boss?" said the Countess. "The exhibition is open for another hour or so."

"I know," said Aidan. "But somehow, I get the feeling that you're not exactly focused on it now. Go on, go – while I'm still feeling charitable. You've worked really hard the last couple of days. Go and enjoy yourself."

"Thanks," said the Countess. She looked across at the roses which she had laid on top of the cupboards. "I'm so excited about tonight. I wonder where he'll take me."

She got the S-Bahn train back towards the hotel. On leaving the station, she decided to check out a department store that was nearby. She found two dresses that she liked and went to try them on. The first one didn't fit right, but the second one, a blue silk wrap dress with paisley patterns on it, looked sensational. Still wearing the dress, the Countess took Mongolian Sheep Pussy out of her bag so that she could see it.

"You look amazing in that," said Mongolian Sheep Pussy. "Why don't you wear it tonight?"

"That's just what I was thinking," said the Countess. She sat down the changing-room stool and put Mongolian Sheep Pussy on her lap. "Thank you for saving me earlier. I nearly blew it. I finally get the thing that I've always dreamed of and then I say no to him. And I'm sorry if I was tetchy with you last night. It all started out so well and then everything went pear-shaped."

"It's okay, Madame. It ended up being a horrible evening. Do you know something though? He *was* there last night. I heard him tell Aidan that he got back there just after one o'clock."

"Really?" said the Countess. "That must have been the exact time I was in the bathrooms with you! So, if I hadn't been such a cry-baby, hiding away in the toilets, I might have seen him. Bugger! You were right. You never lost faith in him. I did."

"I'm not sure that I was right about making you stay," said Mongolian Sheep Pussy. "It was so painful for you. But having seen the way he looked at you in the restaurant earlier, I just knew that he wanted to be with you."

"You're a very clever bag," said the Countess. "And I'm so glad that I have you. But I have to ask. How come you ended up with the MSL today?"

"Now, that would be telling," said Mongolian Sheep Pussy. "Let's just say that I knew that there had to be an explanation for last night, and I took it upon myself to find it."

"Hmm," said the Countess as she smiled at the bag. "Well, you saved the day. Thank you. I can't believe that I have a proper date with him tonight. Not some vague arrangement to meet up but a proper plan."

"I was bursting to tell you," said Mongolian Sheep Pussy. "I couldn't believe it when you said no to him. He's crazy about you, Madame. He loves you, and he wants to be with you."

The Countess touched her heart. "At last. I wonder what made him change his mind."

"No doubt you'll find out later," said Mongolian Sheep Pussy.

The Countess picked up the Queen Mum bag. "And you,"

she said to the bag. "Thank you for taking care of me last night and this morning. I've been such a mess."

"You're welcome, Madame," said the Queen Mum bag. "I'm really pleased that things are turning around for you. But now I think you need to get out of that dress and go and see if you can find a pair of shoes to match it."

"More wise advice," said the Countess as she started to untie the dress.

* * *

The accessories had spent the rest of the afternoon in a very tense silence. Usually, they would have cleared out of the lounge by the end of the day in case the Countess returned with clients, but instead, all four of them sat on the sofa and waited for her return. Pussy Deluxe was concerned for Mongolian Sheep Pussy. He hated to think of a bag of her quality being subjected to horrors of street life in Berlin or the domestic set-up of a thieving cleaner. Pussy With Balls felt bad because American Ted was going to take the rap for his inadequacy. He was still desperate to go out and look for Mongolian Sheep Pussy. Pussy Original was concerned for American Ted after the comments made by Pussy Deluxe.

American Ted felt like a failure. He had struggled to cope with the Countess the previous evening, and now, one of her treasured accessories had gone AWOL. After reporting to the Countess about the tragic loss of Mongolian Sheep Pussy, he would have no choice but to do the honourable thing and resign from her household.

Eventually, they heard the sound of the door being rattled as the Countess fiddled with the electronic key system to gain entry to the suite. A feeling of dread shot through each accessory, even Pussy Deluxe. They had no idea what shape the Countess would be in, and who could tell how she would take the news that American Ted was about to break to her?

Imagine their surprise when the Countess burst through the door carrying a huge bunch of red roses, swinging Mongolian Sheep Pussy around on her finger and shouting at the top of her voice, "I have a date tonight! A date with the MSL! And he loves me. Who wants to come out with me tonight?"

"A date, Madame?" said Pussy Original. "How did this come about?"

"Madame, this is wonderful news," said American Ted.

"I'll come on your date with you," said Pussy Deluxe.

"Mongolian Sheep Pussy, you're safe!" cried Pussy With Balls. "Blimey. I've been so worried about you. Where have you been?"

"Mongolian Sheep Pussy is my hero," said the Countess. "Or should I say, heroine. She brought the MSL to me, and he gave me these lovely roses, and we're going out tonight. Everything is suddenly looking up!"

She put the roses, the Queen Mum bag and her shopping bags on the dining table, and with Mongolian Sheep Pussy in her hands, she plonked herself down on the sofa with the other accessories.

"What are you lot doing in here?" she said. "Is something wrong with the bed?"

"Everything's fine, Madame," said Pussy Original. "We just fancied a change of scenery, didn't we, chaps? I'm sorry though. We should have moved earlier. If you had come in now with some clients, then we would have been in trouble."

"Don't worry," said the Countess. "Who cares about that? I

don't care about anything now. I have my date, and that's all that is important."

"I told you all it would be all right," said Mongolian Sheep Pussy. "None of you believed me. I saved the day. I got them together. Madame, he's going to kiss you and look after you and tell you that he loves you. And you'll be married and live happily ever after and we'll all come to your wedding. And then you'll have beautiful children."

"Okay, stop," said the Countess. "One thing at a time. Let's just go out with him tonight and see how it goes. I'm more than happy with that for now."

"What happened, Madame?" said American Ted. "Please tell us about it."

The Countess relayed the details about her encounter with the MSL and how Mongolian Sheep Pussy had saved the day.

"And I got away just after four o'clock," she said. "So I had time to go shopping, and I don't have to do any work stuff tonight. I am free to spend the whole evening with the MSL. Isn't it all just so wonderful? I think, at last, things might be coming together."

"It does look that way, Madame," said American Ted. "I'm so pleased for you."

"Thank you," said the Countess. "Thanks to all of you. You've supported me so much through all of this. I wish I could take every one of you with me, but I think that might look a bit weird. But really, I can't thank you enough. You're the best accessories a girl could wish for."

"You're welcome, Madame," said Pussy Original. "Now, what time is this date? Do you need to start getting ready, and what are you going to wear?"

"Good point," said the Countess and looked at her watch.

It was just after six o'clock. "Yes, tonight I can take my time to get ready. And at last, I'm going to get to luxuriate in that lovely big bath. I have a new dress to wear. I bought it on the way back here. And the Queen Mum bag suggested I needed a new pair of shoes to match, so I've had a good spend-up."

"Of course, Madame," said Pussy Original. "We can't have you going on a date wearing any old pair of shoes."

"Exactly," said the Countess. "I'm so lucky to have accessories that understand me so well and know what's best for me, sometimes even before I do. I love you all so much for that."

"Why don't you go and run your bath, Madame?" said Pussy Original. "We've really missed Mongolian Sheep Pussy today and we'd love to chat with her."

"Sure," said the Countess. She got up from the sofa, took off Persian Dolly and laid him down over the back of the sofa. Then she went into the bedroom where she called up housekeeping to order a vase for her roses.

As soon as the Countess had left the lounge, all the accessories stared at Mongolian Sheep Pussy.

"Ooooooh, I wouldn't want to be in your shoes right now," said Pussy Deluxe.

"What?" said Mongolian Sheep Pussy as she stared back at them.

"We're really pleased that today has turned out so well, and you've obviously played a very important part in getting the Countess her date," said American Ted.

"Yes, I have," said Mongolian Sheep Pussy. "Without me, she would have rejected the MSL, and she would never have known that he loves her."

"He loves her?" asked Pussy Original.

"Yes," replied Mongolian Sheep Pussy. "And he said that she was the one."

"At last," said Pussy Original. "This is brilliant news. But we've been going crazy here today, looking for you and wondering what the hell had happened to you. Why didn't you tell us or Pussy With Balls what you were going to do? It was really stupid and inconsiderate to leave this room on your own. We had no idea where you were and anything could have happened to you."

"I couldn't," said Mongolian Sheep Pussy. "Not one of you trusted me. You've thought all along that I was a fool for believing that romance was possible. And even right now, in the Countess's moment of happiness, you are still treating me like an idiot. I'm not some naughty schoolgirl, you know. Who do you think you are to talk to me like that?"

"We were worried," said Pussy With Balls. "And this morning, you didn't even have the decency to let me know what you were doing or ask for help."

"I knew you would try to stop me. After seeing the Countess so distressed last night, I just had to find a way to bring them together," said Mongolian Sheep Pussy. "I have never stopped believing that the MSL was the man for the Countess. You weren't out with us last night, when their eyes met across the restaurant, and he jumped up and almost took her in her arms right there and then. I knew he would turn up at the gala ball and, might I say, I was right. He was there, looking for her."

Mongolian Sheep Pussy paused and looked at Pussy With Balls, American Ted and Pussy Original. They still looked annoyed with her.

"It just didn't add up that the MSL had let the Countess down," she continued. "There had to be an explanation, and I had to find it."

"How did you get out of here?" asked Pussy With Balls.

"I slipped out when the cleaners came in," said Mongolian Sheep Pussy. "It had to be a split-second decision or else I would have missed the opportunity. You were asleep. I'm sorry that I didn't tell you and that you've been worried, but it's just something that I had to do."

"We thought your disappearance had something to do with the cleaners. We were worried that you'd been stolen and that we'd never see you again," said American Ted.

"That's why we're giving you a hard time now. You don't know what we've been through today," said Pussy Original. "We've been out of our minds with worry."

"I've said I'm sorry," said Mongolian Sheep Pussy. "And everything is okay."

Pussy With Balls nudged her with one of his pom-poms. "You're a very clever bag. It sounds like you've saved the day. I don't know about the others, but I'm very proud of you."

Mongolian Sheep Pussy looked at Pussy Original. He was still angry about all the anxiety that Mongolian Sheep Pussy had caused, but he couldn't deny that she had been right about the MSL. Despite his frustration, he knew he had no choice but congratulate her.

"Well done," he said and gave her a kiss.

"Thanks," she replied.

American Ted walked up to her and gave her a hug. Then he started to cry.

"What's the matter, Ted?" she said. "I'm home, and the Countess is happy."

"I know," said American Ted. "There aren't words to describe how I've felt about everything since last night, and I was so worried about you today." He grabbed her in his paws and held her to him tightly while he cried into her fur. "Thank goodness you are safe. I'm really proud of you too, but don't ever disappear without telling us again."

"Yes," said Pussy Original. "Next time you head off on a matchmaking expedition, please phone home and tell us where you are."

"Okay," said Mongolian Sheep Pussy. She started to cry too. "I promise I'll do that. I'm sorry that I put you through this. It's wonderful to know that I'm so well looked after here."

"Isn't it fabulous? said Pussy Deluxe to Persian Dolly at the other end of the sofa. "Not a dry eye in the house. People pay good money to see this in the movies, and we have it here in our own front room."

"Thank God it's all worked out okay," said Persian Dolly. "The Countess was really moody this morning. I wasn't looking forward to more of that."

"You should have been here," said Pussy Deluxe. "It has been a meltdown. I didn't think American Ted was going to get through the day without topping himself, especially when they realised that Mongolian Sheep Pussy was missing. Then there was all the heroics as Pussy With Balls declared that he would search Berlin high and low for her and Pussy Original deciding that just because he's been to Switzerland a few times, he could speak German and would use that to go out and find her. And then that pathetic bear stopped them. I think it would have been really great to have offloaded the riff-raff element in the accessories."

"The bear has really lost it, hasn't he?" said Persian Dolly.

"Oh yes," said Pussy Deluxe. "But he still managed to do this honourable speech about how it was ultimately his responsibility that Mongolian Sheep Pussy had gone and that he would tell the Countess."

"Really?" said Persian Dolly. "What an idiot. If she wanted to go running around Berlin playing cupid, then surely that's up to her."

"Yes, but you know how it is around here," said Pussy Deluxe. "He thinks he's in charge, so he has to do all the big talk."

"He doesn't look so big now though," said Persian Dolly. "The MSL loves the Countess, so it's only a matter of time before he is installed in the Countess's bed. That leaves the bear out in the cold."

"Yes, I've already mentioned that," said Pussy Deluxe.

"You never miss a trick," said Persian Dolly. "You can be so spiteful sometimes."

"Hey! Whose side are you on?" said Pussy Deluxe.

"Nobody's," said Persian Dolly. "I just want a peaceful life. At least the Countess is going to be happier now she has the MSL. Let's hope we've seen the end of those awful mood swings."

* * *

Housekeeping arrived with the vase. The Countess, who was still in her bathrobe, took it and arranged her roses in it. She put them on the coffee table in front of the sofa.

"They look great, don't they?" she said.

"Gorgeous, Madame," said American Ted. "But don't linger around looking at them. It's almost seven o'clock. You need to keep getting ready."

"Gosh, you're right," she replied. "Now it's time to put on my new dress."

She went back into the bedroom while the bags discussed

who should go out on the date with the Countess. "You should go," said Pussy Original to Mongolian Sheep Pussy. "You're the one who has never lost faith, and the MSL seems to like you. You go."

"Maybe you should go," said Mongolian Sheep Pussy. "I've had my fun for the day. And if anything should go wrong, you'll handle it better than me."

"No. I'm far too scruffy. He'll take her somewhere nice. It's going to have to be you, the Queen Mum bag or possibly Pussy Deluxe. But I think it should be you. We all think that, don't we?" said Pussy Original.

"So, you mean that I don't get to go with her?" said Pussy Deluxe.

"No!" said Pussy With Balls, Pussy Original and American Ted in unison.

"You don't deserve to," said Pussy Original. "You didn't give a damn about Mongolian Sheep Pussy today, you've been winding up American Ted in a most unfair way, and the Countess is going to be all dressed up, so you won't look right anyway."

Of course, that last statement was most galling for Pussy Deluxe. "I'm a quality bag that looks right in all environments."

"So does Mongolian Sheep Pussy," said Pussy With Balls. "And I do believe that she is of the same quality as you."

"And she is much better suited to a first date," said Pussy Original. "She's all delicate and pretty, whereas you are large, lumbering and…?"

"I think you've lost that argument," said Persian Dolly to Pussy Deluxe.

"It's okay for you," he replied. "You get to go anyway."

"That's the advantage of being a coat," said Persian Dolly. "A woman generally has fewer of them than handbags, especially when she is travelling. Handbags are so ten-a-penny."

"Oh, piss off," said Pussy Deluxe. "I hope she drops you in a puddle. You won't be such a smart arse then."

* * *

A while later, the Countess emerged from the bedroom and modelled her new outfit for the accessories. Pussy With Balls and Pussy Original whistled as she picked up Persian Dolly, threw him around her shoulders and paraded about the room.

"How do I look?" she asked.

"Smashing, Madame," said Pussy Original. "He's not going to be able to resist you, that's for sure. So, are we banished to the closet?"

"No. You can hang out on the bed as usual," said the Countess. "I've made a decision. I'm not going to invite him back here tonight, and I will resist if he invites me to his room. It's our first date, and even though things are looking good, I have no idea how it will all go. I'm going to take it slowly."

"The Queen Mum bag will be very proud of you," said Pussy Original.

The Countess smiled and touched the handle of the Queen Mum bag. "I hate to admit this, but I think you have a point. It's about time I started behaving better. The MSL is really important to me, and I don't want to mess it up."

"Well done, Madame," said the Queen Mum bag. "You're becoming the lady I always knew you could be. I'm sure that tonight will be a very special evening for you."

"Which bag are you going to take?" asked Pussy With Balls. "Mongolian Sheep Pussy would tone very well with some of

269

the colours in your dress."

The Countess picked up Mongolian Sheep Pussy. "Yes, I think so. Without this lovely bag, I'd be sitting here all miserable and eating my dinner from a room-service tray. Would you like to come with me, Mongolian Sheep Pussy?"

"I'd be honoured, Madame," said Mongolian Sheep Pussy. "It's going to be such an exciting evening and a hundred times better than last night could ever have been."

"Enjoy it, Madame," said Pussy Original. "After all the heartache, you've earned it."

The Countess collected her things and placed them inside Mongolian Sheep Pussy. There was a knock at the door.

"That's him," said the Countess. "Right, you lot. Into the other room, quickly." She grabbed Pussy Original, Pussy Deluxe, Pussy With Balls and American Ted, took them into the bedroom and dumped them on the bed. Then she went to the door of the suite and opened it.

There he stood. Wearing the suit he had worn on the first night in Berlin, with a black open-neck shirt. The Countess could have pounced on him there and then.

"Hi there," she said. "Come in for a sec while I put my coat on."

"Wow!" he said as he stepped inside the door. "That is some dress."

"Thanks," she replied and did a twirl for him.

"Are you wearing this coat?" he asked as he picked up Persian Dolly. "It's a lovely soft suede."

"Yes, isn't it," replied the Countess. "I like to call it Persian Dolly, but I'll explain why another time."

"Then allow me," he said as he held the coat out for her and helped her put it on. "So, tell me, do you name all of your things?"

"Thank you," she replied, loving the closeness of his presence. "No. Only my favourites."

She went to the table to get Mongolian Sheep Pussy then turned to face him. He looked her up and down, beaming at her.

"Are you ready?" he said, reaching for the door handle.

"I am," replied the Countess.

"Then let's go," said the MSL.

* * *

They left the suite and walked towards the lift. The MSL's hand brushed against the Countess's a couple of times. She felt the usual bolt of excitement when there was any contact between them.

"Where are we going?" she asked.

"Away from here," said the MSL. "Away from all these conference people."

"Good," said the Countess.

As she got into the lift, he placed his hand in the small of her back. He kept it there while he pressed the button for the ground floor, and she leaned into him slightly, enjoying the moment.

They left the hotel, and the MSL instructed the doorman to hail a taxi. The Countess looked up at the sky. The grey clouds from earlier had dispersed, and now, as twilight fell, it was clear. The doorman seemed to know where they were going, and with no instruction from the MSL, he told the driver their destination.

Once in the taxi, the MSL turned to the Countess and smiled.

He placed his hands on hers. She basked in the warmth of his hand and the security this gave her. Tonight, it was not going to be some drunken antic that she could barely remember. This was the real thing, she was on a date with the man of her dreams, and he had just held her hand!

The taxi swung through the streets of Berlin. It eventually reached Unter Den Linden, one of the main Boulevards in East Berlin, named after the Linden trees that lined it. In front of them was the Brandenburg Gate, recently restored and lit up.

"It's beautiful isn't it?" said the Countess.

"Sure is," he replied. "I guess this really is Berlin. The Brandenburg Gate."

The taxi did a U-turn and pulled up in front of a hotel.

"Ah, this must be it," said the MSL. "The Hotel Adlon. It's the best hotel in Berlin, even better than the Kempinski. We are going to have dinner overlooking the Brandenburg Gate. Is this okay for my countess?"

"Oh yes. I've heard about this hotel, but I've never been here before. Back in Berlin's heyday, this used to be the place to be. Marlene Dietrich used to stay here. Einstein. Charlie Chaplin. Roosevelt. Everyone who was anyone."

"And now, the Countess is arriving," said the MSL, with a smile. "The history of the hotel is complete."

Still holding hands, they stood on the steps of the hotel and looked across at the Brandenburg Gate.

"This is amazing," said the Countess. "Thank you so much for bringing me here."

They turned and went inside.

"I thought we might have a drink first," said the MSL.

The Countess looked around the bar area. The tables were

low with bowed baroque style gilding on the legs, and the soft chairs were upholstered with a similar flouncy design.

"Let's sit over there," said the MSL as he took her hand and led her to the table. He gestured for her to sit down first. "Is this okay for you?"

"This is lovely, thank you," said the Countess. She watched him as he sat down, folding his tall frame into the chair. He noticed her looking at him and smiled back at her, his eyes bright.

"Ladies first," he said as he passed her the cocktail menu.

"Thank you," she replied. She flipped through the first couple of pages, skimming her eye over the cocktails. "These look amazing," she said. "But do you know what, I think I just fancy a simple gin and tonic."

"That sounds perfect," said the MSL. "I'll have the same."

When their drinks arrived, she held the plastic monogrammed stirrer by its top and prodded and played with the ice before gazing back up at the MSL. He was watching her.

"Mmm. That's a lovely G&T," she said as she placed the stirrer on the table.

The MSL held out his glass and clinked it against hers. "I'm so happy we're here. We should have done this a long time ago."

"That would have been good," said the Countess. "But maybe, maybe it wasn't the right time. It could have got complicated when we were working together."

The MSL sipped his drink and looked as though he was pondering what she said. "Maybe," he said. "I guess we shouldn't worry too much about the past. The most important thing is that we take this moment and make it the right time now."

The Countess's stomach flipped. She couldn't believe he was talking like this. "I'd like that," she whispered.

After their drink, they went into the restaurant where the maitre d' showed them to their table. The restaurant was like a giant conservatory with huge palms everywhere and windows on all sides looking out onto the street. Their table was in the corner by a window and had a perfect view of the Brandenburg Gate.

"I like it here," said the Countess. "How did you find this place?"

"I spoke to the concierge at the Kempinski and told them that I needed a very romantic restaurant that was good enough for a countess," replied the MSL, "and they arranged for us to have this table."

"Great planning," said the Countess. "I'm very impressed."

"I'm just pleased that I get to dine with you at last," said the MSL. "Last night was agony. In that restaurant, it was torture to have to take my eyes off you and go back to my table and talk business."

"Wasn't it," said the Countess. "I had to sweet talk those Dutch people, but all I could think about was dancing with you."

"I'm so sad that we never got to dance," said the MSL. "I couldn't wait to take you in my arms. You looked so sensational in that dress."

"And I wanted to dance with you when you were all dressed up in your tux," said the Countess.

"We'll have to make another opportunity," said the MSL. He picked up the wine list. "What would you like to drink? Champagne?"

"That sounds lovely," said the Countess. "But I don't want

so much that I don't completely remember this night with you and the food and this beautiful hotel."

He looked into her sparkling eyes, "Me neither," he said. "I want this night to be etched on my brain for ever. Our first night." He reached across and took hold of her hand. "How about we just have a glass and then see what we feel like afterwards?"

"Perfect," said the Countess.

A waiter gave them the food menu while the MSL ordered the champagne.

"I know I should be more adventurous," said the Countess as she lifted her eyes from the menu, "But my eye has just fallen on Wienersnitzel, and now I want that."

"Then have it," said the MSL.

"But there are so many yummy dishes on this menu," said the Countess.

"Then we'll have to come back here another time," said the MSL, "so that you can try something else."

The waiter brought the champagne and took their dinner orders. When he had finished, the MSL took hold of her hand again and said, "I know that we know each other through work, and we hung out a lot in New York last year. But I don't know your likes and dislikes, or your favourite movies or what you like to do on a Sunday afternoon."

The Countess smiled and twirled her fingers around his. "I don't know that stuff about you either. Where shall we start?"

"Something easy," said the MSL. "Favourite movies."

"Gosh, I don't know," said the Countess. "*Breakfast at Tiffany's* is one of my eternal favourites."

"Ah, I knew you were a closet romantic," teased the MSL.

"Ha-ha, yes, I suppose – I can't help it, really. But I do like edgy stuff too. How about you?"

"I'm more of an action movie man – *Die Hard, Mission Impossible* – and you can never go wrong with a bit of *Star Wars*."

"*Star Wars* is fun," said the Countess and sang the first few bars of the theme.

"I like clever stuff as well," said the MSL, "like *The Truman Show* – have you seen it?"

"No," said the Countess, "you'll have to initiate me."

The MSL caught his breath.

The Countess continued, "But I confess to liking cheesy things too."

"Such as?" asked the MSL.

"Mm, *The Sound of Music*," she replied. "It's on every Christmas. I love it."

"I think we all secretly like cheese. So, if I get a job in London, will I have to watch lots of Merchant Ivory movies to understand British culture?" asked the MSL.

The Countess laughed. "No. We've moved on a lot in recent years. You don't even have to have a butler now." *Gosh,* she thought. *Did I hear him right? Did he say he wants a job in London?*

"Even if you're a countess?" said the MSL.

"I could do with one sometimes," said the Countess. "I can be quite messy. But no. It's not compulsory. *It's just me and my handbags at home.* Are you really thinking of working in London?"

"I am," he replied. "That was one of the good things to come out of last night. I had some very interesting conversations. On our table, at dinner, there were a couple of recruitment consultants who work out of London. They say that there is quite a bit of work going."

"Really?" said the Countess. Things were looking up indeed.

"Yes," said the MSL. "I've been in New York for a long time, and the project at SC Radcliffe is wrapping up. And besides, there's a beautiful countess that I would like to spend more time with."

Her heart lurched. Gosh, he was saying all the right stuff tonight. "Really?" she heard herself saying again.

"Really," he repeated as he reached across the table and placed his hand on hers. "I want us to spend more time together. And I don't want it to be because we work together. We did that for too long."

Her heart was beating fast. This was all going so well. "I'd love it if you were over here," she said. "I've missed you, the last few months. And I'd love for us not to be working together."

"I want it that way too," said the MSL. "Then we don't have to worry about dating."

"Dating?" said the Countess.

"Dating," said the MSL. "I'd like to do more of that with you. Would that be okay?"

* * *

Apart from the Queen Mum bag, the accessories were all sitting on the bed in the Countess's suite while she was out with the MSL. Pussy Deluxe and Pussy With Balls were watching television. American Ted was tired and had curled up between the two pillows and was sleeping. Pussy Original was propped up against one of the pillows.

A loud bang from the television programme woke American Ted. He sat up and rubbed his eyes with his paws.

"Hey, Ted," said Pussy Original. "Are you feeling better?"

"I think so," replied American Ted. "That was a good sleep. Is the Countess still out?"

"Yes, they've been gone a couple of hours now," said Pussy Original.

"We should probably start making ourselves scarce," said American Ted. "I know the Countess said that she wasn't going to bring the MSL back here, but you never know. Passion may get the better of her."

"I don't think she will," said Pussy Original. "She really wants this to work. But we can move in another hour or so, just in case."

"I'm so pleased that Mongolian Sheep Pussy is okay," said American Ted. "It's been such a horrible day."

"Me too," said Pussy Original. "I don't think I could have coped if anything had happened to her."

"Thankfully, everything is going the right way now," said American Ted. "And according to Mongolian Sheep Pussy, the MSL loves the Countess."

"It's good news isn't it?" said Pussy Original.

"It is," said American Ted. "But it changes things. Pussy Deluxe was right earlier. She won't need me anymore."

"In theory, if he looks after her properly, she won't need any of us," said Pussy Original. "We'll just be handbags and nothing else. Having the MSL in our lives is going to change everything."

* * *

When the Countess and MSL had finished dining, they had coffee back in the lounge and enjoyed the ambience of the hotel and the people-watching. Eventually, the MSL said, "Let's take a walk up to the gate."

He helped her put on Persian Dolly and then offered his arm to her to walk out of the hotel. Once outside, he put his arm around her shoulders, and she put hers around his waist. She loved this feeling and knew she would have to try very hard to keep the ever intensifying flutterings of desire under control. It just seemed so right – the two of them, properly together.

They ambled up to the floodlit Brandenburg Gate where a busker was playing a Viennese waltz on the violin.

"Ah! Listen to the music," said the MSL to the Countess. "It looks like we are going to get our dance after all."

He grabbed her right hand in his left, put his other hand on her waist and started to waltz. There were quite a few people wandering around, but the MSL and the Countess were oblivious to them. The violinist was overjoyed that there was a couple dancing to his music, and he played another waltz for them.

"Did you plan this music too?" asked the Countess as she spun around with him.

"No," said the MSL. "But it could not have turned out any better if I had. It had never occurred to me to come to Berlin and waltz at the Brandenburg Gate."

"Me neither," said the Countess. "I've been to Berlin before, but it wasn't anywhere near as romantic as this."

"You like romance, don't you?" said the MSL.

"Oh yes," said the Countess. "I think in a previous life, I must have lived in a fairy tale."

"A fairy-tale countess?" said the MSL.

"Of course," replied the Countess. "Fairy-tale princesses are so common these days. There's one in every storybook."

"There's only one countess for me," he replied. "And tonight, I'd like her to be mine. That's if she'd accept an American who is not a count, an earl or a prince?"

"You are my prince," she replied. "And it feels like I've been waiting for a hundred years for you to arrive."

"Does that mean it's time for me to kiss you?" asked the MSL.

They stopped dancing and stood, looking at each other. The MSL took the lapels of Persian Dolly. The Countess found herself lost in his eyes as he gently pulled her towards him. She had imagined this moment for so long. Softly, almost imperceptibly, she felt his lips brush against hers. He pulled back a little and they looked at each other. And then neither could hold back any longer as their lips met, slowly at first before passion overwhelmed them and they melted into each other.

At length, they released their embrace and for a moment, looked at one another in wonder, before simultaneously bursting into laughter. The MSL took hold of her hand, and they walked up to the gate.

Under the second arch from the left, he stopped walking, pulled her towards him and kissed her again.

"I need to tell you something," he said. He held both of her hands and took a tiny step back.

"What?" she asked, looking directly into his eyes.

He looked down briefly then gazed back at her. "I don't know if it's too soon to say this. But I don't care, because I don't want anything to go wrong between us again. And I don't want there to be any confusion."

The Countess could feel her chest tighten with anticipation.

He continued. "I want you to know that I love you. To be honest, I've always loved you, but I was too scared to do anything about it. But I'm not scared now. I want to be with you. You incredible, amazing woman. I love you."

The Countess thought her heart would leap out of her chest with joy. "I love you too," she said. "I always have."

They hugged each other tightly, his arms around her waist and hers over his shoulders, Mongolian Sheep Pussy hanging from her wrist. The Countess buried her face into the side of his neck, closed her eyes and breathed in. There was the clean laundry smell of his shirt, a trace of aftershave and then one hundred per cent MSL. He smelled perfect. Her MSL. Her love.

They released the embrace just enough to gaze at each other. The Countess tucked Mongolian Sheep Pussy between them. She ran her finger around the side of his eye to the little mark on his cheek and smiled at him.

"I love you," he repeated as he leaned in to kiss her again.

The Countess heard a quiet squeal of delight from Mongolian Sheep Pussy, who was squashed between them. She ignored it and kept kissing the MSL.

"What was that noise?" asked the MSL, his lips still close to hers.

The Countess shrugged. "I've no idea. Maybe it's someone who's really happy for us."

The End

Enjoyed this book? Please help others find it

Thank you so much for reading *Tales of the Countess.* I hope you enjoyed it. It would really mean a lot to me if you would leave an honest review for it, please, at your favourite online book retailer.

Reviews tell the algorithm gods that something good is happening and that they should show my story to more people. Then those people look at the reviews and it helps them decide whether the book is something they might enjoy.

As an independent author, I don't have the marketing budget of the big publishers, so I can't rely on huge billboard ads to get my name out there. However, a review from a happy reader is just as valuable.

Thanks again,
    Cali x

A Message from American Ted – Get exclusive bonus material!

Would you like to know more about what I think of the Countess and the MSL?

Please join the exclusive Countess of Kennington VIP club and get an article written by yours truly especially for fans of *Tales of the Countess*. I tell all on what it was like to come into an adult household, how I cope with supporting the Countess and how I feel now that she is with the MSL.

Joining the VIP club also allows us to stay in contact. You will receive the occasional newsletter (I promise you won't be spammed with loads of emails), more inside info on the accessories and updates on new releases. We at Kennington Mansions love building a relationship with our readers, and it would be fantastic to have you in our club.

Sign up here www.calibird.com/AmericanTedBonus and get my innermost thoughts now!

Ted x

Acknowledgements

I started writing this book twenty years ago when I was a fledgling writer of just a few months. Originally a short story, it grew and grew. The first draft was a tad autobiographical, but with each draft, the characters became truly their own people. Some were dropped, others were added, and *Tales of the Countess* became a genuine story in its own right.

The story then spent a few years sitting in a drawer when I parked the project. Thankfully, three years ago, I felt the Countess twitching in that drawer, and it was finally time for her to make her entrance into the world.

Along the way, lots of very kind friends have read it, given me guidance and recommended courses that would help me make it better. Thank you to Helen Campbell, Angus and Julia Clacher, Allison Phillips, Martin Edmonds, Vida Adamoli, Caroline Gallup, Allan Boroughs, Sue Heron, Rachel Worthington, Nicole DuJardin and Melissa Chapin. I deeply apologise if I have missed anyone off this list. It's been a long project, and my memory of the early days is a bit hazy!

Thank you to my editor, Miranda Summers-Pritchard, who gave me invaluable advice that made the story a much better read. Thank you also to Ampthill Writers' Group. I love meeting up in the pub on the first Wednesday of the month and chewing the cud together.

I would like to thank Joanna Penn and Mark Dawson for

teaching me everything I know about the publishing business. You have played an intrinsic part in allowing the Countess to see daylight.

For most of the time that this book has been on the boil, I have worked part-time as an IT consultant. Thank you to my managers for allowing me to do that, and a huge thank you to my colleagues for putting up with me not being in the office two days a week.

Speaking of putting up with me, a big thank you to my husband, Graham, my close friends and my family. I wouldn't get very far without you all.

While the people in *Tales of the Countess* are entirely fictional, the accessories are real. I own them all, and they already had those names long before I started writing the book.

And yes. In the mid-1990s, fuelled by too much alcohol, I did use to strut up to people in various nightclubs in London, offer them a leopard-print fake fur handbag and ask them if they wanted to stroke my pussy.

About Cali Bird

Cali is in her mid-fifties and lives in Bedfordshire. She was single until she was nearly forty and used to be the archetypal career girl, living in Central London and working in investment banking. One day, she had an epiphany, realised that she needed to honour her creative side and started writing. Since then, she had various side projects including running a life-coaching business, giving self-development talks and blogging about creativity at www.gentlecreative.com. She has practised Buddhism for over thirty years and is a self-confessed tree-hugger.

Cali has known her husband, Graham, since they were at school together. Although they once had a smooch when they were nineteen, they didn't get back in contact for many years. Within a month of their first date, they realised they had found someone special in each other, but it was another few years before they were married at the tender age of forty-six. It's never too late to find love!

Also by Cali Bird

As well as fiction, Cali writes about personal development and creativity. If you feel stuck in your job and wish that there was an escape route, but you don't want to be penniless or rely on winning the lottery, then check out Cali's other book **Don't**

Give Up Your Day Job – *Practical ways to lead a fulfilling life and still pay the mortgage.*

Don't Give Up Your Day Job is full of good news for jaded souls who are on the verge of giving up on their hidden desires. In a pared-down no-nonsense style, this is a practical and realistic 'how to' manual to determine what you really want for your life and how you can go about making a start on that in non-scary and sensible way.

Whether you want to find time for a hobby, start a new business or transition into a new career this book will teach you how to go about doing that while keeping the security of your current pay cheque.

* * *

If you fancy being creative yourself whether that's writing, painting, making jewellery or whatever floats your boat – you'll love Cali's blog **www.gentlecreative.com**. Find a way to scratch that creative itch in realistic bite-size chunks that fit around the other things you have to do in life (like work or taking care of your family!)

Say Hi to Cali

You can contact Cali at www.calibird.com/contact or on Twitter at @calibird

Printed in Poland
by Amazon Fulfillment
Poland Sp. z o.o., Wrocław